MW01133153

Earth Defiant
The Ember War Saga Book 4

RICHARD FOX

For Kristy,

ISBN: 1530155045
ISBN-13: 978-1530155040

CHAPTER 1

The Toth evolved from pack hunters. The smaller, fast-breeding and less intelligent members of the race cooperated with larger warriors to run down the sauropods of their swampy home world. The smaller Toth were always expendable, herded beneath the feet of larger creatures to distract them from a striking warrior, or used as bait to lure out the larger predators when a pack leader desired something more unusual for dinner.

The fleet in high orbit over Neptune held to the pack mentality. Dozens of ships ranging from destroyers to battle cruisers waited in high orbit. The warriors in command of each ship understood their place; they were servants to a larger master.

Hidden within the icy strata of Neptune's methane clouds, a leviathan lurked.

****

A golden sun sunk through bands of red and ochre, its mottled reflection shimmering against the horizon of the Pacific Ocean. Two Marines sat on a boulder lapped by ocean waves, watching the sun's final moments of the day. Puffs of water vapor billowed out to sea on the evening breeze from their e-cigarettes.

"Ain't this something?" Lance Corporal Standish asked. He took a deep breath from his vape stick and closed his eyes, shaking his head slightly as off-white fog exhaled from his nose. "No Xaros drones chasing after us. No insane horde of banshees trying to rip us limb from limb. No—"

"No peace and quiet," Bailey said. She stood barely even with the other Marine's shoulder, her long black hair pulled tight into a bun on the back of her head. She tugged a sleeve of her service khakis away from her wrist and glanced at her watch.

Standish drew in a quick breath to say something else, but Bailey grabbed his arm and he took the hint to stay quiet. Her face, bathed in the final golden rays of the sun, spoke of emotions roiling inside her. One corner of her lip twitched, wavering between a half smile and a frown. A tear glinted from her eyes. Bailey swiped a forearm across her face, leaving a stony countenance in its wake.

"Sorry…" Standish said.

"It's not you. I'm just being a sook," the Australian Marine said. "Just thinking about everyone who's *not* here to see this with us."

Torni. She's still hung up on her, Standish thought. Torni had stayed behind on the planet Takeni, giving up her spot on the last evacuation shuttle so more of the alien Dotok civilians, and a few badly wounded Marines that included Bailey, could reach safety. Torni died on Takeni, killed by other Dotok twisted into monsters by the Xaros.

Standish struggled to find the right words that might help Bailey. Every human being on Earth or in the orbiting fleet had lost loved ones when the Xaros invaded. Less than half a million souls remained. Everyone grieved differently, and in

Standish's experience, it was best to let others volunteer their emotions, not go prying for details.

Standish waited until the edge of the sun touched the horizon.

"You ever do a training rotation here on Hawaii? The training area around Pohakuloa?" Standish asked.

"Did a few low-orbit–low-opening drops off the *Poltova* to the Big Island," Bailey said. "Never got to see the place."

"I heard there's some new R&R complex over the hill from the Dotok camps," Standish said, his voice quickening. "Everybody's cycling through. Hot chow made by actual chefs, VR domes, fishing trips, white sandy beaches. Whole nine yards."

"You asking me on a date, Standish?"

"No! No, Sarge. Just saying that we, the bloodied and battered Marines of the *Breitenfeld,* are due our time off the line. Wouldn't you say?"

"We can ask Lieutenant Hale about it once he and Gunney Cortaro are back from Phoenix," she said. "Come on, our bird's supposed to be wheels up in ten minutes."

They walked past the fenced perimeter of the Dotok camps, row upon row of military tents interspersed with sanitation pods. The Dotok refugees mingled between the rows, gawking at the spectacular sunset and wide sky, sights they'd never experienced on Takeni, a colony world where they'd lived at the bottom of deep, narrow canyons.

Ibarra robots and 3-D printing factories had set up the camp for almost fifty thousand Dotok within days of their arrival, which was not a moment too soon. The ancient generation ship they'd escaped in, the *Canticle of Reason,* was falling to pieces in orbit.

"What're we going to do with them?" Standish asked, nodding his head toward the fence.

"Above my pay grade," Bailey said with a shrug. "Maybe they'll fix their damn ship and help us fight the Xaros when the drones come back."

"Doesn't seem like too much to ask. We did save their bacon back on Takeni," Standish said.

"You hear why we dropped them all on Hawaii instead of Phoenix with all the other civilians?" Bailey asked.

They stepped onto a concrete tarmac and walked toward a Mule transport. Light spilled from the interior down the lowered ramp.

"Beats me. Titan Station locked down the *Breitenfeld's* commo soon as we came back through the Crucible. I haven't heard a word from my contacts—I mean friends—in Phoenix," Standish said. The young Marine was part of the "Lance Corporal Mafia," a suborganization of the larger Marine Corps since the United States Marines formed at Tun Tavern a little over three centuries ago, and he had an ear for gossip and rumors.

The Mule's pilot, Jorgen, sat at the bottom of the ramp, his forearms resting on his knees. He squinted at the Marines as they neared, struggling to make them out in the twilight.

"You're on time," Jorgen said. "But there's a problem. Damn plane's broken."

"Broken? We came down just fine half an

hour ago with a load of orphans," Bailey said. "How is it broken?"

"Well," Jorgen said as he stood up and stretched, "my crew chief found out there's a mess hall just through there." He pointed to a lit path cut into the jungle beyond the landing pad. "And they're serving chow right now. Real chow. Not the rehydrated emergency hardtack the galley's been feeding us for the last six weeks. Turns out, the Mule's computer core took a dump and we've got to wait at least two hours for it to reboot."

"Oh…that kind of broken," Standish said.

"Damned shame, lowest bidders and all that. Let's eat," Jorgen said.

****

The mess hall was a man-made cavern, plastic sheeting stretched across a metal frame large enough to enclose an entire football field. Hundreds of Marines, black-uniformed Aerospace Corps men and women, soldiers and sailors lined up at serving stations. More crowded around banks of coolers holding canned drinks before they found an open seat at the long tables to sit down and eat.

Standish and Bailey, each holding trays of steaming food, watched in awe as the mess hall seethed with activity.

Standish glanced at the shoulder patches on passing sailors' uniforms: *Ottawa, Eylau, Crimea*.

"Sarge," Standish said, pointing to a sailor sitting at the end of a table, laughing at a joke lost in the din, "that guy's on the *Tucson*."

"So?"

"Xaros blew the *Tucson* to pieces. Saw it with my own eyes," Standish said. "The girl across from him? Her patch says she's on the *Ticonderoga*."

"Only twenty-two ships survived the attack on Ceres. Not one of them was named the *Ticonderoga*," Bailey said.

"I know."

"Let's just eat, OK? We've been gone awhile. Things can change." She led Standish to a pair of open seats and sat down, keeping her eyes on her tray as she ate, and not the crowd around her.

"Holy—Sarge, there's five officers over there with *Midway* patches." Standish had gone pale. "*Midway* went down in the mountains south of Phoenix. There's no way it's back in service so soon. The crew complement on that super carrier was almost nineteen thousand squids. Did they empty out half the fleet to-to-to…"

"Standish," Bailey hissed as she leaned toward him. "Eat. Your. Food."

"How long have we been gone?" Standish whispered. "I was on the *Breit* when we had that flash of light and—" he snapped his fingers "thirty or so years gone just like that. What if every time we jumped to Anthalas and Takeni, we lost a bunch of time?"

"Look at your forearm screen. It should've connected to the local network and auto set to the local time and date," Bailey said. She waited for Standish to check the screen on his arm. The Marine's brow furrowed in deep confusion.

"We didn't do the time warp again," Standish said. "Then…who the hell are all these people?"

The lights across the mess hall dimmed several times and silence fell across the crowd.

A naval officer, with the physique of a champion mountain climber and red hair pulled into a bun behind her head, climbed atop the banks of freezers in the middle of the hall, the four stars of a full admiral's rank on her shoulder boards. A petty officer tossed her a megaphone.

"Eighth Fleet." The megaphone whined with feedback as her words boomed through the mess hall. "This is Admiral Makarov. I hate to do this to you, but all shore leave is cancelled effective immediately." There were a few grumbles from the crowd, all quickly silenced by sharp words from chief petty officers and gunnery sergeants.

"There is a threat, an alien race called the Toth, on course to Earth," Makarov said. "I'll give you a complete briefing as soon as I can. Now…I want every last one of you to return to your barracks. You'll muster for transport back to your ships in the next few hours." She lowered the megaphone and shouted her next words.

"Who are we?"

"Eighth Fleet!" thundered hundreds of voices.

"Who are we?"

"Dragon slayers!" Hoots and cheers followed.

Standish and Bailey traded a look, both too stunned to say anything.

Makarov lifted the bullhorn to her mouth. "That's right. And we're going to make these Toth regret ever setting foot, or claw, or whatever alien filth they have, in our solar system. I've got six more mess halls to get to. You have your orders."

The admiral tossed the megaphone to an aide and jumped off her improvised stage, rolling through her landing with the grace of an acrobat, then striding through a gap between tables toward open doors.

A group of sailors stood up from the tables and made for the doors, buffeting around Standish and Bailey like they were rocks in the middle of a stream.

"Hey, Sarge. I thought Admiral Garret was the only flag grade officer left in the fleet," Standish said.

"I think you remember right." Bailey tossed her fork onto her plate of spaghetti and meatballs and sighed.

"Then where did Admiral Makarov come from?" Standish asked.

"I don't know. Let's get back to the *Breit* before things get any weirder."

CHAPTER 2

Captain Valdar sat with his fists balled against his lap, his back straight and his entire body tense. Pictures of Toth starships lay across Admiral Garret's teak wood desk, dozens of pearl-hued vessels dotted with jagged crystal weapon emplacements.

Valdar had sparred with a single Toth cruiser above the skies of Anthalas. The...thing in command of the alien ship, nothing but a disembodied nervous system floating in a tank, had taken some of his crew hostage and demanded Valdar surrender the secret to the "false minds and weed bodies" of the humans the Toth overlords had discovered when they feasted on their human prisoners.

Valdar, clueless to what the Toth spoke of, had launched his own investigation and discovered that some of his crewmen had very young bodies, only a few months old, but each of those with "weed bodies" had no inkling of what they truly were. He'd kept his findings close to his chest, waiting for the day he could share this disturbing news with one of the few men he trusted, Admiral Garret.

But the Admiral knew. He knew and he seemed to accept these abominations without a second thought. Valdar wanted to scream at the admiral, demand to know just why such a thing should be tolerated.

"Ibarra's probe detected their wormhole a few days ago," Garret said. "They sat in space just beyond Neptune's orbit, then set course for Earth. They didn't say a word to us until you—and that damn big Dotok ship—came through the Crucible. We got lucky with your arrival. You made it look like we've got an entire fleet of reinforcements on the other side of that wormhole. Makes the Toth want to negotiate for what they want instead of just killing us for it."

"And what do they want?" Valdar asked, even though he knew the answer.

"They want the tech," Garret said. "They want to make their own procedurally generated humans and they want all our proccies as part of the bargain."

A hologram flared to life behind Garret's desk. A middle-aged man with a full beard formed in the semiopaque light, rendered in shades of blue and white.

"Sorry to intrude," Marc Ibarra said. "I was just finalizing things with the Toth ambassador."

"You want to bring us both up to speed?" Garret asked.

"We're set for a summit on Europa. One vessel per side. We don't move past Mars; they don't move within the orbit of Jupiter," Ibarra said. Ibarra clapped his holographic hands together, but no sound came. "Welcome back, Captain Valdar. You've been *very* busy since I saw you last. Making new friends on Anthalas, taking a detour on your way home to bring back Dotok like they were stray puppies. At least you brought back the omnium reactor—not in time to do any good against the Toth, mind you."

"What are you talking about? A summit?" Valdar asked.

"The Toth want to negotiate a deal. Rather nice of them to be diplomatic instead of just trying to kill us all," Ibarra said.

"Those monsters," Valdar said, rising to his feet, "they murdered my crew and ate their minds. They think we're nothing but meat and you think they really want to treat us as equals? To talk?"

"Not at all," Garret said. "I've had several long talks with our Karigole advisors, Kosciusko and Rochambeau, about their experience with the Toth. You're aware of what the Toth did to them, correct? The Toth, when they were still part of the Bastion Alliance, showed up to the Karigole home world under the guise of helping modernize the Karigole military. As soon as the Karigole began to trust them, the Toth wrecked the entire planet's defenses in a move that made Pearl Harbor look like a low-budget fireworks show."

"Then the Toth consumed the entire Karigole population," Valdar said. "Steuben, he's on my ship. He told me."

"We're not going to give the Toth the same chance," Ibarra said.

"Then why are we bothering to negotiate?" Valdar asked.

Garret sniffed and put his hands on his desk. A fingertip touched the edge of a data slate and called up a picture from a void dry dock, a half-built human assault cruiser held within an encompassing framework. Garret shifted the photo side to side.

"We need more time," Garret said. "We've been on a shipbuilding spree since you left for Anthalas. Ibarra's new and improved construction robots can turn out a new ship in record time. Even got the *Midway* back into service, but a ship without a crew is pretty useless."

"The clones," Valdar said, "you're growing more of them."

"The proccies are a procedurally generated

consciousness inside a flash-grown body. They're not 'clones,' my good captain," Ibarra said. "Don't insult my handiwork with such a pedestrian, and inaccurate, label."

"You two can split hairs later," Garret said. "But, yes. We need more time. A few more days and we'll have the manpower to fully crew Twelfth Fleet. If we have to take on the entire Toth fleet now…" He shook his head.

Valdar remained silent. The hum of Ibarra's hologram droned through the room.

"Why don't we just give them what they want?" Valdar asked. "Give them the proccies. The tech. We can find another way to beat the Xaros when they return. Diluting who we are as a species to almost nothing with the proccies is no different from being wiped away by the Xaros."

Ibarra's hologram wavered with static as his face contorted in anger.

"I've been playing the long game since the day that probe landed in the desert," Ibarra said. "You think I'm going to put everything at risk over your…your ethical objections? The proccies *are* the plan, Valdar."

Ibarra crossed his arms and looked to Garret.

"Why are we bothering with this?" Ibarra asked the admiral. "Promote his XO and send the *Breitenfeld* to Europa. Get the ball rolling."

Garret slammed a palm against his desk. He snapped to his feet and jabbed a finger into—and through—Ibarra's holographic chest.

"You are not in charge, Ibarra! *I* am the commander in chief of every man and woman in uniform. Our deal is to cooperate with you and whatever the hell's passing over instructions through your granddaughter, Stacey. I just had to authorize deadly force to protect proccies from lynching. Do you have any idea how badly the civilians in Phoenix want to do exactly what Valdar just proposed?"

Ibarra looked down at Garret's finger, embedded up to the third knuckle into his hologram, and stepped back.

"The true-born population hasn't exactly

embraced the proccies, I admit."

Garret sank back into his chair and shook his head.

"The truth is, Isaac," Garret said, "that we may have to turn over the proccies before what's left of the human race tears itself apart over the issue. We've got time to figure something else out before the Toth arrive."

"What?" Ibarra asked. "Since when do you think that—" Ibarra's hologram cut out when Garret jabbed a finger against a control screen on his desk.

"God, I love doing that to him," Garret said. He took a data rod from a drawer and rolled it to Valdar. "Those are the instructions for our negotiator. You'll shove off for Europa as soon as your ship is rearmed and refueled. You'll be on tight-beam IR commo with Titan Station your whole trip. This time of the year, it'll take almost two hours for a message to get back and forth from here to Jupiter. We can work the time dilation to our advantage in the negotiations. Squeeze out some more time."

"I don't understand. My ship's been in the void for months. My crew is exhausted. I've traded blows with the Toth and you're sending me to negotiate with them?" Valdar scooped up the data rod and slipped it into a pocket.

"There's a lot you don't know, Isaac. Due to the Toth's…ability…to ingest memories, there's a lot we aren't telling you. If everything goes south, then what you don't know you can't give up. The rest of the fleet—new ships and what survived the assault on Ceres—is integrated with proccies, whether the crews know it or not," Garret said. "Your ship has a handful, but as far as the public knows, you don't have any. That makes it easier for me to deal with the true-born leaders in Phoenix. No one would trust proccies to negotiate their own surrender.

"And you're not the negotiator, Captain. Lieutenant Ken Hale gets that job."

****

Ibarra watched Valdar and Garret shake hands on the holo projection in the middle of the

23

Crucible's control room. The *Breitenfeld's* master and commander left the room and Garret looked to the camera and nodded.

Ibarra snapped his fingers—without any sound—and the hologram dissipated.

Two Karigole, both wearing human shipboard skinsuits and overalls, watched the last few ghostly motes of light die away from the holo tank without a change to their scaled faces.

Ibarra waited impatiently for either Kosciusko or Rochambeau to say something. The two advisors, each several centuries older than Ibarra, had an annoying cultural tradition that demanded the oldest member of any discussion be the first to speak.

Kosciusko, the scales covering his bald head rimmed gray with age, brushed the tip of a clawed finger over his lips.

"You trust him?" Kosciusko asked.

"Do I trust him to do as we ask? No," Ibarra said. "Do I trust him to do what we need him to do? Yes."

"Must you always speak in riddles?" Rochambeau asked. A goatee of straw-colored hair extended down from his face, the long, thick hairs bound at the tip by a dark smooth stone streaked with blood-colored lines.

"Sorry if I don't grunt and scratch myself when I speak, but I mean what I said." Ibarra waved a hand over the holo tank and a model of the solar system flared to life. Dozens of red arrows hovered near Neptune, each pointed straight at Earth.

"How do you know Valdar will act as you promise?" Kosciusko asked.

"Valdar lost his family to the Xaros," Ibarra said. "The only thing he has left are his ideals. He had the choice between returning to Earth right away with the omnium reactor, or saving the Dotok. You know what he did. With these negotiations, he'll see himself at a turning point in human history. True born or proccie. He has nothing to lose but his ideals and his honor; he'll do the right thing, from his point of view."

"I thought humans held honor and integrity

of self in high regard," Rochambeau said.

"The military ones do." Ibarra waved a dismissive hand in the air. "I've been playing this sort of shadow game with generals, dictators, presidents—you name it—for decades. The key to winning that game, my two scaly friends, is to cheat."

"We don't know this word, 'cheat,'" Kosciusko said.

And that is why you are my pawn, Ibarra thought.

****

The overlord's dining hall centered along a trough sunk into the floor. Gilded cradles for a dozen overlord tanks lined either side of the trough. Kren waited for his guest, another overlord with a tank bedecked in jewels and precious-metal inlays across his tank depicting great acquisitions and the death of corporate foes during the Toth's long life. The guest's nerve tendrils were long, pooling against the bottom of the tank, his brain dotted with nodules and crusted over from nearly a millennium inside the tank.

"I hope our facilities are to your liking, Lord Olux," Kren said as he settled his tank into a cradle. Sitting at a lower social position to another while on his own ship annoyed Kren, but this guest was something special.

"This is quaint…almost rustic," Olux said.

"Once this acquisition is complete, I have a number of ideas in mind for a renovation." Kren's claw tips tapped against the deck. Menials vanished into the kitchen at his signal.

"I question your valuation of the human technology. I told Dr. Mentiq your corporation was foolish to lease a *Domination*-class vessel for this expedition, and you agreed to such a high percentage of all future profits…" A tendril rubbed against a barnacle-like growth against the front of his cerebrum.

"You've not tasted the human meat. The procedurals are a unique delicacy like I've never had before," Kren said.

"You're young…and of limited means,"

Olux said.

Kren's nerve endings rolled against themselves in annoyance. *Leave it to one of Mentiq's lackeys to flaunt his wealth whenever possible*, Kren thought.

"For now," Kren said. "But once you sample the procedurals, and what they represent, you'll realize that Mentiq should have demanded a higher percentage from us. Minds made to order, Olux. No need to raise meat from birth to achieve a certain flavor. Delicacies in days!"

"We shall see. You must achieve the humans' compliance first. If they destroy the technology and we return with nothing but cargo holds full of spoiling meat, I doubt your corporation will cover the bond you put up to finance this mission. And you know what happens to lords who default on a debt to Mentiq," Olux said.

"Yes, I am well aware of the terms." Kren pounded a claw against the deck. "Aren't you hungry?"

Menials carried a wooden plank from the

kitchen, a menial tied to pegs along the side. The waiters set the plank in front of Kren and scurried away. The four-legged Toth before Kren had smooth scales, and steam rose gently from its naked body.

"You take your meals sedated?" Olux asked.

"Drugged into a euphoria," Kren said. "My warriors caught them manufacturing recreational narcotics. I find the taste pleasing as an appetizer. Care to try?"

"I cannot taste them anymore," Olux said. Older overlords developed a tolerance to simpler minds as they fed over centuries. Their fix came from more exotic sentients or from specially bred and raised warrior stock. Keeping their addictions at bay only became more expensive as time went on, making them a customer base Kren knew he could sell to once he had the procedural technology under his control.

Kren's feeder arm extended from beneath his tank and poked at the menial. Its tongue fell out of its mouth and it laughed gently. The spiked end snapped open and monofilament tendrils snaked into the menial's skull. The menial jerked against its restraints and went slack.

"Aah, nice." Kren withdrew his feeder arm and shoved the plank into the trough with one of his mechanical arms. The trough opened and the dead menial fell into reprocessing vats beneath the floor.

"I'm afraid I've little else to offer you but my crew," Kren said. "I have a few senior warriors that I'm displeased with."

"I brought my own," Olux said. His claw tips drummed against the deck.

The door to the kitchen opened. A warrior led a cloaked humanoid figure to Olux. A collar attached to a straight pole held by the warrior kept the cloaked figure from escaping. The warrior pushed the cloaked being to its knees in front of Olux.

One of the warrior's mid-arms reached out and gripped the cloak. It tore away with a flourish. A naked alien with midnight-blue skin bent its head toward Olux. A line of quills ran down the center of its scalp and along its spine to a short tail. Overly long arms hugged its torso; its fingertips were covered in raw, puffy flesh where claws had been.

Kren saw the reflection of emerald-green eyes against Olux's tank.

"My, my…is that a Haesh?" Kren asked.

"It is. Taken from Mentiq's own garden." Olux's feeder arm extended and lifted the Haesh's face toward Olux. "Sing for me?"

The alien pulled away and looked down.

"Shame I only brought one," Olux said. "They have the most amazing voices, but they'll only sing when you threaten to consume their offspring." His feeder arm rose like a serpent and struck against Haesh's skull with a snap.

Kren remained silent while Olux writhed in pleasure. It was rude to talk during digestion. Olux pushed the dead alien into the trough once the high passed.

"I've only ever heard rumors about the wonders in Mentiq's gardens," Kren said. "I will peruse his stock once this is over with."

"Mentiq will make anything available, Kren, but only if you can pay the price," Olux said.

Kren felt a thrill go through what little remained of his body. An unlimited source of wealth was right at his claw tips. All he had to do was take it from the humans.

****

Lieutenant Hale hated hospitals. He had no good memories of their sterile halls, worn chairs in the waiting room and the constant air of dread worn by anyone who wasn't walking around in scrubs or a doctor's coat.

As a teen, he and a group of friends were in a car wreck when the vehicle's auto-driver malfunctioned and sent the car rolling down a hillside. Seat belts and crash foam let Hale walk away from the crash with minor cuts and bruises. Two friends in the backseat weren't so lucky. He'd stayed in the ER hours after being treated, waiting for news. When a pair of doctors finally came to see the assembled families, the news had been devastating. One boy was paralyzed from the neck down. The other died in surgery.

That Hale had just finished weeks in the *Breitenfeld's* sick bay recovering from wounds taken on Takeni didn't exactly endear Phoenix's only hospital to him either.

He glanced at his forearm screen: five minutes later than the last time he checked. Fingers tapped at the screen, trying and failing to connect to the local data network. He'd received updates from the *Breitenfeld* since he'd touched down on Earth, yet he was cut off from the rest of the local network by some kind of firewall.

The sound of footsteps echoing down the hallway prompted Hale to sit up and look over his shoulder.

Gunnery Sergeant Cortaro walked toward him, a slight limp in his steps. Cortaro carried a metal peg in one hand and wore a brand-new boot over his left foot.

"I thought you were here just for a checkup," Hale said.

"Robo-surgeon's got one hell of an upgrade

while we were gone," Cortaro said. He raised his right knee to his chest and balanced on the foot in the new boot. "They fit me for a new cybernetic. I'm a cyborg from my shin to my toes. I can even *feel* my boot and socks, sir."

"Not bad for a prosthetic. They going to grow you a new leg?" Hale asked.

"Roger that. They said it'll be a couple days before the proto-cell tank will have it ready. Genetically identical, no risk of rejection." Cortaro set his foot down and spun the peg like a baton.

"I'm surprised you kept that," Hale said. He swiped fingertips across his screen until he found the ride pod icon, which was grayed out.

"I'm attached to it. Was attached to it. I need it in case Standish gets out of line," Cortaro said with a chuckle.

Hale cursed and poked his forearm screen harder. "Can you get network access?" he asked Cortaro.

The gunnery sergeant looked to his own screen and shook his head.

Hale went to the unmanned nurses' station and leaned over the counter. Shadows moved inside an interior office.

"Excuse me," Hale said. "Can you call up a pod for us?"

A short woman dressed in scrubs and with dark skin and hair of very short and thick curls came out of the office. She looked at Hale, eyes wide and lips trembling.

Hale pointed at his forearm screen. "No access. Sorry to bother you."

The nurse nodded quickly. Her fingers danced over a screen and Hale's forearm computer buzzed with a message: a two-person pod would be waiting for him at the entrance in seven minutes. The nurse turned away and hurried toward her office.

"Thanks. Hey, is something wrong?" Hale asked.

The nurse glanced around, then came back to Hale.

"You're from the *Breitenfeld.* I'm not

supposed to talk to you," she whispered. The slight sound of doors thumping open from down the hallway echoed through the waiting room. The nurse chewed on her bottom lip and took quick, shallow breaths.

"Your ship is pure," she said. "Don't let them on board. Don't let anyone else onto your ship. They look just like us so you can't be sure."

"What? Who?" Hale asked.

"The proccies," she hissed. Two Military Police officers strode into the waiting room, gauss pistols at their hips and thin plates of riot armor strapped to their bodies. The nurse backed away from Hale like he'd suddenly became a venomous snake and scurried back to her office.

Hale felt Cortaro tense up, his hand slipping to the base of his peg leg to use it as a club. Hale shook his head slightly and Cortaro relaxed.

"Gentlemen," an MP said, "we'll escort you to your pod."

****

The travel pod pulled away from the

hospital and zipped onto a solar-cell road, the photoelectric hexagons glinting beneath the high sun. The two-person pod was little more than a plastic cabin on wheels, controlled by a central computer core that managed Phoenix's vehicular traffic. The system had been perfected by the middle of the century, eliminating the need for those in larger cities to own a vehicle or even bother with a driver's license.

"What the hell was that, sir?" Cortaro asked.

"Damned if I know." Hale leaned against the clear plastic of the cabin and tried to read a sign scrawled onto bedsheets and hung from open windows of an apartment building. "Did that say 'True Born Only'?"

"I missed it," Cortaro said. He reached down and scratched his new calf.

Hale hadn't spent much time in Phoenix since the Xaros occupying the planet had been defeated. Barely a shell of the city remained; most of the intact buildings were near the Ibarra Corporation's headquarters at Euskal Tower. Those structures that hadn't been deconstructed by the drones into omnium were ravaged by neglect and the elements.

The pod zipped past squat towers alongside the highway, none of which Hale remembered from his time in the city. He kept his gaze on an incomplete building, nothing but a metal frame surrounded by stacked cargo containers. Spider-like construction robots skittered over the frame, spinning additive components into the floors, walls and ceilings of the new building.

Hale remembered an exhibition from a Consumer Electronics Show in Las Vegas where prototype construction robots built an exact replica of Notre Dame Cathedral in less than twenty-four hours. He and his brother, Jared, got to walk through the building before it—in true Vegas fashion—was imploded.

The new construction bots looked like they could build even faster than what he'd seen those years ago.

The pod merged onto the highway and into

the far-left lane normally reserved for automated cargo trucks. Cortaro gripped his armrests as the pod swerved around slower traffic.

"*Madre de Dios*," he muttered as the pod cut between two trucks with only feet to spare.

"Who told this thing we're in such a hurry?" Hale asked.

Black and yellow stripes flashed around the edge of the front windshield.

"Traffic congestion ahead," a pleasant voice said. The pod slowed with the flow of traffic into the far-right lane until it came to a complete stop behind a refrigeration truck. Hale saw an off-ramp ahead of a bend in the road.

"I thought automated traffic wasn't supposed to jam up like this," Cortaro said.

"Pod," Hale said, "what is the nature of our delay?"

A buzzer sounded. "Sorry. This pod is not connected to the local news network."

Hale thrummed his fingertips against his armrest.

"To hell with this." Hale unbuckled his seat belt and ignored the pod's gentle safety message. He pointed to the off-ramp. "That's the exit to 87 South. We're a twenty-minute walk to the space port and I could use some fresh air." He pulled the handle, but his door didn't open.

"I'm sorry," the pod said, "but premature exit of the vehicle is not authorized under section twelve of the Phoenix Autonomous—"

"Emergency override," Hale said. He jiggled the handle to no effect. Hale held his palm up over his shoulder and Cortaro slapped his peg leg into the lieutenant's hand. Hale struck the peg against the handle, breaking it loose with a crack of polymers. A boot to the plastic door sprang it loose from the hinges.

Hale jumped from the pod and into the heat of a Phoenix summer. He felt his armpits and forehead slicken with sweat as he fished his cap from a pocket and slid it onto his head. Hot wind sent grains of sand skittering down the roadway. The *tick tick tick* of the sand mingled with the almost silent hum of idling vehicles.

The burr of a warning buzzer came from the abandoned pod as Cortaro climbed out.

"Sir, somebody's going to be pissed you broke that pod," Cortaro said.

"What're they going to do? Dock my pay? Our Mule back to the ship is supposed to be wheels up in forty-five minutes," Hale said. "Can you run on that new leg?"

"Might as well find out," Cortaro said with a grin.

Hale took off at a jog. Cortaro kept up, but he hadn't run since Steuben blew the leg off to save the Marine from the Toth claws impaled through his shin. Hale kept the pace slow and deliberate as they made for the off-ramp.

"Hey, L-T!" Hale glanced over his shoulder and saw Sergeant Orozco, his strike team's heavy gunner, waving to him from the tiny open window of a cargo truck. Hale skidded to a stop.

"Orozco? What're you still doing down here?" Hale asked.

"I'm about to put down roots, that's what," Orozco said. "Me and big guy went to pick up a part as a specialist fabricator. Caught a ride back in this truck, but we've been sitting here for an hour waiting for this show to get back on the road."

"Get out. Follow me," Hale said.

"The damn door's bolted shut," Orozco said. The Spaniard cocked his head back to whoever he shared the cab with and nodded. Orozco ducked back into the cab and a moment later the door distended outward with a *whump*. A second blow sent the door flying off the hinges and clattering to the ground.

Steuben's clawed hands grabbed the doorframe and swung him out of the truck. The Karigole picked up the battered door and tossed it into the cab once Orozco was clear.

"Steuben, you're finally learning how to be a Marine," Cortaro said.

"One does not accept obstacles when given an order," Steuben said. The alien's yellow eyes ran up and down Cortaro's new leg. "You are whole?"

"Whole enough to get back in the fight. Don't think I'm not pissed about you blowing a chunk off me." Cortaro pointed the tip of his peg at Steuben's chest. "I'm also grateful you saved my life."

"These emotions are in contradiction," Steuben said.

"I'm a complex man," Cortaro said.

"Girls," Hale said, "you can hug it out once we're back on the ship. Let's go, double time."

****

The four jogged down the off-ramp, and then Hale ran to the side of the other column. His eyes darted along the road as it curved beneath the highway, over decrepit buildings that looked even worse for wear than he'd remembered.

The suburb of Chandler, just outside the spaceport, used to be the industrial section of the city, and the long decades of neglect during humanity's absence weren't kind. Caved-in roofs and collapsed walls made the once seedy section of town look like a felled tree rotting in the forest.

New double walls of fences topped with razor wire surrounded the spaceport, their smooth chrome finish glittering in the sunlight.

A giant mass of people clustered around the main entrance, and rows of them blocked the road leading through a four-lane gate as they swayed to a chant that Hale could barely hear. Travel pods and cargo trucks were backed up bumper-to-bumper from the crowd on either side of the gate.

"So that's the hold up," Orozco huffed.

"Lieutenant Hale, can you explain this behavior?" Steuben asked.

Hale slowed to a walk and the rest followed suit.

"It looks…like a protest," Hale said. More and more people filtered through the ramshackle buildings beyond the spaceport and joined the protest.

"Humans will gather in large numbers to air grievances?" Steuben asked.

"That's our custom. What do the Karigole do when a group is upset like this?" Hale asked.

"Ritual duels between champions," Steuben said.

"That does not surprise me. At all," Orozco said.

Steuben cocked his head to the side. "Why are they chanting 'True born for Earth' and 'Proccies out'?" The Karigole's senses were a good deal more sensitive than his human allies, a trait that had saved lives on more than one occasion.

"'Proccies'? That's the second time I've heard that today," Hale said, "and I still don't know what it means." He put his hands on his hips and peered into the crowd. "That gate's the only way in or out. Anyone see service uniforms in that mess?"

The other Marines and Steuben shook their heads.

"We might not be real welcome down there," Cortaro said.

"You think Steuben's the proccie they're talking about?" Orozco jabbed a thumb at the Karigole.

"The last four of us are in this solar system.

Our presence and involvement has been overt from the beginning. I even gave an interview to a journalist," Steuben said. "There is a group of humans cutting into the fence."

Hale scanned along the fence line until he found a small knot of protestors huddled around the chain-linked wall. Another group, all carrying signs, stood between those cutting their way in and the guards posted at the main gate.

They set up a screen, Hale thought. *There's more to this than some mass of angry people.*

"Your security is lax for such an important facility," Steuben said.

"The fence is supposed to keep coyotes and other wild animals out, not determined people," Hale said. "But we can use this to our advantage. We'll piggyback and get in that way. If security shows up, they should let us in." He found a street without much of a presence leading to the saboteurs.

"I've got a route. Not too many people on it," said Hale, looking at Steuben, "but we bring you down there and I doubt anyone'll be happy to see you."

Steuben pulled on a necklace chain of spun wire and fished out a crystal, set into an intricate mesh of gold and platinum. He pressed the medallion to his chest and light curved around his body. Steuben vanished with a slight pop.

"My refractor field will hold," Steuben's disembodied voice said, "so long as I do not move too quickly or come into contact with anyone."

"I saw you use that in Tucson," Cortaro said. "Why've you kept that hidden until now?"

"The field gives off an enormous energy signature," Steuben said, his voice moving down the ramp. "Any advanced civilization, like the Xaros and Toth, can detect it easily. The human eye is easily fooled."

The saboteurs cut through the first row of fencing and moved on to the next.

"Let's hurry," Hale said.

****

Hale scrambled over a crumbling wall and

rushed across the remains of a convenience store in a low crouch. His hands twitched, aching for the familiar heft of a weapon. Trying to infiltrate through the ruined neighborhood without his usual panoply of graphene-reinforced ceramic armor, strength-boosting pseudo muscles and IR communications made him feel like he was missing a part of himself.

Marines didn't need all those bells and whistles in Korea or Vietnam, he thought. *Neither do I.*

A pack of protestors ran past the convenience store, whistling and shouting, "True born for Earth!"

"Sir." Cortaro knelt against the wall beside Hale. "What're our rules of engagement?"

"I don't know if these guys are a bunch of shitheads who'll give us trouble or not, but we've got the right to self-defense. We're here to get back to the *Breitenfeld,* not pick a fight with the people we're supposed to protect," Hale said. "So don't pick a fight."

Pulverized concrete puffed around Steuben's large footprints. The air shimmered slightly as the cloaked alien approached.

"They're through the second gate," Steuben said. "A small group ran into a nearby building, but the rest are just standing outside the perimeter waving their arms."

Hale took a slow breath, trying to cover his indecisiveness with a mask of calm. Trying to stop a mob armed with nothing but his fists and a few good Marines wouldn't end well for any of them, but if the infiltrators had bombs or firearms, they could do immeasurable damage in the spaceport.

He glanced at his forearm screen—still no contact with the local network and that meant no contact with the spaceport's security forces.

"What kind of building was it?" Hale asked.

"Barracks," Steuben said.

"They're going to kidnap someone?" Orozco asked.

Hale stood up and crammed his cap into a pocket. He unzipped his fatigue top and shrugged it off his shoulders. "Turn your uniform tops inside out. That could buy us a couple seconds before they realize we might be what they're after. Steuben, can you clear us a path?"

"My cloak could fail," he said.

"Get us through the second fence line. After that, we're gravy," Hale said.

"Gravy?"

"Just go. I'll explain later," Hale said.

Once his Marines had modified their uniforms, their tops now showing dull gray fabric instead of the desert-pattern camouflage, they followed Hale out of the building. Cortaro kept his peg-leg club held flush against his arm.

The crowd's attention focused on the main gate, where lights atop security vehicles flashed in the midday heat.

Hale made a beeline for the breach in the fence. Protestors, men and women in Ibarra Corp overalls and a few in civilian mufti, murmured as he slipped past them. He was ten yards from the gate when the first cry went out behind him.

Two large men in spacer overalls stood flush with the hole in the fence. One held his hand out to Hale.

"Hey!" The guard's challenge sent a hush through the nearby protestors. "What do you think you're—" The guard jerked to the side as unseen hands tossed him through the air. He slammed to the ground and rolled like a log dropped from a moving truck.

The other guard stared on, dumbfounded. The air in front of him shivered and a shove sent him into the dirt.

Hale ducked into the hole and continued on through the other fence. With a quick glance over his shoulder, he saw Orozco and Cortaro right behind him. None of the protestors chose to follow them into the spaceport.

"Sir, look at that," Orozco said, pointing to the barracks.

Three men hustled a soldier out of the building, shoving and kicking him toward the breach in the fence. Hale changed direction and ran toward the soldier, who wore black and gray urban camouflage fatigues and stood head and shoulders over his captors.

"How'd they take that guy without a fight?" Cortaro asked.

"Let's go ask them," Hale said. He stepped up his pace into a full run.

The captors came to a stop. One with a thick black beard that reached down to the middle of his chest punched the soldier in the kidneys and stomped the soldier's feet until he came to a stop. The soldier, who didn't show any sign that the strikes hurt him, held his head low.

"That's close enough," the bearded man said to Hale. He reached a hand behind his back and kept it there.

Hale slowed to a stop and raised his hands.

"What's going on here?" Hale asked.

"We're taking this freak to trial, that's what," said a lanky captor with pitted skin. "You true born or you proccie?"

"He's military, got to be a proccie," the third

said.

"I don't know what the hell you guys are talking about," Hale said. "But I know you're not taking that soldier anywhere."

The soldier raised his head. His face was thick boned, a countenance so atavistic it was almost Neanderthal. His skin was a mottle of copper and green hues. Dull eyes sparkled to life as he recognized Hale's uniform.

Hale took a step back. "What'd you do to him?"

"'Do to him?' They make them like this," the bearded captor said. "You know what? I don't have time for this." He pulled his hand from behind his back and brandished a pistol. The weapon wasn't a military-grade gauss pistol, but a crude lump of 3-D printed polymers, a ghost gun popular with revolutionaries and criminals ever since that particular technological genie had been loosed from its bottle and spread over the Internet. Homemade guns weren't accurate or reliable, but they could kill just the same.

"Now you jarhead proccies get out of our way before I get antsy." The bearded man held the gun up in the air. When Hale and the other Marines didn't move, he lowered the weapon toward Hale.

The man's arm halted in the air, then shook as the gunman strained to move.

"What the—" The bearded man's forearm snapped in half with a sickening crunch. He howled in agony as broken bones tore through his skin and blood spurted from the compound fracture. Red droplets sprayed into the air, sticking against Steuben's shimmering outline.

Steuben's cloak collapsed. The Karigole held the screaming man's broken arm in his grasp. Steuben bared double rows of pointed teeth at the bearded man, whose cries of pain shifted to terror as he tried to yank his arm away from Steuben.

The gun fell to the ground, and Steuben released his grip.

"No hurt!" the soldier roared. He lowered a shoulder and plowed into Steuben. The sudden impact sent Steuben stumbling backwards. A left cross from the soldier's meaty fists snapped Steuben's head back. The Karigole fell into a roll and back onto his feet.

The soldier wailed at Steuben with a haymaker. Steuben ducked under the blow and slammed a fist into the soldier's stomach. The punch earned a grunt from the soldier, who hammered a fist against the top of Steuben's head.

Steuben went down to a knee and swayed out of the way of the soldier's next blow. Steuben reached an arm behind his back and launched an uppercut that should have knocked a man's head right off his shoulders. Steuben's knuckles hit the soldier in the armpit, dislocating the shoulder with a sickening pop.

The soldier roared and swung his good arm at Steuben. Steuben leaned back just enough to feel the whiff of the soldier's mottled fist across his face. Steuben snapped a kick into the soldier's crotch hard enough to knock the soldier's hips back and his head jutting forward.

Steuben hooked a punch into the soldier's

jaw. The soldier's head bobbled on his neck as he looked at Steuben, the lower half of his mouth askew from the rest of his face. The soldier growled, eyes filled with rage as bloody spit bubbled over split lips.

Steuben hit the soldier in the temple, knocking him to the ground.

The soldier slammed a hand into the dirt and tried to push himself back up.

"Indigo! Stand down!" someone shouted. The soldier seemed to relax, but he kept his eyes fixed on Steuben.

Steuben kept his guard up and turned his claws away from the soldier. Steuben caught a glimpse of Hale with the makeshift weapon, pointing it at the would-be captors. An open-top truck had arrived, carrying a team of armed security robots.

A Marine in combat armor ran between the two fighters, the name "Hale" stenciled on his breastplate, palms raised to them both.

"Indigo, are you OK, buddy?" Jared Hale

asked the soldier.

The soldier tried to answer, but his dislocated mouth mangled his words.

"Fix yourself," Jared said. Indigo grabbed his jaw and snapped it back into place.

"Enemy hurt little one," Indigo said, his words slow and deliberate.

"Not enemy, Indigo," Jared said. "Karigole, remember? Karigole are our friends."

"Ugly friends," Indigo said with a nod. The soldier's face grimaced and he pawed at his dislocated shoulder. "Hurts…"

Jared grabbed Indigo's bear paw of a hand and kept it away from the injury.

"I'm sorry," Jared said over his shoulder to Steuben. "They're not conditioned to you yet. He saw an alien threat to a human and reacted to his training."

"Why didn't he defend himself from the others?" Steuben asked, still not lowering his guard.

"They're loyal. Completely loyal to human beings, incapable of intentionally harming one of us. You…sorry," Jared said.

"Indigo bad?" the soldier asked, panic in his voice.

"No. Indigo you're a good soldier," Jared said.

Hale ran toward them.

"Steuben, are you OK?" Hale skidded to a halt when he recognized his brother.

"Jared?"

"Ken?"

"What're you doing here?" they asked in unison.

"Hold on." Hale shook his head and pointed at Indigo. "What happened to him?"

"He's a doughboy," Jared said. "Where have you been?" he asked with derision. "Wait, where *have* you been?"

"Hale," Steuben said and both brothers looked at him. "My Hale."

"Steuben," Ken Hale said, "we've got a Mule waiting for us on pad ninety-four. Go with Orozco and Cortaro. I'll catch up."

The Karigole backed away from Indigo, not turning from the doughboy until he was a dozen yards away.

Hale looked over Indigo, who was breathing heavily. Blood dripped from his mouth.

"The last couple months have been pretty crazy," Ken said.

"You don't say. We need to compare notes later," Hale said. He wasn't sure what he'd share with his brother first: the mission to Anthalas, coming face-to-face with the Qa'Resh aliens behind the Alliance against the Xaros drones, or the nightmare on Takeni trying to evacuate civilians in the middle of an invasion.

"He's a doughboy, Ken," Jared said. "Ibarra makes them by the bushel. Command's trying to figure out how to use them best, so I got assigned a platoon of these meatheads for evaluation. They're dumber than a sack of hammers, but they can fight like demons. They're defenseless against the true-born thugs running around Phoenix, which is why they're all locked up on the spaceport."

"Ibarra…makes them?"

"They're bio machines, technically. Xaros can't hack them…Wait, you don't even know about the proccies, do you?" Jared asked.

"There's that word again."

Jared's lips tugged down into a frown. He gave his brother a look that Hale hadn't seen since Jared told him that their grandfather passed away.

"These people aren't real," Jared said. "Not like you and I. They're grown in a tube and given some kind of procedurally generated consciousness. Thing is, none of them know it. They all think they're perfectly normal. They have memories from before the Xaros invasion and everything."

"False minds in weed bodies," Hale said, remembering what a Toth overlord had demanded from him when he was their prisoner. Hale didn't have an answer for the Toth, and he'd watched as it murdered two human beings right in front of him because of that.

"Kind of," Jared said. "People in Phoenix went nuts over this. There's a true-born movement causing all sorts of havoc in the city, demanding to know who's real and who's…not. The doughboys are just icing on the cake. Every last doughboy's getting transferred to Hawaii, and I'm going with them."

"Why two sirs?" Indigo pointed a finger at the Hale brothers.

"Not that smart, like I said." Jared glanced at his forearm screen. "I've got to get him to a doc and my commander wants an update. You staying here long?"

"I'm on the first thing smoking back to orbit," Hale said. He realized that this chance encounter with his brother wasn't going to last much longer.

"Well," Jared said, "glad you made it back in one piece. You keep it up, OK?"

"Stay safe." Hale embraced his brother and remembered what home felt like.

CHAPTER 3

Doctor Accorso walked through the *Breitenfeld's* sick bay. He shrugged off his lab coat and tossed it onto a hook outside his tiny office then stopped to survey his domain. As the ship's chief medical officer, the sick bay was his to command and his to control. The slight smell of sterilization wash and ozone from UV lamps was his personal favorite; it meant the room was clean.

There were no patients. The last of those badly injured fighting the Toth and the Xaros banshees were on Earth, recovering in the new military hospital. Peace and quiet. Accorso knew to appreciate moments like this; someday it would fill with cries from the wounded and reek of spilled blood.

He opened the door to his office and found someone in his chair. The woman wore the usual void skinsuit and coveralls, but her loose black hair and calm demeanor wasn't that of a sailor.

"Come in, Dr. Accorso," she said. Her face was almost ageless, wavering somewhere in her thirties with flawless skin too perfect to be anything but the result of plastic surgery. She half smiled at him, and Accorso felt fear creep into his chest.

"Maybe not." He backed away and felt something hard against the small of his back.

"Don't make this difficult," a voice rasped into his ear.

The woman wiggled fingers at an empty chair and a firm hand guided the doctor to the seat. Knight, the ship's counterintelligence officer, stood in the doorway; he spun a blade in his hand before sliding it into a sheath on his belt.

"What is this?" Accorso asked. "What are you doing in *my* seat?"

"I'll be out of here soon as we've everything settled. I'm Shannon. You know the good Mr. Knight," she said. "We need to discuss your findings, the paper about your crewmen with telomere abnormalities."

Accorso swallowed hard. On Anthalas, an alien entity possessed a young Marine medic named Yarrow. Accorso had done extensive tests on the Marine and discovered that the telomeres in his cells were as long as a newborn baby's. Somehow, Yarrow's body was much younger than the age in his medical records but the abnormality wasn't caused by the encounter with the alien. It was present from the moment Yarrow set foot on the *Breitenfeld.*

After sharing the news with Captain Valdar, he'd secretly examined blood samples from the rest of the crew and discovered dozens more like Yarrow. Accorso had neatly documented and packaged his findings for release to the truncated medical community in the fleet and in Phoenix, but the communication's blackout kept him from sending it.

"I don't know what you mean," Accorso said.

Knight rested the knife edge of his hand

against the base of Accorso's neck.

"Now, now, doctor," Shannon said. "Medicine is your strong suit. Spotting liars is mine. We have your paper from the ship's archives—the rough drafts saved on your workstation and the print copies you hid in your golf bag. We need to know if there are more."

"What? Give me back my work or I'll have Valdar—" He tried to stand up but Knight slammed him back into the chair. The counterintelligence officer looked to be in his mid-fifties, but his grip sent pain shooting down Accorso's arm.

"Doctor, exactly who do you think we work for?" Shannon asked.

Accorso considered the knife on Knight's belt and just how far away the nearest crewman would be during the ship's rest cycle. He found cooperation the easiest road to survival.

"Ibarra," the doctor said.

"You may know a little of what Ibarra's done for the sake of humanity," Shannon said. "I'll let your mind wander in your free time to all the things he's truly capable of. Back on point. Are there any other copies?"

"A data rod in the base of my chair and another in the lining of my surgical kit," Accorso said, his shoulders slumping in defeat as Knight loosened his grip.

Shannon wiggled her fingers and the two rods appeared in her hand with a flourish.

"Good, you know when to be honest," she said. "Mr. Knight, would you please?"

Accorso heard a hiss and felt a sting against his collarbone. Knight held a small pneumatic applicator in his hand; the device was disguised as a stylus.

"What'd you do to me?" Accorso asked. He touched his collarbone, but felt nothing amiss.

"An insurance policy," Shannon said. "You now have a tiny explosive device sitting on your subclavian artery. It will pop if it's disturbed, exposed to air, or if I push a button. You're a trauma surgeon. I think you know how many seconds it'll take you to die once that artery gets turned to hamburger." She raised an eyebrow, and Accorso nodded.

"Terms are simple. Never recreate that research. Never tell anyone about that research. And deny that research ever happened if someone questions you about it. If you ever even hint that someone's telomeres are off for any reason, you'll be dead before you hit the ground. We clear?" Shannon asked.

Accorso opened his mouth to speak, but no words came out.

"I'm serious." Shannon held up her hand, thumb and middle finger pressed together. "One wrong move and…"

A snap in Accorso's ear scared an unmanly shriek from him. Knight snapped his fingers again with an evil chuckle.

"I…got it," Accorso said. "Can I ask why?"

"You can ask, but we won't answer. Maybe we'll remove the explosive in the future. Maybe we won't. It'll last inside a human body for decades." Shannon stood up, stretched her arms over her head, stepped around the desk and gave Accorso a pat on the head as she left the room.

Knight pointed to his eyes, then at the doctor and then shut the office door.

****

Shannon bundled her hair into a void-ship standard bun as she and Knight walked down a passageway.

"Just like old times," she said.

"How're things on Earth? Does the boss need me?" Knight asked.

"Difficult, the Toth are a disruption we hadn't planned for, but the boss…he never saw a crisis he couldn't twist to his favor."

"The Toth aren't some Chinese bureaucrat or Russian general we can bribe or scare into submission," Knight said.

"We've been with Ibarra for fifty years. Trust him." Shannon stopped at an intersection and waited for a sleepy-looking Marine to pass between them and turn down a hallway before speaking again. "He's the same man, even if he is a hologram now."

"He kept that probe and the Xaros invasion from us the entire time we did his dirty work. You ever wonder what he's still hiding?"

"Ignorance was always bliss, Eric," she said. "I've work to do dirtside, not in this box. Which way to the shuttle bay?"

****

Hale stood on the Mule's ramp as it descended. He ducked down and jumped from the opening as soon as his frame could fit through it. Chief MacDougall shouted at Hale from the other side of the *Breitenfeld's* flight deck, words so laden with Scottish brogue that Hale wasn't sure if he was being insulted or complimented for his little maneuver.

"Sir," Standish, waiting just beyond the yellow and black warning at the edge of the flight deck, called to Hale. The lance corporal gave Hale a salute as his lieutenant jogged toward him. "Sir, Bailey and I were in Hawaii, doing total legitimate Marine Corps things that you shouldn't ask about, and we…" Standish leaned toward Hale and spoke in a loud whisper, "we saw some really weird stuff going on there."

"I'm sensing a trend," Hale said. "What did you see?"

"I don't spend much time worrying about what happens in officer country, but have you ever heard of Admiral Makarov?"

Hale shook his head.

"Maybe Eighth Fleet?"

Another shake.

"Sir, did we come back to the right planet? Maybe something went bonkers in that alien jump-engine thingy. Since I've got on this ship, I've seen giant killer robots, fricking six-armed lizards that want to eat my face, a giant…globe…thing that possessed new guy. You tell me that we accidentally jumped into an alternate timeline or something and I'm open to the possibility."

Cortaro limped over to the two Marines.

"Problem?" the gunnery sergeant asked.

"Standish thinks we're in an alternate

timeline," Hale said.

"That's not the dumbest idea he's ever had…this week." Cortaro lifted his cybernetic foot off the ground and rotated his new ankle. "Doc said take it easy for a few days. I think I might have rolled the ankle."

A bosun's whistle blew "Attention" over the loudspeakers.

"Now hear this. Now hear this," Commander Ericsson's voice bellowed through the flight deck. "*Breitenfeld* will raise anchor from Titan Station in two hours. I repeat: *Breitenfeld* will disembark in one hour. All sections make ready. Lieutenant Hale to the bridge, ASAP."

"But we just got back," Standish whined.

Hale turned to Cortaro, dozens of instructions on the tip of his tongue.

"I've got it, sir," Cortaro said. "Go see what they need."

****

Hale knocked three times on the door to Valdar's ready room.

71

"Enter."

Hale slid the door aside and stepped inside. The captain sat at his desk, cluttered with piles of data slates and printouts in ringed binders. Valdar looked years older than the day he took command of the *Breitenfeld* a mere six months ago.

"Sit down, son," Valdar said.

Hale picked up an enclosed food tray, which felt cold and heavy, from a chair. The captain was skipping meals again.

"Uncle Isaac, I was just in Phoenix and witnessed…the city's not the same as when we left it," Hale said.

"It's the proccies," Valdar said. "A procedurally generated human consciousness implanted into a flash-grown body. That's what the Toth wanted from us, and that's why they're here."

"The Toth…are here?"

Valdar brought Hale up to speed on everything he'd learned from Admiral Garret and the intelligence gathered about the Toth's arrival.

"Garret and Ibarra agreed to a summit with

72

the Toth," Valdar said. "We're weighing anchor as soon as we're resupplied. Ibarra has an old research facility on Europa. He mothballed it years ago and it escaped the Xaros' notice. Robots are getting it back up and running. That's where we'll meet the Toth."

"Meet with them? Sir, I watched them murder two sailors right in front of me. Why aren't we forming up with the rest of the fleet to blow them out of space?"

Valdar pushed his chair away from his desk and leaned back. His moustache, now shot through with gray hairs, twitched.

"Ken, because of your unique situation, and the Toth's ability to absorb memories, you're going to be kept on a very short leash. A lot of things will be need-to-know for you, just like they are for me, in case there's a breakdown in negotiations," Valdar said.

"I don't follow," Hale said.

"You're the ambassador. You broke out of the Toth's ship, gave them a bloody nose on

Anthalas too. That gives you a lot of…*wasta, mianzi,* credibility, however you want to look at it…in Toth culture. It makes you, and only you, the best choice to handle these talks."

"Uncle Isaac. I'm a Strike Marine. I shoot people and break things. I don't…negotiate." Hale felt a tightness in his chest at the idea of being close to a Toth overlord and not being able to blast it into pieces.

"Your grandfather—who I met, great man— he ever tell you about his work with the Awakening movement in Iraq, way back in '07? He was a Marine in Ramadi and got the locals to stop being shitheads and turn on Al Qaeda. Worked great until we let it all slip away, but that's a different discussion. You can do this, Ken.

"Ms. Lowenn stayed on board. She's become something of an expert on the Toth since we encountered them. She'll prep you with more cultural knowledge—teach you which of their buttons to push and which ones not to touch," Valdar said.

Hale ran a hand over his short hair. "This is a lot to take in."

"There's more," Valdar said and Hale rolled his eyes. "My crew has been infiltrated. Ibarra snuck proccies onto this ship. They've been with us since we left for Anthalas. I'm telling you this because they're a bargaining chip in these negotiations."

"How so?" Hale sat back, mentally and physically recoiling from the implications of what Valdar just said.

"Handing the proccies over to the Toth is a valid course of action if it'll save Earth from another war. The fleet is in shambles. We have one—*one*—city. A single point of failure for the future of humanity. Giving up those things might just make us stronger when the Xaros arrive, and there's no way to reason with the drones." Valdar nodded as he spoke, evidently convinced of what he was saying.

"Besides," Valdar said, "it's not like these proccies are real people. It'll be like trading cattle."

"Hold on," Hale said. "This is coming straight from Ibarra and Admiral Garret? They understand what the Toth will do with the proccies? The Toth aren't going to put them in a zoo. They're going to…" Hale remembered the Toth overlord pressing feeder tentacles into a Mule pilot's skull—and her screams as she died.

"Don't fall into the trap of thinking the proccies are like us, Ken. They're not. They're Ibarra's Trojan horse to take over the human race. Ibarra can't be trusted. He already doomed everyone we love—my boys, my wife." Valdar choked up. His jaw clenched and anger filled his face. "Ibarra let them all die for his plot. We can't let him win. These proccies are almost perfect. You've even had one right under your nose for months."

"What? Who?"

Valdar opened his desk and took out a folded piece of paper. He slid it across the table to Hale.

****

76

Bodel pushed Kallen over the low ramp leading into the cemetery. Three suits of armor stood in their coffins, ten-foot-tall machines with a singular purpose: death. Bodel glanced up at his armor, so new it still smelled of the factory where it was made. Elias and Kallen had to rip him out of his last suit on Takeni to save his life after his armor was badly damaged in battle. He hadn't hooked up to a suit since.

Lafayette greeted them with a nod. The Karigole stood next to a large open case.

"You have it?" Bodel slurred. The right side of his face was slack, a consequence of the many strokes he'd suffered from being forcibly removed from his armor. Neural spikes from battle damage were normally fatal; most considered Bodel lucky that he wasn't catatonic or crippled even more.

"If I had asked you to meet me here," Lafayette glanced around the cemetery, "without the nerve-jack, I do believe Elias would have ripped my limbs off."

"Only one," Elias said through his armor's

speakers, "I kind of like you."

"Hurry." Bodel kicked a foot against the brakes on Kallen's wheelchair and snatched up a cane hanging from the back of her chair. He stabbed the deck with the cane as he lumbered toward Lafayette, dragging a lame leg behind him.

"How did you compensate for the degradation along his spinal cord?" Kallen asked.

"I used a stem-shunt." Lafayette tapped at the base of his skull, his metal fingers clinking against the metal of his cybernetic skull. The Karigole was heavily cyberized; only his face still had the appearance of flesh, and even that was a vat-grown replacement. The rest of his body was constructed of polymers and composite materials, replacements for a body horribly maimed by a Xaros disintegration beam. Kallen didn't know how much of the original Lafayette was left beneath the bionic components, and he'd never offered the information.

"Karigole nervous systems aren't the same as human," Kallen said.

"Yes, I am well aware. Ibarra's probe caught a few errors in my original prototype, but this model should function as designed." Lafayette reached into the case and pulled out a flexible metallic pad that looked like a spine protector she'd seen motorcyclists use.

"I wear it all the time?" Bodel asked.

"No, it will stay in your tank as part of your interface," Lafayette said. "But I need to attach it to your plugs this one time."

"Will it help with…" Bodel touched the slack half of his face.

"No, I'm afraid not, but the advances your doctors are making in neural-regeneration are—"

"Don't care." Bodel tried to undo his coveralls, but one hand refused to grasp the zipper properly. "Ugh, damn thing."

"You keep skipping your physical therapy and it won't get any better," Kallen said.

"Thank you, Mom," Bodel said.

Lafayette undid Bodel's coveralls and tossed it aside, revealing the armor skinsuit he wore beneath it. Lafayette pulled the suit away to expose Bodel's back. Plug holes started at the base of his skull and ran down his spine.

"This will be unpleasant," Lafayette said before pressing the nerve-jack into Bodel's plugs. The soldier moaned in pain, half his face contorting in agony. Lafayette pulled Bodel against his chest and connected the rest of the nerve-jack into Bodel's spine, each new connection triggering a small cry from Bodel.

"Hans?" Kallen asked. Her hands remained folded across her lap, but her face was full of concern.

"It's…all right," Bodel said. He stumbled back from Lafayette and tried to open his left hand. "Still the same," he slurred.

"I told you—I could fix your body or you could wear your armor again," Lafayette said. "That's all I can do on such short notice."

"My armor is ready?" Bodel asked.

"Unit 02," Lafayette raised his voice, "don armor."

80

The brand-new suit of armor reached down, grabbed Bodel by the waist and lifted him in the air. The chest plate swung open, revealing the oval-shaped armored womb within. The lid of the womb slid down and the armor pressed Bodel into the padded enclosure. Bodel grabbed a pair of handles and tried to smile at Kallen as the womb closed and neural connectors reached for his skull and spine.

"Bodel?" Kallen asked as she craned her neck to try to read the status screen by his armor's knees.

Lafayette pushed her wheelchair closer to the screen.

"I'm in," came from the armor. "Juice is coming in. Wait until I'm fully connected before I can talk again." Bodel's voice was happy, almost jubilant as the womb filled with the hyper-oxygenated fluid that would replace his need for air.

Kallen watched as his system booted up.

"I turned down Elias' audio receptors," Lafayette said quietly, "so this is between just us. Your condition was the baseline I used while engineering a solution to Bodel's problem."

"Why? I synch with my armor just fine," she said.

"Karigole habit. We try to solve a bigger problem than the one presented, makes things seem easier. The damage to your spinal column is significant, but I believe I can make a nerve-jack for you that will restore your mobility."

Kallen looked up at Lafayette with wide eyes.

"I've been in a wheelchair since I was four years old," she said. "You could help me walk? Feel?"

"You'd need a fair amount of muscular-regeneration work, but yes, it could be done," Lafayette said.

Kallen's mouth pressed into a thin line. "But."

"But you would never wear armor again," the Karigole said. "The amount of rewiring, so to speak, that you need would render you incompatible with the armor interface."

"I could run again…" Kallen looked up at Bodel's suit, then to Elias. "No," she whispered.

"Odd," Lafayette said. "I thought you would accept the offer."

"They need me, Lafayette. I am an Iron Heart. I am armor."

"As you like." He tapped her on a withered shoulder. "Perhaps when the war is over."

"That is a day that will never come," she said. "Don't tell Elias or Bodel, please."

"It will stay between us."

"I'm in!" Bodel's mechanized voice came through his armor's speakers. The armor's left hand rose in front of its helm and the digits tapped against the thumb. "My synch rate…that can't be right."

"You're at twelve percent," Kallen said, "and rising…slowly."

"You aren't going into the field with anything less than eighty percent," Elias said.

"The software needs time to adjust," Lafayette said. "Give it a few more days of wear and you'll be fully functional. I'll monitor your progress from the Crucible."

"You're not coming with us to Europa?" Elias asked.

"No, I don't trust the human engineers with my omnium reactor. They look at it wrong and they might break my new toy," Lafayette said.

"We'll see you on the high ground." Elias knocked his fist against his breastplate in salute.

****

Yarrow sat on an ammo crate, his head hanging between his shoulders, staring at his empty hands. A slightly open door let in a fan of light, casting a dim glow through the cargo container he'd taken refuge in.

The sound of footfalls approached. Yarrow sniffed, uncaring.

The door opened with a creak and light spilled over Yarrow.

"There he is," Standish said. Yarrow glanced up and saw Standish, Orozco and Bailey standing in the doorway. "New guy, where you been? Hale calls you and Gunney off the range and then Gunney gives us this 'Don't ask where he is' routine when he comes back without you."

Yarrow kept his gaze on his hands as the three Marines came toward him.

"Hey," Bailey said, putting a fingertip on Yarrow's chin and lifting it up, "I know Standish can be a bit of a prick with the 'new guy' routine, but we're all squaddies. What's eating you?"

Yarrow took a deep breath.

"I'm not real," the medic said.

The three Marines traded quizzical glances.

Standish poked Yarrow on the shoulder. "Seem pretty real to me."

"Hale called me into his office," Yarrow said, shifting on his seat, "told me I'm 'procedurally generated.' Ibarra grew my body in a tube. My mind is the result of a computer simulation. All my memories from…before I got on the *Breit* are all fake. All part of Ibarra's plan to crew a larger fleet when the Xaros come back. Just…shake and bake a bunch of fake people."

"Are you a clone of some Yarrow that died on Earth?" Orozco asked.

"No. I'm brand new. A test-tube baby on steroids with a head full of lies." A sob went through Yarrow as he spoke. "My mom's not real. My dad's not real. Neither's my sister. I used to just think that they're dead, killed by the Xaros. Now…they-they never *were*." Yarrow sobbed and pressed his head into his hands.

"Hey, c'mere." Bailey wrapped an arm over his shoulder. "Just let it out."

Yarrow shrugged her arm away.

"I don't even know what I am anymore," he said.

"You're a Marine," Orozco said. "Remember when you saved the life of that sailor who'd had her arm ripped off by that banshee?"

"Or when you dragged my dying ass to the last Mule off Takeni?" Bailey touched her side where an explosion-propelled hunk of rock had ripped through her side. "You patched up Hale and me while you were bleeding all over the place."

"You passed out soon as we landed on the *Breit*," Standish said. "I carried you to sick bay. Oro and I both gave you a pint of blood to keep you going. Doc Accorso said you're lucky your blood is AB positive."

"I know what I did…just don't know what I am," Yarrow said.

Standish pressed a finger against the name tape on Yarrow's uniform, then touched the globe and anchor crest on his chest.

"You're telling us who and what you are," Standish said. "We've seen who you are. So what if you came out of a tube with an installed personality? Sure, that's a bit weird, but—" Bailey jammed an elbow against Standish's ribs. "I don't care. You're a great medic. Brave Marine. Even if you are the frigging new guy."

"We've all had to give up what we had before the war," Bailey said. "It's gone—our homes and families, but we've got each other and we've got this fight. I don't want any other medic but you with us."

Yarrow sniffed a last time and nodded quickly.

"Hale say if anyone else was a...like you?" Orozco asked.

"There are a couple others but he didn't say who. That team of Rangers we picked up before Anthalas were all proccies," Yarrow said. "We're all made after the invasion."

Standish fiddled with his hands as he thought hard. "I've been with Gunney and Hale since before we were assigned to this ship. No way I'm a proccie."

Bailey went pale. Her eyes darted from side to side before widening.

"Melbourne!" she pointed at Orozco. "Before the war, we were there on an exercise. Went drinking together with a bunch of my mates. Remember?"

"I got a tattoo that night," Orozco said. "And I had my *sardinas*. Got them awhile back in San Sabastian and kept them with me until Takeni. I'm not a proccie."

"Everybody on the ship's going to have an existential crisis when this breaks out," Standish said. "No wonder we were on a commo blackout when we got back to Earth. Wait...so Yarrow's a virgin?"

"What?" Yarrow snapped to his feet. "No, I had a girlfriend in high school and we...but that didn't happen." He looked at Bailey in confusion.

"Don't you fucking look at me like that," Bailey said. "We're in the same squad. Never."

"No, no I..." Yarrow turned his attention to Orozco.

"Hell no," Orozco said with a definitive shake of his head.

"That's not what I'm—"

Standish broke into a chuckle, followed by Orozco and Bailey.

"Bunch of dicks," Yarrow said indignantly.

"Come on, new guy," Standish said. "Gunney wants our void armor inspected and serviced by showtime or there'll be hell to pay."

****

Steuben tapped his knuckles against a bulkhead as he entered Lafayette's workshop. He'd given up on successfully sneaking up on his fellow Karigole; Lafayette's cybernetic implants made the game unwinnable for Steuben.

Empty space had replaced the massive omnium reactor that Lafayette had spent months studying and experimenting with. What had been a seemingly disorganized mess of tools and incomplete projects had been packed into crates, ready for transport.

Steuben stepped around a stack of boxes and found the remnants of his entire species—Lafayette, Kosciusko and Rochambeau—talking to each other.

"Brother," Kosciusko said to him, "you know they are here? The Toth?"

"I do," Steuben said. He touched knuckles to Kosciusko's and Rochambeau's temples, a Karigole gesture of fidelity and affection. "I shed their blood on Anthalas."

"Now we've the chance to hurt them," Rochambeau said.

"After we learned what the Toth did to our home, to our people," Kosciusko said, "we all swore the oath. *Ghul'thul'ghul.* I will not be the last. Our centurion made that vow so that we could reach this day, so that we could stay alive until we had our chance to strike the Toth. It is time."

"What is our purpose?" Steuben said.

Kosciusko dipped his head slightly. "The human shade, Ibarra, summoned us once he learned of the Toth threat. We've created a plan with him. One that will allow us to strike at the Toth overlords, one in particular."

"No, it can't be," Steuben said.

"Stix is with the Toth fleet. The Toth that came to our people with promises to aid us, the Toth that earned our trust. He betrayed us. Our race was doomed to extinction on his order. He must die by our hands," Rochambeau said.

The four Karigole slapped their forearms together, each agreeing to the objective.

"You will stay with the *Breitenfeld,*" Kosciusko said to Steuben. "Guide the humans.

Don't let them fall for Toth lies. Wait for the right chance to strike."

"We aren't going to attack?" Steuben asked. "The humans have a fleet. The Dotok will lend what support they can."

"We do not have the strength of a broadsword in morning's light," Rochambeau said. "We must be a dagger in the dark. We will be the instrument that defeats the Toth—that is assured."

"What of the humans? Do you really trust Ibarra?" Steuben asked.

"You and Lafayette witnessed them deal with the Toth without Ibarra's influence," Kosciusko said. "What are their true motives?"

"The Marines are warriors," Steuben said. "Inexpert, but they fight with passion. They will die so that others may live. If they'd been part of the Alliance before the Toth's betrayal…more of us might have survived the fall."

"Not all of them are Marines," Lafayette said, his voice tinny as it came through his augmented throat. "Some are craven, like the Toth.

I find it difficult to believe Ibarra when he says he means to aid us."

"I've worked with Garret and Makarov." Kosciusko brushed his hands together, an old gesture to ward off evil spirits. "They are honorable."

"The humans, we must turn them against the Toth," Rochambeau said. "Make them enemies. They may build the strength to defeat the Toth, and the Xaros."

"The humans have a clan, Americans," Kosciusko said, "known for destroying foes that strike without honor. The Toth will make that mistake. It is their nature. Lafayette will go to the Crucible with the omnium reactor. Use it to aid the humans' technology."

"What?" Lafayette asked. "You want me to sit out the last battle of our people?"

"No, old friend," Kosciusko said. "The three of us will fight this battle. It is up to you to win the long war." All the Karigole but Lafayette touched their wrists together.

"If the three of you could do anything but kill things, I wouldn't see the wisdom behind this decision." Lafayette touched his wrists together.

"Steuben," Kosciusko looked to the tallest of the Karigole, "your relationship with the one called Hale, is it strong?"

"We are battle brothers."

"Good," Rochambeau said, "because everything depends on him."

****

Valdar pressed his knuckles against the side of his head, fighting the onset of another headache. He initialed a supply reacquisition and tossed the clipboard to the right side of his desk, where a growing pile of paperwork waited to go back to fleet headquarters.

No matter how urgent his ship's mission to Europa, the desk jockeys beneath Camelback Mountain wanted complete reports on every quadrium round expended and death of a sailor and Marine under his command.

One hand reached into the mass of folders

on the left side of his desk and grasped a tiny box. Valdar peered down at the box. A name was written across the lid, David Valdar, his oldest son, with the words "Play Me."

Valdar took the top off, revealing a black square with a thumb-print scanner. He pressed a shaky thumb against the reader.

A hologram swirled to life over the box. Valdar set it on the desk and watched as a face coalesced, a face that wasn't his son's. A man with coal-black skin, a lion's mane of white hair and strong features looked around Valdar's office before turning his gaze to the captain.

"Are we alone?" he asked.

"Who the hell are you?" Valdar demanded.

"I am Claude Fournier, leader of the true-born movement. I must apologize for using your son's name, but I had to get your attention," Fournier said.

"You have my attention but you're testing my patience," Valdar said.

Fournier smiled. "I've spoken to many naval

officers who know you. They tell me you're honorable, trustworthy…and a patriot. Our race is under attack, subverted from within by Ibarra's abominations. These proccies aren't true humans, and they will be the end of us if we true born don't fight back."

Valdar and Fournier regarded each other for several seconds. Valdar shook his head.

"This is a trick," Valdar said. "Ibarra and his probe can tap into any communication device we have. They've broken into our systems before. You must be some sort of loyalty test or a complete idiot for thinking you can talk without Ibarra listening."

Fournier laughed. "You're smart and security conscious. That's why I came to you, Captain. The device you have in front of you is a tangle box. Quantum dots within that box and mine are entangled; there is no in-between the dots for Ibarra to tap into. I can't say I understand the technology, but it works."

"Quantum encryption was only ever a rumor," Valdar said. "How did you get it?"

"Back during Ibarra's rise to power, we suspected he had some way of cracking our communication systems. So we developed the tangle boxes to keep our discussions private from him—much easier than meeting in person," Fournier said.

"'We'?"

"The governments of the world. I was once an intelligence agent of the South African government. Myself and a few others—CIA, KGB, Chinese Ministry of State Security—infiltrated Ibarra's colony mission. Had to keep our eyes on that old bastard and we had tangle boxes to keep in touch with each other and our handlers back on Earth. We are without masters but not without purpose. So, will you hear me out now?"

Valdar found everything Fournier said both plausible and believable. He nodded.

"The Toth are the key to our salvation," Fournier said. "We can use them. Have them remove the cancer for us."

"I wouldn't put out the welcome mat for the

Toth just yet," Valdar said. "I'd just as soon blow them out of space as talk to them."

"I know your dealings with them were difficult, but consider this. They came here to talk, to negotiate. Ibarra and his probe have been pulling our strings for decades, and they still are. The true-born resistance has kept him off balance. He can't take us out without turning every last human against him. I'm not afraid to become a martyr, but there's a lot of good you and I can do before that happens."

"What do you have in mind?" Valdar asked.

"The proccies. We give them—all of them—to the Toth," Fournier said.

"Easier said than done. The proccies I've encountered don't know what they are. There's a blood test." Valdar shared Accorso's method for identifying the proccies by their unnaturally long cell telomeres.

"We considered that," Fournier said. "Ibarra controls every lab in Phoenix and his technician robots have been altering blood tests. The two scientists I used to do our own tests died in rather convenient accidents, but there's another way to find the proccies, one Ibarra can't dispute or interfere with."

"The colony manifest," Valdar said, "a list of every man, woman and child that was part of the fleet going to Saturn."

"That's right. It was on a True View data rod, and all of those are time-stamped and unalterable," Fournier said. "Everyone on that manifest is true born; the rest must be proccies. We give the Toth everyone *not* on that list. Problem is, we can't find the list. That's one of the reasons I need you."

"I have some ideas where we can find one," Valdar said, coming up with a mental list of officers he knew were loyal and discreet. "What else do you need?"

"The negotiations…can you influence them?" Fournier asked.

"Everything from Earth goes through me to the officer who'll be face-to-face with the Toth," Valdar said.

"Get us a treaty that rids us of the proccies," Fournier said. "Do that, and I'll make sure Phoenix welcomes you back as a returning hero."

"If I go against Admiral Garret...that's treason," Valdar said.

"Who're you fighting for? Ibarra and his alien masters, or the human race?"

Valdar glanced at the framed photograph of his dead family and closed his eyes.

"I...I am with you."

"Good. Contact me once you've found a manifest. Make sure your officer gets us the right treaty." Fournier's hologram faded away. Valdar slid the communicator into his desk.

As Valdar straightened his uniform in front of a mirror, he finally saw a man with a true purpose staring back at him.

CHAPTER 4

Ibarra cycled through the camera feeds monitoring the tank farms until he found Thorsson meandering between the rows of cylinders. The blond-haired man stopped at a tank and cupped his eyes to get a better look at the voluptuous—and naked—woman floating in the amniotic fluid. Electrodes stuck to her bald head fed her nearly grown mind with memories as her closed eyes quivered in synaptic REM.

Ibarra fired up a holo-projector in the ceiling and popped up behind Thorsson.

"Busy?" Ibarra asked.

Thorsson jumped away from the tank, dropping a data slate to the floor with a clatter.

"Must you do that?" Thorsson asked, his face red.

"Spare me the indignity," Ibarra said as his hologram tossed a hand in the air. He leaned toward the tank that Thorsson had taken an interest in, Ibarra's head half-disappearing into the tank. He straightened up and asked, "This is one of the mark III's?"

"That's correct. All military personnel with cross-referenced memories of fleet training," Thorsson said. "No need to do a shakedown tour with the other units. We're growing starship crews, not individuals."

"And the rejection rate?" Ibarra asked.

"Higher. Almost six percent have to be recycled due to suicide ideations and depression that come up during the procedural creation. We identified a code segment that can cut that in half, but it would impact their empathy coefficient and that—"

"Unacceptable," Ibarra said. "I want human beings, not unfeeling brutes."

"Of course, sir." Thorsson picked up his data slate. "The new data-processing facility is almost online. We can fire up the east fields in another…thirty hours. That will bring our individual unit count to eighty thousand. The numbers on the *Lehi* remain static. We'll be well ahead of schedule, even with the demands of doughboy quotas."

"Where are we with the specialists? The ones designed to lead those brutes?"

Thorsson shrugged his shoulders. "The test subjects are under constant surveillance. We can design procedural memory scenarios once we have that data."

"Which means we need to get them into combat," Ibarra said, tugging at his lip.

"We have data from the Gallipoli experiment, but there were some…issues." Thorsson rubbed his right shoulder.

+They're here+ came to Ibarra from the probe at the heart of the Crucible.

"Shift your production queues to the lance ships. I want them crewed as each one comes off the lines. Understood?"

"I thought the larger capital ships were—"

Ibarra cut his projection and shifted to the Crucible. His holo materialized in the control room where Kosciusko and Admiral Garret were waiting for him in person. Admiral Makarov's holo floated next to the central dais and a map of the solar system.

"Sorry for the wait," Ibarra said. "Busy, busy, busy."

"We're here to finalize the defense of Earth," Makarov said. "What is so important that it kept you away?"

"An error in the repair yard on Titan Station," Ibarra said. "My robots almost installed the *Tour's* rail cannons without the backup pneumatic runners. Always have analogue backups to every digital process. World War III taught us that."

"Can the Toth hack our computer systems?" Admiral Garret asked.

The probe slid up from the dais, a needle of light surrounded by bluish motes of light. Makarov backed away, her hand automatically reaching for a pistol that should have been at her hip.

"If the Toth possess that capability, I've not detected their presence on any of our networks," the probe said. "Did I startle you, Admiral Makarov?"

"No," she snapped. "Remind me to get an in-person tour of the Crucible once this issue is resolved."

"Moving on," Ibarra said with a shake of his head, "can you access the Toth networks, Jimmy?"

"Negative, the Toth seem to be operating under analogue conditions, and there's nothing on the electromagnetic spectrum to suggest they're using any sort of communication but point-to-point IR," the probe said.

"They're coming at us like we were Xaros," Kosciusko said.

"So? All we know is that the Toth aren't fool enough to win the battle for us with their own stupidity," Garret said. "What're our chances now that Admiral Makarov's Eighth Fleet is coming online?"

"It has been a century since the Alliance severed ties with the Toth," the probe said. "They have either created their own jump drives or found a way to repair the Qa'Resh drives they possessed before we lost contact with them. Their military capabilities have improved, based on the brief engagement between the *Breitenfeld* and a Toth cruiser over Anthalas. In a fleet-to-fleet engagement, the Toth sustain unacceptable casualties in seventy percent of the scenarios."

"And what about us?" Garret asked.

"Titan Station sustains heavy damage and Phoenix is decimated. The Toth make no distinction between military and civilian targets," the probe said.

"Win the battle, lose the war," Ibarra said. "We have to conserve what we can for the Xaros."

"Better to deal with the wolf on your doorstep before the wolf on the other side of the hill," Makarov said. "My fleet will be fully operational in two days. Any chance we can get more Q-rounds? Would those make a difference?"

"I have robots constructing quadrium harvesters beneath Europa's ice right now," Ibarra said. "But they won't make a difference here. We're installing the omnium reactor on this station as we speak, but it won't be online in time to produce much."

"Then we will have to kill the Toth ship to ship," Kosciusko said, punching a fist against the dais.

"Simple, inelegant, expensive...and true," Ibarra said.

"Show me a least-time plot for the Toth fleet to Earth," Garret said. A red line traced from the enemy fleet over Neptune to Earth. "Give me an overlay of the lancer squadrons and the graviton emplacements." Blue fleet ship icons popped up through the asteroid belt between Jupiter and Mars, along with solid blue dots that formed an evenly spaced ring through the belt.

"The graviton mines were meant to slow down the Xaros, but they should foul the Toth Alcubierre drives just the same," Garret said. "If we redeploy the lancers to this point," he pointed to where the red line intersected with the asteroid belt, "we could knock out enough of their ships to make an attack on Earth a suicide run."

"We agreed to keep our ships within Mars' orbit," Ibarra said. "If they detect the lancers trying to sneak around the asteroid belt, we'll have a shooting war on our hands. I say we keep the lancers where they are—snug against big chunks of rock where the Toth can't see them—until we really need them."

"Ibarra speaks sense," Kosciusko said. "We array our forces defensively, put the *Midway* and the rest of Eighth Fleet over Phoenix to protect the civilians. Wait for the time to strike."

"We'll be ready," Makarov said. "Kosciusko, you'll join me on the *Midway*? Along with the expeditionary squadron the Dotok offered?"

"Correct, I will join you soon," Kosciusko said.

"Then let's get to it," Garret said.

Makarov nodded. She looked to her side and waved her fingertips across her throat. Her hologram faded away.

"She, and her entire fleet, are unaware that they're proccies," Ibarra said. "We need to keep them ignorant until this is resolved. Can't have the Eighth descend into chaos like Phoenix."

"The commo blackout between the Eighth and Earth has held," Garret said with a thankful nod to the probe. "Can you maintain it?"

"Don't insult my probe, Admiral," Ibarra said. "We'll do our job—you do yours. Use *Breitenfeld* to keep the Toth talking until Twelfth Fleet is out of their tubes. We'll have a nice surprise waiting for the Toth."

"Fair enough. I'm going to evacuate civilians out of Phoenix. They'll be pissed, but at least we won't lose everyone to one Toth attack," Garret said. "When will Stacey return from Bastion? Any word on what reinforcements she can bring with her?"

"I do not have an open channel to Bastion,"

the probe said. "She ferries any and all communications from the Alliance, and she is not scheduled to return for another thirty hours."

"In the meantime, we'll plan for the worst and hope for the best," Ibarra said. "I thought we'd have decades before it came time to defend Earth. Yet…here we are. Let's make it happen."

CHAPTER 5

Stacey Ibarra inhaled quickly, then slowly blew the air from her lungs. She repeated the breathing exercise several times, keeping her eyes closed.

"No problem, Stacey," she said to herself. "You're just addressing almost every sentient species left in the galaxy." She opened her eyes and saw herself in her bathroom mirror. She patted her cheeks, then grasped the edge of a porcelain sink.

A wet rumble went through her stomach.

"No! I'm fine, just fine." She grimaced and opened an eye. Her skin was pale and moist with sweat. "Come on, girl. You went *mano y mano* with a Xaros drone and won. Sure, I had a bunch of Marines with me, but who else in the Alliance can say that?" She glanced up, trying to find an answer. "Lafayette. Lafayette fought a drone, but look what happened to him. Me? I'm still in one piece. Take that, all the rest of you judgmental aliens."

"Ambassador Ibarra," came from the ceiling. Stacey let out a startled cry, then recomposed herself.

"Yes, Chuck?"

"Congress begins in seventeen minutes," the station's AI said. "At your normal pace you will arrive on time, if you leave now. You are scheduled to address the entire body in regards to—"

"I know damn well what I'm supposed to be doing," Stacey said. She ran a finger through her straight black hair, knowing full well that her appearance was irrelevant. The station broadcast a hologram around each ambassador. For Stacey, it meant every ambassador appeared human, and she appeared as the species of whatever ambassador looked to her.

"Let's do this," she muttered.

The corridors of Bastion glowed yellow, alerting each ambassador to the approaching session in the main hall. Stacey did her best to look assertive as she walked past others, her head up and shoulders back. Looking confident didn't go very far in quelling the riot of butterflies in her stomach though.

Holo-panels on the walls flashed with arrows, directing her to a human-sized doorway. She stepped into a pod, a circular anti-gravity sled with an opaque dome and a waist-high bank of controls. The dome would remain dark until Congress officially started.

"Chuck, give me something for my stomach," Stacey said. She waved a hand over a sensor and the text of her prepared speech appeared on the dome like a teleprompter. A panel opened beneath the control banks and a cup fell from a dispenser. Carbonated water poured into the cup.

"You arrived ten percent faster than usual," Chuck said. "Should I adjust your standard-pace model?"

"No." She downed the liquid, which tasted sweet with a chalky aftertaste. "Ugh, what is that?"

"Does your stomach feel better?"

"It does, actually."

"Ibarra personal setting, four hundred thirty-seven," The AI's voice changed to Stacey's "Don't tell me the details if it'll make things worse." The voice switched back to normal. "Do you still want to know?"

"Skip it." She scrolled through the agenda for the council meeting and frowned. "Chuck, why is the Vishrakath ambassador requesting equal time to respond to my address?"

"Unknown."

The Vishrakath ambassador held significant sway with many of the other ambassadors. The Vishrakath held twelve major systems and colonies on hundreds of planets on the outer rim of the galaxy that they'd settled with sub-light ships over the course of thousands of years. They were one of the founding members of the Alliance. That Ambassador Wexil chose to involve himself in her request didn't help her stomach. At all.

The black dome faded away until it was transparent. Hundreds of domes floated around her, each with an ambassador inside. Many were looking right at her.

Stacey swallowed hard and smoothed out her simple tunic.

In the center of the Congress hall, a gigantic slab of rock jutted from the floor. Its flat top looked like it had been shorn away by a laser. An enormous face of a woman with a long braid of hair running down her left shoulder came into being, the Qa'Resh.

Stacey was one of the few ambassadors who'd ever seen the Qa'Resh in their true form: crystalline jellyfish with long tentacles, natives to the upper atmosphere of the gas-giant planet that Bastion orbited. The Qa'Resh always addressed the council masked as whatever species looked upon it.

"Members of the Alliance," the Qa'Resh "woman" said, "we are gathered here on a matter of grave importance. The humans, the newest member of our Alliance, are under threat—not from the Xaros, but from those we once called allies, the Toth."

115

Rumbles of disquiet came from the ambassadors.

"To address this matter is the human ambassador." The Qa'Resh vanished as Stacey's pod floated toward the rock mesa without any sensation of movement.

"Set rotation on my pod to slow," Stacey said quietly. She waited until the climb over the mesa was complete, then began speaking.

"Honored intelligences of the Alliance. Three days ago, I returned from Earth with news of the Toth presence in our solar system. The Toth brought sixty-five star destroyers and battle cruisers, not a trade fleet. That they wish to negotiate is a farce. They betrayed the Karigole. They violated the sanctity of Bastion's predecessor. They cannot be trusted now.

"Earth's defenses are meager, but expanding rapidly thanks to the…repopulation techniques perfected by the Qa'Resh and member species, but we cannot guarantee success against the Toth. I do not believe the Toth will be satisfied with seizing the procedural technology for themselves. They may conquer our planet and humanity risks the same fate as the Karigole.

"The Alliance has more to lose than one member. The only Crucible jump gate in Alliance space orbits Earth. The single greatest strategic asset in our long war against the Xaros is as stake.

"Earth needs reinforcements. Even a few ships could convince the Toth of our resolve and send them from the system without loss of life. What races will pledge forces? I am scheduled to return to Earth soon, and I will ensure the Crucible is ready to assist your journey."

Stacey stepped back from the edge of her pod. A holographic billboard sprang up above her, a white plane ready to record what races would send aid to Earth.

A single icon from the Dotok appeared, Ambassador Pa'lon pledging the *Canticle of Reason*. The gesture was more symbolic than anything as the ship was already in orbit around Earth.

Stacey stared at the billboard for almost a minute…but no other icons appeared.

"Chuck, is that thing on?"

The billboard vanished, replaced by the Qa'Resh.

"Ambassador Wexil of the Vishrakath," she said.

A pod with a dark haired "man" with a patrician face floated up level to Stacey. Wexil gave her the briefest of glances before speaking.

"While the threat to the humans is unfortunate," he said, "we cannot risk complete annihilation, not while other options remain viable. While the incomplete Crucible is a great asset, it cannot mitigate all risk from using the jump engines."

"Would the esteemed ambassador please explain what the hell he's talking about?" Stacey kept her face stern, but she regretted the un-diplomatic words.

Please let some of that be lost in translation, she thought.

"The jump engines on your little ship, the *Breitenfeld*," Wexil said, "recorded fluctuations in the fabric of the quantum space with each jump. These fluctuations, while slight, could lead to a subspace rift, a rift that would tear space apart at the quantum level and expand at the speed of light. We lack the technology to repair a catastrophe of that magnitude. Even one rift would eventually annihilate all matter in the galaxy, stopping only at the edge of the dark-matter halo."

"I've reviewed that math," Stacey said, her mouth dry as fear crept up her chest. "The chances are miniscule when used in conjunction with a Crucible, even an unfinished one like that near Earth. We're more likely to encounter a naturally forming rift as a matter of quantum flux—and we'd have to wait several times the known age of the universe for that to happen—than if ships come through the Crucible. Your concerns are unfounded."

Wexil swept his hand across his chest and a dark filter passed over the vast majority of Alliance space. Only six inhabited star systems were unaffected, all centered on Earth.

"These are the only star systems that can reach Earth without risking a rupture," Wexil said. "While the individual risk is low with each jump, sending hundreds of ships to Earth's defense creates an ever-growing probability of disaster. Once the Crucible is complete and we fully understand its capabilities, it should allow risk-free access to the entire Alliance, but until that day…"

Wexil looked at her and sneered. "Perhaps an analogy you might understand, Ambassador Ibarra. One of your ground cars on a highway in a major city has little risk of an accident. Put many more cars on that highway and there will be an accident most every day. And it takes only one such accident to destroy everything."

"Then only those fleets within range can assist," Stacey snapped, unable to come up with a valid argument against the logic Wexil presented. She turned her attention back to the assembly. "Is this Alliance going to let the Toth seize the

Crucible? Do you think they will use it to defeat the Xaros or raid your worlds?"

A pod carrying a young man who looked barely older than sixteen floated level with Stacey and Wexil.

"Ambassador Shinx of the Gan," the Qa'Resh intoned.

"The Gan home world lies near Toth space," the boy said without fanfare. Not every Alliance species cared for the pleasantries of politics. "Hours before my scheduled return to Bastion, a small Toth ship arrived at the edge of my system and self-destructed once it delivered this message."

A Toth elite in an ornate tank appeared in the holo field above Stacey's head. A disembodied nervous system floated in pale pink liquid as strands of tiny bubbles shimmied through the liquid.

"Worlds of the Alliance," the words came out mechanical, translated by a machine without inflection or emotion, "I am Chairman Ranik of the Tellani Corporation. We desire the meat species on planet Earth. We will have them. The system remains yours. Their meat will satisfy us. Interfere and we will find sustenance from the rest of you." The message repeated twice before the hologram blinked away.

Wexil's pod rose above Stacey. "The gift we gave the humans to repopulate is fortuitous. The Toth will have a nigh-unlimited food source, and another threat to our Alliance will be neutralized."

"You would feed us to the Toth as a matter of convenience?" Stacey jabbed her control station and brought her pod level with Wexil. Were it not that Bastion kept all the ambassadors separated by force fields, she would have launched herself into the Vishrakath's pod and strangled him.

Wexil looked at Stacey with indifference, then turned his chin up.

"The human request has been decided," he said. "I motion to move on to further business until an alternate course of action is proposed."

Stacey screamed, but her words remained trapped in her pod as votes tallied in the air.

CHAPTER 6

As Hale swiped pages aside in a thick binder, he glanced up from his assigned reading to scan around the *Breitenfeld*'s library. Bookshelves bolted against the deck with bars across the shelves stretched from floor to ceiling around the metal table where he sat.

The need for physical books was almost an anachronism in the modern age, when every scanned piece of human learning was available to anyone with a li-fi connection to the Internet, but with the rampant use of malware and electronic warfare from Chinese and other nations—and now the Xaros—the Atlantic Union military took no chances, refusing to rely on databases that could provide a digital attack vector.

"Are you skimming again?" a woman's voice came from deep within the stacks.

"No." Hale flipped the pages back. "I still don't understand why you want me to read about what *I* experienced with the Toth."

"Because," Lowenn said, stepping around the corner of a stack, holding a pile of binders against her stomach, "several scholars on Bastion added notes to your account. Don't think you're the first one to ever deal with them." With her loose hair and thick-rimmed glasses, Lowenn looked every inch a librarian.

"This is pointless," Hale said as Lowenn dropped the binders on the table. "We know what the Toth want: the proccies. Done. Let me get back to my Marines."

"No, Ken, it's not enough to know what they want. You need to understand why they want it," Lowenn said. She pulled out a chair and sat across from him. "I admit that alien psychology and sociology are a new field of study for me, but the answers are there."

"The Toth elites, the ones in the tanks, they need to...consume nervous energy to stay alive,"

Hale said.

"It's more than just food for them," she said. "Whoever designed their tanks hacked into the pleasure centers of the Toth's brains. Every time an elite feeds, it gets high. The greater the neural energy, the bigger the high."

"That's why they targeted the Karigole. They were long-lived...better eating," Hale said. "I tried to ask Steuben about this, but he gets all kinds of pissed off when anyone mentions the Toth. Can't say I blame him."

"He promised to rip my face off if I asked him about the Toth a second time," Lowenn said.

"Me too. Those exact words," Hale said with a nod.

"The Toth elites," Lowenn said, picking through the stack of folders, "can get by with eating the warriors and the menials we've encountered, but their addiction to newer, more varied sources of neural energy doesn't have any known treatment. The Alliance sent a probe to the Toth home world centuries ago and found them on the verge of extinction because the elites were going through the rest of the population faster than they could breed."

She teased out a thin folder and opened it. "Here we are. Progress reports from the probe showing how it found a way to clone the Toth and caused a population explosion." She slid the folder to Hale, showing an exponential growth chart with smaller dark bars that levelled off with time.

"The darker bars…that's how many elites there are?" Hale asked.

"See, I knew you weren't that dense," Lowenn said with a smile. "Seems the Toth got their act together and limited how many elites their society would have, but those that were in the tanks weren't satisfied with eating just their own kind."

"How could the Alliance go along with this? The Toth are cannibals. Those ambassadors on Bastion wanted…this?"

"Don't judge another species by our standards. Moral relativism fails whenever we apply it to something with a completely different biology and history. As for Bastion, it seems that the Toth were incorporated into the Alliance before there was such a thing as Bastion."

"I don't follow," Hale said.

"The records I received are incomplete, but there are several references to someplace called Communion. It disappears from the official narrative right around the same time the Toth betrayed the Karigole," Lowenn said. "Then Bastion enters the scene."

"Right, another intergalactic mystery for another time. I still don't know why I'm learning any of this," Hale said.

"Because, Ken, you've…you've never dealt with an addict before, have you?"

"I had an aunt. She overdosed on heroin before I was born. Other than that, no."

"Addicts, you can't reason with them," Lowenn said. "They are trapped by whatever their brain is screaming at them to get. Booze, gambling, opiates, whatever. The procedural technology that Ibarra's using, apparently it can produce a fully grown human with a lifetime of memories in less than two weeks. If the Toth get ahold of this, they'll have a virtually unlimited, variable fix to their addiction."

"The difference between living off nutrient paste or eating real food," Hale said. The last month the *Breitenfeld* spent waiting for its jump engines to recharge after the retreat from Takeni was spent on emergency rations—nothing but combat paste to eat and water to drink. He and his Marines were used to austere living, but the navy had a reputation for fine dining. The *Breitenfeld's* sailors had complained about the eating situation loudly, constantly, and with enough colorful metaphors to make even the saltiest old chief blush.

"Now do you get it?" Lowenn asked. "Now do you understand why the Toth are here? This isn't some sort of trade delegation."

"The weapons on their battle cruisers told me as much," Hale said.

"OK, let's talk about Toth corporate structure."

Hale groaned and opened another binder.

****

Lieutenant Durand snapped the tip of a pointer stick against an exploded wire diagram of an Eagle fighter. A ready room full of pilots watched their commander as she moved the tip from place to place on the diagram.

"The new vectored engines have a twelve percent increase in thrust-to-mass ratio. Combine this with the upgrades to the maneuver thrusters and our new birds can outrun, and out dance, what we're used to." Durand waggled the pointer stick in the air. "The new specs are loaded into the simulators, so I want everyone to log no less than nine hours per day. If you're scoring less than ninety percent on the graded runs, I'm upping your time to twelve hours."

Pilots shifted in their seats, but none dared voice a complaint.

"Your first dogfight with the Toth, if it comes to that, is not the time or place to realize your Eagle flies like a bronco with a poker up its ass," Durand said.

"Why don't we just use Dotok fighters? They're superior to your Eagles even with the upgrades," someone said from the front row. He was taller than most in the room, with thick strands of hair bound into a ponytail. He wore the same flight suit as the rest of the squadron, but his sallow gray skin and blunted beak marked him as an alien Dotok.

"Thank you, Lothar," Durand said, calling the Dotok by his call sign. "Remember what we said about waiting to speak until called on?"

"You didn't answer the question," said a second Dotok, almost a carbon copy of Lothar but a good foot shorter.

"Same point, Manfred, wait until you're called on," Durand said to the second Dotok.

"You didn't even let us bring our own fighters from the *Canticle of Reason*," Lothar said. "Now my brother and I have to fly your human ships that handle like rickety kites."

Durand breathed through clenched teeth. It had been Captain Valdar's idea to incorporate

Dotok pilots into her squadron while the *Breitenfeld* and the *Canticle of Reason* sat in space in orbit around a brown dwarf, waiting months for the jump drive engines to recharge. Her squadron had lost too many pilots, and the Dotok had too many pilots for their few remaining fighters.

Durand had had a few cultural misunderstandings while in the Atlantic Union fleet. Her French heritage hadn't always meshed perfectly with the mores of other member nations. Dealing with the Dotok brothers had found the limits of her patience on more than one occasion.

"Because—as I've told you many times—Squadron Leader Bar'en needs every Dotok fighter plane for his unit, and the chance of fratricide is greatly reduced if we're all in the same type of fighter," Durand said.

Manfred's and Lothar's heads jiggled slightly, a Dotok gesture for annoyance.

"In other news," Durand said, "the hot water heater for the showers are still down." Groans came from the pilots. "Except for the stalls on deck twelve, and I have one hot shower chit. Whoever scores the highest number of kills on today's sims gets it. Get to your holo pods and show me who wants it the most."

****

Durand pulled a tray from a slot in the mess hall dispenser and looked around for her pilots. A table full of black jumpsuits stood out from the mass of sailors clad in deep blue and Marines in green camo.

Her pilots had kept a seat open for her in the middle of the table. The men, women and the Dotok brothers barely acknowledged her with more than a nod as she joined them; all were focused on eating.

"It's real," Mei "Glue" Ma said as she slurped down a noodle from a steaming bowl of reddish-brown soup and shoveled more into her mouth with chopsticks. "It has to be real," she said with her mouth full.

"Still reconstructed, soy-fortified with vitamins and minerals," said a pilot named Landas as he bit into a bacon cheeseburger and closed his

132

eyes. "But at least it's not nutrient paste."

Durand slid a plastic lid off her plate and smelled wine and spices of beef bourguignon. She dabbed the tip of her spoon into the sauce and tasted it.

"It isn't chalky, for once," she said. The first bite tasted like something she could have ordered at a restaurant in Brettone.

"I think they upgraded the dispensers," said Choi "Filly" Ma.

"Who needs better Eagles when we can have chow like this?" Landas asked. "I'll fight harder just to come back to this goodness."

The crack of a shell cut across the table. Manfred, sitting shoulder to shoulder with Lothar, crunched down with his thick beak, shattering whatever was in his mouth. Two bowls sat before the Dotok brothers, one containing a pile of dark-skinned nuts, the other full of pulverized shells. Manfred leaned over the bowl of broken shells and spat out fragments with a quick shake of his head.

The human pilots stopped eating, their eyes

on the Dotok.

"Manfred…" Durand said.

Lothar popped a nut into his mouth and broke the shell with a loud snap.

"Lothar!" Durand snapped.

"What?" Manfred asked. "Isn't cracking how you compliment the chef? These are the best *kushny* nuts I've had in years."

"The chef is a 3-D printer, not a person, and it doesn't need your compliments," Durand said.

Lothar's jaw clamped down, with much less noise.

"Thank you," Durand said.

"Durand called Gall," Manfred said, "what are…'proccies'?"

Durand suddenly lost her appetite.

"Yeah," Landas said, "we've been meaning to ask you about that." Other pilots nodded.

Durand sighed and unscrewed the cap on a small bottle of alcohol-free red wine. "What have you all heard?"

"While we were gone," Filly's voice

dropped to a conspiratorial whisper, "Ibarra came up with some way to make…people—with memories and everything, but none of them know what they are, and there's no way to tell them apart from the rest of us."

"First off," Durand looked each of the pilots in the eye, "none of you are proccies."

"Told you we had nothing to worry about," Manfred said to Lothar.

"Captain Valdar knows about it, and there's been some issues on Earth because of this," Durand said.

"I heard the Toth are here because of them," Glue said.

"We'll know exactly what the Toth want when we get to Europa," Durand said. Pilots shifted in their seats and looked over their shoulders at the sailors and Marines around them. The aviation wing on the *Breitenfeld* had always been insular, a step apart from the rest of the ship. She could sense where this conversation was heading.

Better strangle this monster in its crib, she

135

thought.

"But let me tell you all something." Durand pointed at Glue. "*She* tried to shoot me down when she was flying for the Chinese." Glue shrugged her shoulders as her two cousins looked away from Durand in embarrassment. Durand pointed fingers at the Dotok brothers. "You two were sent to goad me into alcoholism."

"Bar'en said we were supposed to teach you hairless apes how to fly," Lothar said.

Durand's hand squeezed into a fist.

"Despite all of this, I am still honored to have you all on my wing," Durand said, "and I will shed my last drop of blood for each and every one of you." Durand looked to each side of the table, letting all the pilots know they were included in her pronouncement. "I wouldn't care if any of you were proccies, so long as you could do your damn jobs and fly like aces."

Durand took a plastic chip from her pocket and slid it toward Manfred.

"Manfred earned our one and only hot

136

shower for the week with six kills in the sims," Durand said. She hoped the misdirection would end the proccie discussion. Captain Valdar had told her and the other section chiefs more, but she was ordered to keep that knowledge confidential.

Manfred pocketed the chip with a shrug.

"But, Durand called Gall, you said each time we fragged you in the sims was worth two kills," Manfred said. "Shouldn't my score be ten?"

"Shut up and eat your nuts, Manfred."

"Yes, ma'am."

CHAPTER 7

Jupiter loomed through the windows of the *Breitenfeld*'s bridge. Valdar, strapped into his command chair at the center of the bridge, watched as the gas giant grew larger as the ship came out of its acceleration.

"Alcubierre drive powered down," said Ensign Geller, the ship's navigator. "Switching to thrusters in thirty seconds."

"Gunnery," Valdar said, pointing to Lieutenant Commander Utrecht seated to his right, "we have visual on the Toth ship?"

"Aye-aye, Captain. One cruiser analog in orbit around Europa," Utrecht said. "Nothing else on the scope or from the spotters."

"Comms, send an IR pulse to Titan Station. Tell them we've arrived without incident and will begin negotiations directly," Valdar said.

The *Breitenfeld* rumbled as the thruster banks came to life. Void ships always felt more alive to Valdar when they ran under their own propulsion. His ship felt like a hunting dog pulling against her leash, eager for the chance to do what instinct and design demanded.

"Sir, we have video feed on the Toth ship," Utrecht said.

"Show me." Valdar pulled up a screen from the arm of his command chair and brought it to life with a tap. The Toth ship was long and thick, its pearl-white hull warping the sun's reflection into a wavy line. Toth fighters, shaped like serrated daggers, flew around the cruiser in groups of three.

Europa, a ball of ice riven with cracks and uneven plains from Jupiter's punishing gravity, mirrored the Toth ship's flawed beauty.

"Same size as the one we saw on Anthalas," Utrecht said.

"And that one had teeth," Valdar said.

"Their laser weapons are tough, but their effective range is limited compared to our rail batteries," said Ericsson, the ship's executive officer. "The amount of particulates in and around the Jovian system should cut that range even further."

"Find us an anchorage over Europa at the outer edge of Mule range," Valdar said. He craned his neck to look over his shoulder at Hale, seated beside the holo table behind Valdar. "Don't worry, Lieutenant. We'll be close enough to get you out if diplomacy falls through."

"This ship and everyone on it is more important than me and my two allowed bodyguards," Hale said.

"No one gets left behind," Valdar said. "Not to the Xaros. Not to the Toth. Not on my watch."

"Sir," said Ensign Erdahl as he spun around in his work pod, "the Toth are hailing us. Audio only."

"Patch them through," Valdar said.

"Thieves..." came over the speakers in a deep baritone, "thief ship from Anthalas. Bright-enfeld. Did you bring what you took from us?"

Valdar touched his data screen and opened a private channel to Hale. "Time to earn your paycheck, Ken."

Hale got out of his seat and cleared his throat.

"Anthalas is in unclaimed space. No Toth corporation or human organization of equivalent legitimacy announced ownership of anything within the…" Hale looked down at his forearm screen "effective gravity well of Anthalas or its satellite. What we took is by right of salvage. Which Toth insults us?" Hale asked.

"Our names are not for meat."

"I demand standing as *bealor*. I killed your thralls with my hand and wiped their blood on the doors of my corporation. You will address me as an equal," the Marine said.

"Hale…you are the Hale," the Toth said.

Hale's eyebrows perked up and his pulse quickened. The speech Lowenn prepared for him was actually working as intended.

"Correct, now who addresses me so that my

time isn't being wasted with an underling," Hale said.

"I am Kren, of the Tellani Corporation and immortal of the Toth."

Only the elites, whose nervous systems had survived for hundreds or thousands of years inside the tanks, referred to themselves as "immortal."

"Kren, you have come to my domain and rendered insult," Hale said. "You will await me for…one-tenth of Europa rotation at the summit site."

"My apologies to the *baelor*," the Toth said.

"One-fifth a rotation," Hale said. He waved his hand in front of his neck in a cutting motion and Ensign Erdahl ended the transmission.

"Is it wise to make him wait?" Valdar asked.

"We're supposed to buy time. I bought us another seventeen hours before the negotiations even start," Hale said. "We're lucky he apologized to me. It gave me a reason to make his punishment even worse."

"I don't follow," Valdar said.

"A Toth apology is always disrespectful," Hale said. "I'll look weak if I don't try to slap him around a little bit."

"I'm with you on this mission, Hale," Valdar said, "but if you piss that thing off, it'll be awhile before I can pull your feet out of the fire."

****

Kren's tank bubbled with anger. Tendrils attached to his thick spinal column quivered as the tank twisted from side to side on its six-armed palanquin. The Toth warriors and menials manning the bridge's workstations cowered, knowing full well that one of them would pay for their master's disquiet.

"You were foolish to antagonize them." Olux appeared on a wall screen. "You've cost us progress."

"Would you have me ignore the *haelor*? Doctor Mentiq maintains our code of conduct. The price for breaking his laws is severe," Kren said.

"I do not criticize your adherence to tradition. I find your lack of foresight disappointing.

The humans have Karigole pets and access to their Alliance. You should have anticipated their sole *baelor* would come to parlay and acted accordingly," Olux said. "I still question why Chairman Ranik sent you on this expedition."

"The discovery of the humans and their weed bodies was mine. This position is my right!" Kren pointed his feeder arm at a menial. The creature scampered to Kren and lowered its head.

Kren stabbed the feeder arm into the menial's skull with a crunch. Mono-filament tendrils snaked through the menial's brain as it convulsed, its claws skittering against the deck. Kren felt a fleeting moment of euphoria, then flung the dead menial against a bulkhead.

"Regardless," Olux said, "if you can obtain the human's technology without further expense, Dr. Mentiq will be most impressed. If these negotiations fail, then Stix and the *Leverage* had best succeed…for your sake."

Olux's screen switched off.

Kren spun around on his palanquin and

pointed a claw-tipped leg at an armored warrior guarding the turbolift doors. "Prepare my shuttle," he said, snapping the claw toward the dead menial, "and replace the bridge crew with fresh menials. That one tasted stale."

****

The Mule trembled as it cut into the thin Europan atmosphere. Hale leaned against the acceleration seat and tapped the back of his head against the cushion. This wasn't a combat drop, but the familiar press of maneuver gravities, the rumble of the ship's engines and the whine of the gauss turrets through the gunner's open IR channels were all the same.

He felt the ice-water shock of adrenaline spread through his limbs and his heart pound in his ears as his autonomous nervous system prepped him for battle.

"Just a discussion," he muttered.

"What was that, sir?" Standish asked from the dorsal gauss turret.

"Nothing. Nothing. You have eyes on the

landing zone?" Hale asked.

"I've got eyes on a whole lot of ice and some more ice. Wait…nope, that's just ice," Standish said through the Mule's IR network.

"Sir," Orozco said from the ventral turret, "you sure it's a good idea for *you* to be doing this? Don't the Toth remember you from Anthalas?"

"It's a curse and a blessing, Orozco."

"I'd really appreciate it if you'd not mention that I'm out here too," the Spaniard said. "I offed a couple of those lizards when we escaped from their ship. Don't want any of them to come looking for me because I killed their father and now I have to die. Anything like that."

"You really think that brain in a box is going to tell the L-T it wants a significant percentage of the human population…and the head of Orozco the Slayer?" Standish asked.

"Hey, maybe they hold grudges. I do," Orozco said.

"The Toth—from what I understand—don't really care about the menials or the warriors. Only the ones in the tanks have any kind of pull in their culture," Hale said.

"I've got visual on the facility," came from the pilot. "Prep the armor for drop."

"Roger." Hale released his harness and got to his feet. A pair of yellow handles connected to cargo runners flanking each suit of armor. Hale knelt next to the end of a folded block of armor and mag-locked his feet and knees against the deck.

"Elias, Kallen, you ready?" Hale asked.

"Always ready," Elias said.

The Mule's crew chief mirrored Hale's position at the head of Kallen's armor and grabbed one of the yellow handles.

"They're linked," the crew chief said. "Give my suit a five-count head start when we hit zero-zero."

Hale flashed a thumbs-up.

The pilot opened his channel, and a green light appeared next to his name a full second before he said, "Stand by for zero-zero...mark." Maneuver thrusters flared from the Mule's forward hull and

Hale swayed forward with momentum. The rear hatch lowered, revealing the icy expanse of Europa's horizon.

Hale felt a chill creep through his armor, even though he knew it was all a trick of his mind.

The Mule went nose up, pointing its open cargo bay directly to the moon's surface. A zero-zero maneuver meant the ship had found equilibrium with a ground target, zero relative speed up or down, nor side to side.

The crew chief pulled the handle and it snapped from the cargo runners. Kallen's armor slid loose and accelerated down the rails. She flew free of the Mule and unfolded her armor in midair as she floated toward Europa, pulled by gravity barely a seventh as strong as Earth's.

Hale snapped the handle and released Elias. The armor soldier followed Kallen down.

"Good luck, sir," Standish said. "Wish I could go with you."

"No you don't," Orozco said.

"You mind? I'm trying to make him feel

148

better."

"I'm loose." Hale disengaged his magnetic locks and pushed against the deck. He floated through the open cargo bay and finally saw Europa in all its glory. Sunlight glared off the icy crust, the glacier-like surface broken up by dark striations of *linae* and deep-blue patches of compacted ice.

A dome the color of fresh concrete, its perfect symmetry betraying its unnatural origins, stuck out from the surface. Hunks of ice crept along the edges. Hale saw several bright-orange robots working along the ice line, pushing back decades of Europa's attempt to subsume the structure.

"Landing zone is clear," Elias said.

"Any sign of the Toth?" Hale activated the anti-gravity linings in his boots, accelerating him toward the surface where he saw Elias and Kallen approaching the dome.

"Saw some thruster scorching against the ice on the other side of the dome," Kallen said. "Has to be them."

Hale swung his feet toward the surface and

let his arms float above his head. He reached for his rifle and grasped nothing. He pawed at his back again, then remembered that he'd left the gauss rifle behind. Showing up armed for a battle wasn't diplomatic by human or Toth standards.

He made tiny corrections with his anti-grav linings and slowed his downward momentum. His feet struck the ground without a sound; Europa's atmosphere was far too thin to carry noise. The Mule soared overhead, waggling its wings as it flew back to a rendezvous point where Eagle fighters waited to escort them all back to the *Breitenfeld*.

Jupiter, half-hidden in shadow, hung large in the sky. Its roiling bands of clouds looked almost hostile to Hale.

"I know it's pretty," Kallen said, "but the rad linings in our suits are good for only so long." The radiation coming from Jupiter, combined with Europa's lack of protective atmosphere or magnetic field, could kill an unshielded human being in less than a day. Hale's armor could keep him safe for a time, but no one liked the idea of sitting around in the open.

"Coming," Hale bent his legs and leaped toward the two armor soldiers. Hale had plenty of practice moving across the lunar surface, and Europa's gravity felt nearly the same. He bounded toward the dome, with much less efficiency and grace than Elias and Kallen.

"I'm surprised this place survived for so long," Kallen said. "Thought the Xaros would have picked it clean like everywhere else in the solar system."

"Ibarra closed down ops on Jupiter when the Chinese took Mars," Elias said. "Made it too expensive to keep things going. Looks like he had the place covered in ice to hide it. Could be why the Xaros missed it."

"Or," Hale huffed as he stretched out his stride, "Ibarra wanted to keep something else hidden from the Xaros."

"You think he's got more squirrelled away somewhere?" Kallen asked.

"Would it surprise you if he did?" Hale

asked.

"No. I trust that guy about as far as I can throw him…when I have my armor off," she said. Kallen, a quadriplegic since childhood, could do little more than turn her head from side to side when out of her armor.

"What is this place anyway?" Elias asked. He slid next to the edge of the dome and knocked it with his armored knuckles. A yellow arrow flashed to life, pointing to his left. Lines of light cut through the surface of the dome, forming a set of double doors.

"It was supposed to be a quadrium mining facility," Hale said. "Europa's got more water than Earth beneath all this ice. Lots of quadrium shells to shoot at the Xaros. Don't really need this place now that we've got—" He stopped before he could mention the omnium reactor they'd recovered from Anthalas. Speaking about that while the Toth were nearby struck him as foolhardy.

The doors flush with the surface of the dome opened, sliding aside and revealing an airlock with plenty of room for both armor soldiers and Hale.

Hale tried to bound inside first and nearly ran into Elias as the soldier stepped in front of him.

"What're you doing, crunchy?" Elias asked. "You're the VIP. We're the muscle. Let's act like it."

Hale let Elias enter the airlock and stood between the two soldiers as the doors closed behind them. Hale felt like a child, flanked by suits of armor almost twice his height, as if he was about to see a doctor for a bunch of shots.

The doors closed and red lights warbled around them. Jets of air blew into the chamber, re-pressurizing it to the point that Hale could hear the hiss out of the nozzles.

"Remember," Elias said, "you give us the signal and we'll start shooting."

"Let's hope it doesn't come to that," Hale said. "We're a long way from the *Breitenfeld*." His hand brushed across the gauss pistol and holster mag-locked to his chest. It wasn't much in the way of a self-defense weapon, not against the big Toth warriors, but it was better than nothing.

The lights switched to green. The inner doors opened slowly, and gentle white light flooded into the airlock. Elias raised his arm slightly. The *click-clack* of gauss rounds chambering into the double-barreled cannon attached to his forearm brought a sibilant growl from beyond the airlock.

"This was not the retinue we agreed," Kren said, his voice amplified by speakers.

Elias stepped to the side and Hale strode into the chamber, a wide space of bare concrete and gleaming white walls. Square, plain columns ran from floor to ceiling every few dozen yards.

In the center of the room, the Toth elite was flanked by two crystalline armored warriors, but holding rifles that looked like they were made of metal vines twisted into the shape of a weapon. A single rectangular table with a stool stood between the Toth and humans.

"You agreed to two bodyguards, did you not?" Hale asked as he took a careful step over the threshold. Earth-normal gravity greeted him as he made his way to the table.

"I didn't anticipate you'd bring...those," Kren said.

"I'm not responsible for your assumptions," Hale said. "Would you like to go back to your ship and fetch two of those little ones you have crawling all over the place? I can come back with Marines more my size, but it'll take me some time to pick the right ones."

Kallen and Elias followed Hale, joints whirring as they stomped the ground.

Hale had rehearsed this little ploy with the two armor soldiers several times. A little theater could go a long way in negotiations, and the soldiers could back up the bluster.

"No. No need," Kren said. "I bring you a gift. A sample of the wealth I have to offer."

A warrior hefted a black metal case onto the table and unfastened a pair of latches with flicks of its claws. The front of the case fell open and gold coins cascaded across the table. Hale picked one and examined it—a lion on one side, a seated man holding a long-necked bird on the other.

"Is this all?" Hale asked. Insulting a gift, or even accepting one while on official duty, grated against his sensibilities and training, but the Toth had a certain set of expectations. They obviously weren't familiar with how humans expected to carry out diplomacy, the first rule being not to show up at the doorstep with an invasion fleet.

A warrior clicked a switch on the case and the coins flew back inside and into neat stacks. It shut the case and pushed it toward Hale.

Hale waved his hand at Kallen and she scooped the case up.

"May we begin?" Kren asked.

Hale grasped his helmet and twisted it to the side. It came off with a puff of air and Hale breathed in chill, stale air. He put his helmet on the table, and sat down.

****

Durand shifted in her cockpit. A quick glance at a mission clock showed she'd been motionless in space for an insufferably long fifteen minutes. The Mule that had dropped Hale on the surface had only just linked up with her and three other Eagles. They'd all wait in geosynchronous orbit over Europa until Hale signaled his extraction...or the Toth made a move.

She squinted her eyes and scanned over Europa's horizon, looking for the glint of silver from the Toth ships serving the same purpose as she and the human ships. Everything, thus far, about these negotiations had been equal. Same number of ambassadors, bodyguards, escort ships...everything except the number of ships in the human and Toth fleets.

Few ships survived the assault on Ceres unscathed. Even with a few months of repairs, Durand didn't know how they could beat the larger Toth fleet if it came to a war.

Bad enough to fight the Xaros...now the Toth, she thought.

A chill went up her spine as she remembered being held captive by the Toth elite and seeing it murder her pilots right in front of her.

"Gall?" Manfred's question snapped her out of the bad memory.

"Go."

"My brother and I, we still don't understand why you call us Manfred and Lothar. These words aren't in the Dotok-English dictionary," Manfred said.

"I told you, it's part tradition and part necessity. Not every pilot has a name that short and easy to say over the radio. Plus, it kept the enemy from learning true names if they listened to radio chatter. So...call signs," Durand said.

"Yes...quaint," Lothar said. "But why am I 'Lothar'?"

Glue joined the conversation, her voice clipped and angry "I told you both—it is arbitrary and not at all fair or relevant."

"You two are brothers," Durand said. "The younger one is taller. You're both...decent pilots. Manfred does better in sims. Your call signs fit you perfectly."

"And this connects to pilots from human

158

history?" Manfred asked.

"Yes. Every human fighter pilot knows Manfred von Richthofen. Isn't that right, Glue?"

"I grew up in China, not under a rock," she said.

"See," Durand said.

"And my namesake was famous for his red plane?" Manfred asked.

"More for the eighty planes he shot down, but the plane was why they called him the Red Baron," Gall said.

"What did they call Lothar? The green arrow? A red blade?" Lothar asked.

"He was always just the Red Baron's brother," Gall admitted.

A *kek-kek-kek* sound of Dotok laughter from Manfred mixed with Dotok speech from Lothar that Durand couldn't understand, but was sure were an impressive series of insults directed at his brother.

"I told you it isn't fair," Glue said with a pout.

"So what're we supposed to do out here?"

Lothar asked.

"We hurried up to get here," Durand said, "now we wait."

****

Hale's hands balled into fists.

"Absolutely not," he said with a shake of his head.

"Perhaps I've not made this point clear," Kren said, the tips of his nerves quivering. "Our survival depends on new and varied sources of sustenance. We must have your proccies—as you call them—and the method of their creation."

"The proccies are not cattle, not livestock, for trade. They are human beings in the eyes of many of us."

"Many? Not all?" Kren said, his tank bending toward Hale.

"Humans have many dissimilar beliefs." Hale's mouth went dry as he chided himself for making such a foolish error. He'd just given the Toth information it hadn't needed, or asked for. "You'd be surprised how few of us can agree on something so simple as what to have for dinner."

"Curious that the Alliance would aid such a divisive species. Yet you managed to defeat the Xaros and capture one of their star gates. My knowledge of that event is convoluted. Perhaps you could tell me more?"

Your "knowledge"...you mean when you ripped the memories out of the brains of the humans you killed, Hale thought.

"We aren't here to discuss history," Hale said.

"No. The Toth offer humanity the following: Human space will be considered Toth territory, and we will provide military protection against the next Xaros incursion. In return you will turn over the means to create the proccies and ten percent of your adult population now, and one percent per Earth year as tithe. Also, you will demilitarize your navy and accept a permanent Toth military presence in orbit."

"Did you offer the Karigole the same?" Hale asked.

"We aren't here to discuss history," Kren said. "Several species on the fringe of Toth space have accepted protectorate status. All are thriving. The annual tithe is a convenient opportunity to remove undesirables and criminals from the populace."

Hale picked up his helmet and stood up from the table.

"What are you doing?" the Toth asked.

"I must take your offer to my superiors and communicate it to Earth," Hale said.

The clawed arms of the Toth palanquin squealed as they tore into the concrete floor.

"You aren't able to make a deal?" Kren asked.

"I can finalize whatever agreement we make, but the decisions will be made on Earth. Unfortunately, we're limited to light-speed communications and it will take at least two hours for me to get an answer to any question I send back. In a rush?"

A deep ululation came from the tank, just

like the Toth battle cry Hale'd heard on Anthalas. The hair on the back of his neck stood on end as the two warriors joined in the predator's call.

"You think my patience has limits?" Kren asked.

"You are guests in our solar system," Hale said. "Behave yourselves or you'll see just what our allies have waiting just beyond the Crucible," Hale said. "The Dotok battleship is the tip of the spear."

A trickle of sweat ran down Hale's back. He slid his helmet over his head before the Toth could notice a flaw in his poker face. So long as the Toth stayed far enough from the *Canticle of Reason*, the bluff might hold.

"I will return in eighteen hours," Hale said. "Don't be late."

CHAPTER 8

Stacey stepped up to a large arched doorway and waited for it to open. She stepped back and forth from the door, then waved a hand up at the sensor at the top of the arch.

"Are you kidding me? Chuck, where is Ambassador Wexil?"

"Ambassador Wexil is in his quarters," Bastion's AI said.

"Does he know I'm standing out here waiting for him?"

"He is aware but has declined to allow your entry."

Stacey banged her fist against the door until it slid aside. Bars lined a long oval room. The dark metal segments were of uneven lengths, attached to each other without a discernable pattern or regard for symmetry, like a web spun by an insane spider.

Wexil floated near the ceiling on the far end, his human illusion incapable of mimicking whatever position his true form used to perch on the wire frame. Some alliance species were not humanoid. She'd seen their human illusions floating through hallways while others had a buffer space around their immense forms.

Wexil waved his hand across a holo projection in front of his face, not paying any attention to Stacey.

"You want to explain your game, Wexil?" Stacey asked.

"Whatever do you mean, Ambassador Ibarra?" Wexil cast the projection aside with a flick of his hand and floated to the ground.

"I've been to the Gann, Aelnolli and Enuur ambassadors—all the species that could send reinforcements to Earth without risking a quantum tear," Stacey said. "They all said they can't help me."

"All are in the path of the Xaros tendril maniple that scoured Earth several decades ago.

They're wise to conserve their forces," Wexil said.

"The leading edge of that maniple won't reach Enuur space for ten years. Ten years! I need a couple ships to come through the Crucible to convince the Toth that Earth isn't worth the price they'd pay to take the proccie technology." Stacey's fists pressed against her thighs. "You know what every one of those ambassadors also told me? They said *you'd* come to see them first. Don't tell me it's a coincidence."

"No, certainly not. Little Miss Ibarra, you're new here. I've been an ambassador for seven hundred years. I have built relationships with the others that you can't fathom. Not since the Toth betrayal has a single species been as decisive as humanity." Wexil shook his head. "You would have been just another fringe group of barbarians erased by the Xaros, but we had the chance to get our hands on a Xaros jump gate. Pa'lon, your Dotok friend, convinced the rest of us to take a chance on you all, and despite my opposition and mathematical probability, it worked.

"We have a nearly complete Xaros gate, and we can complete its construction with the omnium reactor from Anthalas. We truly live in exciting times."

"The gate, the reactor, all bought with human blood," Stacey said. "My people are on the verge of extinction because of this plan, yet we fight your battles and are a part of this Alliance. Why are you so determined to let the Toth finish the job the Xaros started?"

Wexil reached out to the cage and seemed to swim up the wall.

"You can't be trusted—that's why. That Valdar character ran off to help the Dotok against the Congress' decision," he said.

"The Qa'Resh overrode that decision!"

"That was not their right. The Qa'Resh are many things, but they are not our masters. I hoped the rescue mission would have failed, showing the wisdom of the Congress to those who'd let foolish notions threaten the survival of all, but, the *Breitenfeld* prevailed." He scowled at her and swung across the other side of the room.

Unease crept into Stacey's limbs. She had no idea what his true form was, but she suspected it would make quick work of her if he chose.

"The Toth were our greatest mistake. We brought them back from the brink of extinction and gave them the tools to thrive, ignoring their…eccentricities. We almost repeated that mistake with you. Humanity will be brought to heel. The Toth will have their treats and we will remold your people as proper soldiers and servants to the Alliance," he said.

"We will never be slaves!"

"I find your presence tiresome. Save your strength for the next Congress when we decide your fate." He looked to the ceiling. "Bastion, remove her."

Stacey rose an inch off the ground and an invisible force swept her out of the Vishrakath quarters. She stumbled into the hallway as the doors snapped shut behind her.

Stacey stayed in the middle of the hallway,

heedless of the stares and whispered comments of ambassadors filing past her.

I'm failing, she thought. *What little we have left is being swept away, and there's nothing I can do to stop it.*

****

Hale sat with Valdar in the captain's ready room. Hale still wore his armor, which wasn't designed to take advantage of comfort. Hale scooted to the edge of the chair, trying to shift the spare magazines and equipment on his belt from sticking into his lower back.

"They're crazy," Valdar said. "What makes them think we'd ever throw open the gates and welcome occupiers?"

"Greed. Maybe they think they're a lot stronger than us," Hale said.

"I'll send this back to Titan Station," Valdar said. "They'll send back not 'no,' but 'hell no.' Any observations I should include for the big brains back on Earth?" Valdar winced at his comment. If Hale thought it was a joke about the Toth elite's appearance, he didn't bother to laugh.

"The Toth…they're here for the proccies first and foremost. Anything else they can wring out of us seems like a bonus. Kren never mentioned the omnium reactor, the entity that possessed Yarrow. No interest in the Crucible or how we beat the Xaros."

Valdar leaned back and laced his fingers behind his head. "We've got some more time to play with. Just need to keep them talking."

"And if they figure out we're stalling?" Hale asked. "I still don't understand the point to this rope-a-dope."

"It's not if, but when, Ken," Valdar swallowed hard. "Things have to stay need-to-know with you…given the Toth capabilities. You're under a unique threat."

"No matter how you put it, it doesn't make me feel any better about having to sit within arm's distance of something that wants to eat…" Hale tapped his temple.

"Go. Get some chow. Sleep. I'll have

instructions from Earth before you're due back with the Toth."

Hale got up and left.

Valdar waited until the door shut behind his godson and pulled out the small box from Fournier. He pressed his thumb against the sensor and waited until a sleepy-looking Fournier appeared in the holo field.

"Captain," Fournier rubbed his eyes. "Sorry, bit early in Phoenix."

Valdar passed on everything Hale shared.

"Bold bunch of lizards, aren't they?" Fournier asked.

"It's the first round of talks," Valdar said.

"We want the Toth to get rid of the proccies. That's all. We need Hale to get an agreement signed in the next four days. My spies in Garret's office tell me they're making proccies as fast as they can to crew another fleet, one that's nearly twice the size of what we've got in space now. If Ibarra and Garret have that, they'll never agree to a settlement with the Toth."

"With that many ships we could probably win a stand-up fight," Valdar said. His eyes glanced at a data slate that showed projected travel time and routes for the Toth fleet to Earth. Delaying the negotiations for four days seemed possible but doubt about working with Fournier scratched at the back of his mind.

"That's why we need an agreement soon. Don't let those two think they could win if it comes to a fight," Fournier said. "Do you have any leads on a manifest?"

"I do." Valdar took a scrap of paper from his pocket. "In the boneyard, the warehouse where equipment recovered from ships destroyed in the battle above Ceres is kept, there's a lot with the personal effects from the *London's* captain. There should be a manifest in his safe. Every captain had a copy prior to the invasion…but we had to hand them in during the fleet's reorganization." Valdar read off the lot number.

"That's Ibarra's doing, keeping the truth hidden from the true born," Fournier said. "The manifest would be in a data rod, gene-locked to the *London's* captain. I thought she died in the battle."

"She did," Valdar said, "but Lawrence, the civilian head of the colony mission, could override the lock with his gene code."

"Yes." A smile spread across Fournier's face. "Yes, that would work. We could know exactly who the proccies are before the Toth get to our doorstep. I'll let you know once we have the manifest."

"I'll contact you once I know more," Valdar said.

"Same. Well done, Isaac. You are a hero to all true-born humans."

****

Stacey lay on her bed, curled into a fetal position. Her fingernails dug into her scalp as she tried and failed to process everything that had just happened in Congress. The Vishrakath plan. The passionate speech from Pa'lon decrying the vote. His praise of humanity for saving the Dotok population on Takeni. Everything else fell into a blur until the final vote, Wexil would have his way.

She hated herself for failing Earth like this. She was only twenty-two and trained in celestial mechanics and physics, not xeno-diplomacy. None of the rationalizations she'd come up with made her feel any better.

"Ambassador Pa'lon is here to see you," the station chimed.

"Send him away," she mumbled into her pillow. This was his third attempt to see her; she wasn't sure if the Dotok was stubborn or didn't know how to take a hint.

Stacey sobbed as she imagined breaking the news to her grandfather and the rest of the people on Earth. The tears grew stronger and she didn't stop them; it wasn't like anyone could see her.

"Stacey Ibarra," a woman's voice boomed through her quarters.

Stacey sat bolt upright. Her room had become a starless abyss, her bed the only piece of remaining furniture. The giant head and shoulders of the Qa'Resh that ran the Congress meetings hung in the air beyond the foot of her bed.

Stacey shrieked.

"Our apologies," the Qa'Resh said.

"For scaring the hell out of me or throwing my people under a bus?" Stacey asked. She ran a sleeve across her eyes. "You even know what a bus is?"

"We do. Humanity is in a difficult position, one we regret."

"Then why didn't you do something to stop it?" Stacey peered over the edge of her bed and into darkness.

"We are ancient. We are wise compared to many species, but we are few. We exist only on Qa'Resh'Ta," she said. Stacey nodded, having seen the great floating city within the clouds of the gas giant that Bastion orbited. "We cannot defeat the Xaros on our own. This Alliance is our galaxy's only chance at survival."

"So what if you have to sacrifice a few pawns along the way, right?"

"All intelligent life is precious to us," she

said as sadness swept across her face. "We saw your true nature when the Dotok were in danger. You are not monsters like the Toth, but your history of civil wars worries many in our Alliance. The parallels between you and the Toth are too many to ignore."

"What? Last time I checked humans don't have a habit of *eating* each other for fun and profit...not for a long time, anyway."

"You are fractious—violent toward each other up until the very moment we saved you from the Xaros, but you are not the Toth. Wexil's plan would destroy your spirit, the core of what drove you to save another species," the Qa'Resh said.

"If you came here to give me a pep talk, this isn't working. The Alliance wants me to go back to Earth and push the reset button on humanity," Stacey said.

"Only if you lose," the Qa'Resh said.

Stacey raised a finger, then an eyebrow.

"What're you getting at?"

"You will return to Earth with instructions for the probe that controls the Crucible, instructions

176

from the Congress," the Qa'Resh said. "We will…amend those instructions. Give you time to defeat the Toth, but you must keep this a secret between you and the Qa'Resh, if you can, then we will give you another gift."

"I'm listening," Stacey said.

The Qa'Resh laid out their plan.

****

Hale watched the ship's flight deck from his vantage point in a duct flush with the ceiling. Flight crews tended to Eagles and Condor bombers on ready alert. The pilots lounged nearby, dressed in their flight suits, ready to be wheels up in less than two minutes of any alert.

The sound of footsteps carried through the air vents. The ducts were designed to rid the flight deck of smoke from a crash or battle damage and were all large enough for a crouching adult to move through them easily.

Hale listened, sure the faint steps belonged to who he was waiting for, not Steuben, the only other person who know about his hideout, but, he reasoned, he wouldn't hear Steuben creeping up on him unless the Karigole warrior wanted to be heard.

Durand came around a corner and rolled her eyes when she saw Hale.

"*Vachement? Ici?*" she said in French.

"What?"

"You piss me off," she said. "You always piss me off. Couldn't we just meet at our old place?"

"The Cemetery's occupied. Elias is fused into his armor. We wouldn't have any privacy like we used to," Hale said.

"Whatever." Durand sat across from Hale and fished a beat-up pack of cigarettes from a pocket on her flight jacket. "I smell smoke. Are the sensor's down in here?"

Hale nodded. Durand pressed the tip of the cigarette against an induction patch on the bottom of the pack until it glowed red with burning embers. She took a long drag and exhaled smoke from her nose.

"You wanted to talk," she said. "Talk."

"Got you a little something." Hale reached into a pocket and handed Durand a gold coin. "A gift for me from the Toth. Whole case of them. We left most of it on the ice, figured Knight the intel squirrel would shit a brick if we brought the whole thing back on the ship. He was still pissed I brought up a couple coins, but he put them through the ringer and said they're nothing but 24-karat gold. Not a Toth listening device or some sort of bomb."

"They bribe you from the very beginning?" Durand ran her finger over the raised lion on one side of the coin.

"That's how they do business," Hale shrugged. "What do you think it's worth?"

"Maybe a month's pay before the invasion. Now it's worth jack squat. What good is gold? No one needs it...we don't even have an economy anymore. Ibarra's robots handle all the dirty work. Everyone's either focused on rebuilding Phoenix or still in uniform."

"Right, so why did Kren think we'd want this?"

"You're on a first-name basis with them now?"

Hale looked away. "Stop. It's not like I asked for this. I got the by name request for this assignment because I escaped from their ship. Makes me a *baelor* or something, some kind of honor feud or vendetta that Lowenn tried to explain."

"Do I have that too? I was right beside you when all that happened."

"Want me to ask?"

"Oh, God no. I have enough to deal with." Durand flipped the coin over. "I wonder why they used this design. Could have just given you a blank coin…but I doubt this is why you dragged me up here."

"I got instructions back from Earth," he said. Hale's jaw worked from side to side. "High command says I'm to give up the proccies. All the tech, too."

Durand held the cigarette to her side and flicked it.

"That can't be right. Don't they know what the Toth will do to them?" she asked.

"I tried to explain that to the captain, but...he said they're not human. We can't treat them like they are. He kept going on and on about how they're some sort of Ibarra plot to erase what's truly human...and it looks like Ibarra and Garret agree with him." Hale wrapped his arms around his chest and leaned back against the bulkhead.

"Do you agree with him?"

"I...one of my Marines is a proccie, Yarrow. Just a kid, but he's as brave as any man or woman I've ever met. He didn't take it well when I told him what he was," Hale said.

"Jorgen told me about a medic that dragged you off a mountain on Takeni, same guy?"

Hale nodded.

"Even knowing what he is," Hale said, "I don't...I don't feel like he's some kind of imposter, some 'inhuman abomination' like Uncle Isaac calls him. I just don't feel like this is the right thing to do."

181

"Maybe it's not," she said. "My grand uncle, Pierre—I don't think I ever told you about him—he lived in Marseille when the *daesh* took it over. He and his wife were poor, had nothing but the clothes on their backs and three children. One day the *daesh* knock on their door, tell them to pay *jizya*. He has no money, so they say they'll take his daughter as payment.

"This is when the Crusade was finally getting off the ground. Pierre knows he could give up his daughter, maybe find her again in a few months when the city is liberated, but he says no. 'My blood is not worth my honor,' he told the *daesh*. So, the *daesh* beat him to death, but they left his daughter, Alizee, behind.

"Was he pigheaded? Yes. Stupid? A little, but my family doesn't remember him for that. Other families, they gave up their daughters. They may have lived, but their hearts died the moment they chose a moment's safety over love."

"I liked my job a lot easier when I just had to kill aliens," Hale said.

"It's your own fault. No one asked you to get so famous. So what will you do?"

"I don't know."

CHAPTER 9

Air scrubbers rattled against their housing high over Hale's head. Condensation grew around the fine mesh covers, forming into drops of water that fell to the conference table.

A drop splashed against Hale's data slate. He wiped it aside with a flick of his finger and glared at the vent above his head.

"To be bothered by such things," Kren said, "how quaint." His tank rested on the concrete floor, the disembodied brain floating level with Hale's head.

"I doubt much of anything can bother you in your…condition," Hale said.

"Sometimes my fluid viscosity turns a bit too thick for my tastes, but the advantages to my ascension far, far outweigh everything I knew when I was imprisoned by flesh," the Toth said. "The ecstasy of my life now…I can't believe I waited so long to make the purchase. I wonder if we can do the same for humans." Tendrils pressed against the tank, as if they wished to reach out and caress Hale. "We could make you the first…"

"I'm fine, thanks. I doubt any human would take you up on the offer either, given what you have to do to others." Hale concentrated on his data slate, hoping the Toth would take a hint and leave him alone.

"Don't be such a hypocrite, *baelor*. All life feeds on life. Your species industrialized the production and slaughter of semi-intelligent animals. The Toth merely evolved beyond your limited capabilities. The price lesser beings pay for our ascended to achieve immortality and guide our race is acceptable."

Hale set the data slate on the table. He stared hard at the knobby mass of gray tissue in the tank, wishing the Toth had eyes he could stare down.

"Not to those a few rungs lower in your food chain," Hale said. "I must reject your counterproposal. We do not accept a long-term Toth military presence in our solar system."

"What if the Toth established a trade delegation on some place inhospitable to human settlement? Australia, perhaps?"

"Don't measure the drapes yet. We haven't agreed on anything else yet."

"Drapes?" Kren's nerve tendrils curled in on themselves. "Do not overlook how important our military aid would be. The Xaros…how long until they return? You think the Alliance will save you from the Xaros maniple? A Xaros invasion has been defeated only a handful of times in recorded history. Only one race survived the second wave, and they did not survive the third. Don't think that humanity's place in their little club is so high that they'll put their own safety at risk for your little blue ball of a planet."

"The Alliance saved us from extinction," Hale said. "Forgive me for being skeptical of your promises."

"They never told you about us, did they? Or

showed you the Belt, our great space dock that surrounds our home world. The hundreds of thousands of starships that will crush the Xaros and save the galaxy once the Toth can…better provide for themselves." The nervous system inside the tank bobbed up and down.

"The Karigole told us enough," Hale said. "Your demand," he tapped the data slate, "for one hundred percent of the proccies is not possible. We don't even know who they all are. Loss of records during the Xaros invasion, you understand."

The feeder arm extended from the palanquin and folded over the table. Hale recoiled slowly, remembering the last time the Toth brandished the bloody tip in front of him.

"I can tell," Kren said. "Do you know what you really are? I can answer the question with just a little…taste." The tip sprung open. Filament wires quivered like a snake's tongue.

Hale snapped to his feet and drew his gauss pistol. He leveled the weapon at Kren as a warning hiss erupted from the warrior bodyguards. The whine of Elias' and Kallen's weapons set Hale's teeth on edge.

"I have a better question," Hale said. "Is your tank bulletproof?"

The feeder arm retracted.

"It is an honor among lesser Toth to nourish their betters," Kren said.

Hale slowly slid the pistol back into the holster, but didn't sit down.

"You have some saying about preferring to die on your feet than living on your knees, but every race—every sentient species—will choose survival over extinction. You are doomed without us. Don't think that little trick with temporal displacement will work again. The Xaros are wise to it and they will search it out, just as we did when we arrived," Kren said.

"And how…did you do that?" Hale asked.

Kren's tendrils froze.

"Let's not focus on minutia," Kren said, its tone becoming gracious as its tendrils loosened to sway in the emulsion. "Let us return to arranging our grand alliance."

****

Durand checked her altitude meter and glanced down at the summit dome, a deep-gray blister against the sea of ice on Europa's surface. She looked to her left and right, making sure her wingmen hadn't strayed. Holding orbit over the moon was easy; waiting was proving more difficult than it should have been.

"We're still here, Gall," Manfred said.

"I thought the Dotok military had a lot of hurry up and wait," Lothar said. "Nice to know humans suffer too, makes me feel closer to you all."

"What about the Toth? Think they're just as bored as us?" Landas asked.

Durand searched the horizon and saw the glint off the dagger-shaped fighters. Each side of the negotiations kept their shuttle and escort craft in low orbit, separated by enough distance to dissuade the temptation of a sneak attack. One of the blades slid toward the human fighters.

"Whoa, everyone see that? Got one coming

for us," Landas said.

"Guns going hot," Lothar said.

"No, everyone, stay calm," Durand said. She reached up to her canopy and enhanced the image of the approaching Toth fighter. It had red echelon marks around the canopy and its weapon's ports were closed. "Maybe he's coming over to take a closer look. Manfred, maneuver back and get in a guard position over the Mule. Let this guy know we're ready if he wants to play."

Maneuver thrusters flared on the Eagle to her right and pushed it out of view.

The Toth fighter slowed, but continued its approach. She'd passed by the fighters on Anthalas, shot down several in the space above the planet. The serrated dagger shape with stubby wings were designed for speed, and they held their shape when in the void or in atmosphere. Her Eagle would reconfigure as needed, extending flaps, ailerons and rudders to better fly when surrounded by air, breathable or otherwise.

The Toth angled straight for Durand. She

flipped the safety off her Gatling cannon and put a hand on the power switch for her weapon systems. She wouldn't be the one to fire the first shot that wrecked the negotiations, not while Hale and the armor were still down there.

"Gall, are you going to move?" Lothar asked.

"You ever heard of a Mexican standoff?"

"Well…no."

"Watch and learn," she said.

The Toth fighter came to a stop mere yards from her nose. She saw a shadow moving from side to side inside the alien's cockpit, the sun's glare fouling her view. The dagger ship's tail rose over the nose, flipping the fighter on top of her Eagle.

"Gall!" Landas shouted.

"It's OK," she said. She looked up and watched as the Toth fighter slowed with remarkable precision until the two canopies were separated by mere inches.

A Toth warrior peered at her, lither than those she encountered on Anthalas. Four of its six arms grasped control sticks in the stretched cockpit. The Toth lay belly down, strapped to a cushion, not in a sitting position like Durand.

Bet that tail gets in the way, she thought.

The pilot cocked its head from side to side, its eyes darting over Durand. It curled its lips back and bared shark-like teeth at her.

Durand raised a hand to the canopy and extended her middle finger.

The Toth's nostrils flared and the fighter moved past her canopy. It inverted and blasted away. Durand's Eagle rocked slightly as the Toth returned to its companions.

"What do you think those red markings mean? Flight leader?" Lothar asked

Durand looked at the side of her Eagle where kill marks for destroyed Xaros drones and several Toth fighters were stenciled in bright paint beneath her name and call sign. The Toth pilot had to have seen them.

"I bet it means he's an ace," Durand said. "Got a couple kills to his name, and he's looking for a few more."

****

A man wearing little more than a flimsy T-shirt and boxer shorts was strapped to a wooden plank. The man's hands were bound and tied against his stomach. Whimpers came through a black hood over his face, wet fabric puffing with each labored breath.

Fournier checked his watch and pointed to the two men standing near the captive's head.

One man pressed against the captive's shoulders. The hooded man struggled, thrashing his head from side to side. Fournier's other man lifted up a bucket and poured ice water over the black hood, sending chunks of ice skittering across a wide puddle seeping into a moldy floor.

The captive couldn't scream during the waterboarding; the saturated fabric of his hood blocked out all air that might have fed his starving lungs. The bucket emptied, Fournier's men stood back, letting the captive flail about.

Fournier snapped his fingers and the hood

came off with a wet pop.

The captive gawped like a fish before he finally managed a soggy breath.

Fournier came over to the captive, and looked at him like he was a naughty toddler. "Mr. Lawrence, we've been at this for hours, and I must say that I'm impressed with how well you've held up. This little interrogation technique is tried and true, but it isn't meant to permanently damage you. You understand? You're true born. You belong on Earth. You're not an abomination…and I don't want to hurt you."

Fournier took a data slate from his back pocket, then plucked a data rod from his jacket. He snapped the data rod into a reader attached to the data slate and turned the screen toward Lawrence.

"I just need your thumbprint and your voice authorization. Open the manifest for me and then we'll know who's true born and who isn't. That's all I need from you. What do you say?"

"Piss…off," Lawrence said through quivering lips.

Fournier sighed and pointed to a far wall. "Look over there."

Lawrence's lips pulled into a snarl, his eyes boring into Fournier.

Fournier dug his fingernails into Lawrence's cheek and twisted his head toward the wall. Dozens of buckets lined the floor, all full of water.

"You'll break," Fournier said. He took his hand off Lawrence's face. "Everyone breaks. No shame in it. What's it going to be?"

Lawrence's body shivered as his eyes locked on the instruments of his torture.

Fournier smiled. A career in the spy game taught him when a subject like Lawrence was close to breaking. *Any second now*, he thought.

"Give…give it to me," Lawrence said.

Fournier pressed Lawrence's thumb against the slate's screen.

"Voice print validation required," chirped the slate.

"Lawrence, John Enrique, X-ray two niner sierra."

The slate dinged.

Fournier snatched the slate away, turned from Lawrence and beckoned a lieutenant over. The lieutenant held a camera over the screen as Fournier swiped through crew and passenger manifests from every ship in the Saturn colony mission.

Lawrence started crying.

Fournier slowed down to read through the list for one ship in particular, his face darkening. He whispered instruction to his lieutenant, then pressed the slate into his back pocket.

The lieutenant tapped one of the torturers on the shoulder. The two left the room together.

"Thank you, Lawrence," Fournier said. He knelt beside Lawrence and gently ran his fingers over the sobbing man's forehead. "Now, tell me where Ibarra makes the proccies."

"What?" Lawrence's eyes widened. "You said…"

"That you'd be done?" Fournier stroked his fingers through Lawrence's hair. "No. I need more from you. Where does he make them?"

Lawrence looked at Fournier with vacant eyes, then shook his head from side to side.

"Hood him," Fournier said to the remaining torturer. "Two buckets in a row." The assistant picked up two buckets, purposefully rattling them together and sloshing water onto the ground.

"The *Lehi*!" Lawrence screamed. "It has to be the *Lehi*. I never knew what was on that ship...Ibarra wouldn't tell me. No crew. No passengers. She's been at anchor with the rest of the navy ships for months. He must be making them there. No more! Please no more of the water..." He broke down into a mess of sobs.

Fournier went to the assistant and whispered, "You know what we need. Don't stop asking questions until you've squeezed him dry. I have business to attend to."

He stepped out of the torture chamber and into a dilapidated hallway. The old commercial building was a few blocks from the Ibarra Corporation headquarters in Euskal Tower. That Fournier and his trusted operatives had set up shop right under Ibarra's nose gave him great pleasure.

Fournier went up a flight of stairs two at a time and shoved a set of double doors open. Applause rose as he entered a ballroom. Dozens of men and women cheered as he raised a fist in victory.

"True born!" Fournier waited for the noise to die down. "What a day. We have the manifest, and *we* alone will share this truth to our last city. The proccies are among us. They think like us, look like us…but they are products of an alien plot. A plot so intricate that they managed to infiltrate *our* organization."

Murmurs spread through the crowd.

"Shannon!" Fournier called out to his assistant. A side door banged open, and his lieutenant shoved a man in front of her, his hands bound behind his back and his mouth gagged.

Shannon kicked the prisoner and sent him to his knees next to Fournier. Those assembled spoke in hushed whispers as one of the true born's founders tried to plead through his gag, an old red cloth napkin crammed between his jaws.

Fournier ripped the gag away.

"What's your name?" Fournier asked.

"Sir, it's me, Njoroge," he said. "There must be some mistake, I can't be a—"

"What ship were you on when Ibarra stole everything from us?"

"The...the *Johnson Atoll*," Njoroge said. "Cabin thirty-seven."

Fournier whipped out his data slate, looked at it, and shook his head.

"You're not on the manifest," Fournier said. He handed it to Shannon, who nodded in agreement.

"No!" Njoroge cried. He tried to get to his feet but Fournier kicked him in the chest, sending him to the ground. Fournier held out a hand to Shannon, who pressed a crude pistol into his palm.

Fournier put two rounds in Njoroge's chest. The proccie struggled to sit up as blood seeped through his shirt. Fournier shot him in the forehead.

"Everyone else..." Fournier said, "everyone else here is true born. There is a city full of people—real people—full of doubt over the truth of what they are because of Ibarra. We have the manifest, and we'll use it to tear through Ibarra's web of lies, but first…we need the upper hand. Now we need to prepare for the endgame."

****

Shannon rolled Njoroge's corpse into a section of carpet cut up from the floor. She didn't have to dispose of the body properly, just keep it hidden for a few more days until Fournier's plan played out. The building was large, with plenty of places to stash a body until the smell became too noticeable.

She ducked her head into the hallway, running her eyes up the blood trail leading from the little office where she'd wrapped up the body back to the ballroom. She and the dead man were alone, and she knew Njoroge wouldn't divulge any new secrets.

Shannon stuck the butt of her pistol against a molar and pushed. There was a painful click as it dislocated. She swallowed blood and counted to ten, waiting for the beacon in her tooth to connect to her employer and open a secure IR line.

"C'mon, c'mon c'mon." She tapped her fingers against her thigh, waiting for the connection. Shannon tapped her forearm screen and swiped through manifest lists.

"Shannon?" Ibarra asked. The tooth sent vibrations into her inner ear, keeping his words for her and her alone. "What have you got?"

"Boss," she said quietly, "they've got the manifest. Already executed a proccie too."

"Your cover must have held if we're talking," Ibarra said.

Shannon's eyes skimmed over the passenger list of the *Doughty* and found Shannon Delacroix's name. That woman was dead. She'd thrown herself out of an airlock soon after the Battle for the Crucible, evidently distraught about the loss of her family on Earth, but her demise was kept hush-hush, and Shannon stepped into the woman's life…after Ibarra adjusted some records.

"Fournier has total confidence in all his

people now," she said. Shannon tabbed over to the manifest for the *Endeavor* and started reading the names. "They know about the *Lehi*. He's prepping an assault on it now."

"Lawrence did well," Ibarra said.

"He doesn't know what's going on," Shannon hissed. "They tortured him for hours before he broke."

"Lawrence is a fine administrator, but a horrible actor," Ibarra said. "He's done exactly what I needed him to. Can you get him out alive?"

Shannon's brow furrowed as she read over the manifest. She scrolled back up and read it again, slowly and carefully.

"Shannon?"

"I'm not on here," she said. "My alias isn't on the *Endeavor's* manifest. This can't be right. Unless…"

"No, listen to me, my darling," Ibarra said.

Shannon sank back on her haunches, sitting on Njoroge's carpet-wrapped body.

"I had you scrubbed from that manifest the

second you set foot on that ship, you understand me?" Ibarra said. "You were going to slip away from the rest of the fleet and come back to me as soon as things settled down. That was always the plan."

"I can't be a proccie. I remember so much…" Shannon said. There was an electric shock from her false tooth. Shannon's eyes unfocused and her head lolled to the side.

"Override," Ibarra said firmly. "New imperative: I was on the *Endeavor*."

"I was on the *Endeavor*," Shannon said slowly.

The tooth shocked her again, and Shannon looked down at the body beneath her, somewhat confused.

"What were you saying about the *Endeavor*?" Ibarra asked.

"Nothing. I was there. My cover is secure…The *Lehi*. Fournier's going to make a move, destroy the production lines we've got supplying the fleet," she said.

"You're not going to believe this, but we've got bigger problems up here," Ibarra said. "I'm working on a miracle…but even I've got limits."

CHAPTER 10

Golden motes of light swirled in the center of the command center. They condensed into an almost incandescent globe, then faded away, leaving a kneeling Stacey in their wake. She pressed her palms against her temples, wincing with pain.

Admiral Garret, Rochambeau and Ibarra's hologram waited for Stacey to come to her feet.

"God, I hate this part," she said. "Like a damn ice-cream headache."

"Stacey," Ibarra said, "I can't help but notice that you've returned without a couple squadrons of reinforcements."

"No, but I've returned with plenty of bad news," she said.

"They're not coming," Rochambeau said.

Stacey shook her head.

"Why the hell not?" Garret asked. "I thought

we, and the Crucible, were the damn lynchpin to their entire war effort against the Xaros."

"We are, sir," Stacey said, "just not on the terms we thought."

The probe rose from the plinth in the center of the command center, a long thin iris of light.

"I've received new instructions from Bastion," the probe said. "This is most unfortunate."

"Bastion, the Congress at least, decided that *not* preserving the Crucible is more important than us," Stacey said. "The probe will cooperate with the Toth, send them back to their space without risking a quantum rupture—more on that later—if we surrender. It will give them everything they need to start producing their own proccies. The computer banks, sperm and ovum depositories. The whole thing."

"What about us?" Ibarra asked. "What's to stop the Toth from just…" He looked at Rochambeau.

"Nothing," Stacey said with a shake of her head. "But the probe will keep a production line, which can be scaled upwards, on the Crucible. The new humans will be…less willful. Obedient to Bastion's orders. Earth will be repopulated, just not by anyone who can truly think for themselves."

"I believe," Rochambeau said, "the human word for this situation is 'bullshit.'"

"Bastion thinks we're just going to roll over and play dead for the Toth?" Garret asked. "I have warships ready to hold—to hell with what they expect from us."

"Let me stress…*if*…if the Toth get to the point where the Crucible is in jeopardy, then the probe will run up the white flag," Stacey said. "If there's one silver lining to this whole mess, it's that the Qa'Resh gave us a chance to save our species on our terms. Let me show you."

Stacey walked over to a holo board listing each human void ship on one side and the Toth ships on the other, all given designations by their relative size compared to human ships.

"What happened with the Dotok…" Stacey looked up and down the Toth ships, then frowned.

"This can't be right. The sheer tonnage of this many ships using Bastion jump technology would require dark-matter capacitors larger than any of these ships."

"Ms. Ibarra, English please," Garret said.

"How many jump gates did they use when they entered our solar system?" Stacey asked the probe.

"One," the probe said. "The wormhole measured—"

"Then where is the ship with the jump engine?" Stacey asked. "The *Breitenfeld* could barely bring the *Canticle of Reason* back from Takeni, and the Toth fleet masses nearly four times the Dotok ship."

"They're hiding something from us," Ibarra said. "How?"

"I'm more concerned that our probe didn't pick up on this to begin with," Stacey said. "Did the Toth initiate contact when they arrived?"

"The Toth designated Kren sent a multifrequency standard greeting three seconds after their fleet translated," the probe said.

"Show me." Stacey turned from the board and a hologram appeared in front of her. Separate lines of transmissions ranging from energy levels just above cosmic background radiation to the upper bands of the near ultraviolet wavelengths.

"The Toth know what frequencies we use," Stacey said. "This mess they sent us is hiding something." She scrolled through bandwidths until she found one that was spikey with energy waves.

Stacey went pale.

"Probe, initiate command line red dash alpha," Stacey said. The probe's sliver of light wavered. "I want you to create a memory partition for the Ibarra matrix. Now."

"Done," the probe said. Ibarra's hologram flickered.

Stacey pressed her palm against a command console. She closed her eyes and the probe faded away.

"It's been hacked," Stacey said. "I sent it into hibernation before it could cause any more damage."

"That's impossible," Ibarra said. "The probe's programming language is—"

"And yet," Stacey snapped, pointing to the rogue transmission, "here is an override code degrading the probe's logic functions. The probe should have realized something was off when the Toth arrived."

"Why did they send a simple override code? Why not take over the whole system?" Ibarra asked.

"Your ships are still rigged for analogue, no computers to take over," Rochambeau said. "If the Toth seized control of the probe, they'd still have to deal with the fleet. They're buying time to get close to Earth."

"Get close? Their fleet is still at anchor over Neptune," Garret said.

"Anthalas," Stacey said. "The *Breitenfeld* said the Toth ship they encountered was cloaked."

Rochambeau and Lafayette spoke to each other in high-pitched whistles and clicks that hurt Stacey's ears.

"The Karigole had experimented with larger cloak fields before the Toth betrayal," Lafayette said. "The technology could, in theory, be scaled upwards. We abandoned the research once field tests failed against the Xaros. A simple lepton pulse would collapse the cloak instantly."

"Do we have a lepton emitter…somewhere?" Stacey asked.

"No, but I can build one in about an hour with the omnium reactor here on the Crucible," Lafayette said.

Stacey looked at Lafayette for a second, and the Karigole just smiled at her.

"Go! Go make a lepton emitter, for Pete's sake," Stacy said. Lafayette spun on his heels and ran from the command center.

"What do you think we're going to find?" Ibarra asked.

"I'm not sure, but we'd better warn the *Breitenfeld*," Stacey said.

****

Valdar looked at the cooling plate of food on

his desk. He picked up a fork and pushed a scoop of fried rice around the plate.

"What's wrong? It actually has taste now," Hale said. The Marine stripped a plastic wrapper off a piece of carrot cake from his own tray and gave it a sniff.

"Can't say I have much of an appetite," Valdar said. He opened a desk drawer and pulled out a bottle of whiskey and two paper cups.

"Uncle Isaac, where'd you get that?" Hale asked.

"There seems to be a lot of booze on my ship," Valdar said. "A couple other captains suggest there's a black marketer aboard the *Breitenfeld*. Each time we leave orbit, the amount and availability of quality alcohol dries up for Phoenix and the fleet. You wouldn't know anything about that, would you?"

"Rumors is all," Hale said. He made a mental note to have a conversation with Standish once this dinner was over with.

Valdar poured a double shot in each cup and

returned the bottle to his drawer.

"Cheers." Valdar held the paper cup up as a toast and tossed back the drink. Hale managed a sip and coughed. "Drink up. It'll help make this next part go down easier."

"We have instructions back from Earth?" Hale forced down the rest of his drink, warmth spreading through his chest.

"High command wants this resolved immediately," Valdar said. "Riots in Phoenix, serious discipline issues in the fleet—the proccies are going to tear us all apart before the Toth or the Xaros get the chance. You're to agree to hand over the proccies—and the tech—at the next session. They were never our choice or our idea. This mess is on Ibarra."

"No, we can't do that," Hale said. "The Toth will...they will make human beings by the millions and slaughter them. Slaughter. Them. Where do we get the right to just condemn so many souls to—"

"They don't have souls!" Valdar slapped a palm against his desk. "They are mockeries. A false front by Ibarra to mask everything that we've lost. Where did Ibarra get the right to doom my family to death? Huh? Now Ibarra wants to replace everyone with something that follows his plan, his vision. We're not going to have it, Ken. Earth is ours. Our future belongs to us and we can't let Ibarra take it away again."

Hale looked away from his godfather.

"I saw his body on Earth. Ibarra's," Hale said. "He went beneath Euskal Tower, loaded up his mind into that probe and died. He could have been on the fleet, sidestepped the Xaros invasion with the rest of us. He chose to die there. That's not the action of someone who doesn't care. Ibarra made the proccies so we'd survive the next fight with the Xaros, and he made them as real to us as he could. I don't understand why we're just throwing them all to the wolves."

"You don't have to, Ken," Valdar said. "Orders are orders. Make this counterproposal to the Toth." Valdar slid a data slate across his desk.

Hale read through the text, his face slack as

the sheer score of the agreement with the Toth became clear.

"We're going to lose more than the proccies with this," Hale said. "We're going to abandon everything we believe in ourselves."

****

The door to an armory locker slid aside. The empty armor attached to a magnetized wall plate formed a human-like shape. Hale, already in his pseudo-muscle layer, grabbed a sabaton from the locker and stepped into it. It tightened around his foot and lower leg, automatically adjusting to his usual fit.

He put the rest of his armor on in silence, his mind working on autopilot.

"Hale," a low voice came from the doorway. The Marine glanced over his shoulder and saw Steuben. Hale slid a mail shirt of linked graphene-ceramic chains over his head.

"Help you?"

"The negotiations aren't going well," Steuben said. The Karigole sat on a bench between the lockers.

"They're going well in that an agreement is close," Hale said. "But that agreement…"

"I am here to apologize," Steuben said. "You desired my counsel several times. I was too blinded by hatred to help you."

"No harm, no foul, Steuben. The decisions are all made back on Earth, and they've got three Karigole there that I'm sure no one's listening to." Hale touched his collarbone through the mail shirt, triggering a sensor. The shirt melded against his pseudo muscle layer. He picked up his breastplate and looked over the interior connection sensors.

"I had a wife," Steuben said, "beautiful, strong, but from a different clan. We had to give up our family support to marry—little worry for those too young to realize they're being foolish. Without our family backing, we had to save for many decades before we could petition a *geth'aar* so we could have a child."

Hale had no clue what a *geth'aar* was, but he wasn't going to interrupt the first bit of personal history Steuben had ever shared for clarification.

"My centurion's mission off world was to be my last. After I returned, we'd have more than enough for the *geth'aar* and a home. My wife...she had the nest already prepared. No more war for either of us, but the Toth put an end to all that.

"Do you know where the Toth struck first? They kidnapped the *geth'aar* from their enclaves. Every last one of them. They ordered our military to surrender, promised to consume a *geth'aar* each deca-turn and broadcast the feeding. Without the *geth'aar*, we'd be extinct anyway...so they surrendered immediately.

"We would have given the Toth anything to get them back...but they took everything. Slaughtered every last Karigole. Even the hatchlings. I saw the fields, Hale. The fields full of our dead."

"Why are you telling me this?" Hale asked.

"Don't trust them. The Toth are prisoners to an insatiable hunger. The more they have, the more they want. They won't stop with just the proccies,"

Steuben said.

"It's not up to me." Hale fixed his breastplate to his chest and grabbed his shoulder plates. "Your military had their orders. I've got mine. What am I supposed to do? Shoot the Toth in the face—or whatever—and tell Earth we're in a war because my personal beliefs got in the way?"

"It is a mistake, a fatal mistake, to trust the Toth," Steuben said.

"You think I don't know that? You were right beside me on that Toth ship. I've seen what the Toth really are." Hale fixed armor to his thighs, hammering the plates with his fist to get the fit tight enough. "This whole situation is shit. It's been shit since the day I landed in Phoenix's hollowed-out shell and fought my first Xaros."

Hale backed into the locker, and his back plate snapped onto his frame.

"What am I supposed to do, Steuben? I know you're a couple hundred years old, but I'm a twenty-four-year-old lieutenant put in front of a god damn brain in a jar…and told to negotiate the fate of the whole planet. All because I managed not to get eaten by them when they had the chance. Thanks, Atlantic Union Marine Corps, but this wasn't covered in the Basic School at Quantico."

"What is the right thing to do?" Steuben asked.

"We beat the piss out of these lizards," Hale said. "Hurt them so bad the one ship we let limp home tells every other Toth that humanity is not to be fucked with. That's what I want to do, Steuben, but wiser heads than mine say violence isn't the answer here."

Hale jammed his hands into his gauntlets and took his helmet from a hook.

Steuben stood up and touched his knuckles to Hale's temple.

"You have a warrior's heart," Steuben said. "If there had been more Karigole like you...things might have been different."

****

Hale bounded over Europa's icy crust beside Elias and Kallen.

"We're going to wear a rut through this ice," Kallen said. "How many more times do I have to look at that nasty fish tank before this is all over?" she asked.

"This might be the last trip," Hale said.

"You don't sound confident," Elias said. "Anything else you want to share with us?"

"Stay intimidating," Hale said. He planted both feet and bounded higher, giving his anti-grav linings a burst to lengthen his arc. He came down at the dome's airlock. When the inner doors opened, the Toth was already waiting for him at the table.

****

Despite the cold, dry air, Hale was sweating. The Toth held a data slate in one of its six clawed legs and was silent for many minutes as it read over the proposed treaty sent from Earth. The Toth's newfound silence unnerved Hale more than the repulsive mass inside the tank.

The Toth set the data slate on the tabletop with a snap.

"I believe we've found common ground,"

the Toth said, and Hale's heart sank in his chest. "Surrender of every procedural growth tank, all stored seed stock and the computer servers for memory generation. Also, deliver every identified procedural human being to my ship once it takes orbit over Phoenix."

The clawed leg rose next to the tank and beckoned a warrior over. The warrior lumbered over and laid an ornate golden tube on the table. The tube unfolded into a large piece of paper. English script and dense Toth cuneiform materialized. The words shifted around, expanding and collapsing as the text rewrote itself.

"The initial agreement," Kren said. The golden sheet fluttered toward Hale.

Hale read it carefully, finding no discrepancies between it and what Valdar had given him.

"Sign it," Kren said. The fluid in his tank shifted from red to deep blue. "Sign." A tiny panel flipped open on Kren's leg and a tapered cylinder spat onto the table. Hale picked up the golden object, a tiny dark tip at one end.

Hale swallowed hard and reread the subsection on the immediate surrender of all known procedural human beings. Signing this meant that Yarrow, his Marine, would be handed over to Kren. Hale looked up from the document and to the mechanical housing just beneath Kren's tank, where he stored the feeder arm.

He imagined that bloody spike opening up over Yarrow's head…

A sea of anger rose in his chest. Hale set the pen down.

"This inspection clause," Hale said. "I don't see the size or any other details of the inspectors specified. Nor do I see a list of locations."

Nerve tendrils twisted against themselves.

"We must be sure you aren't hiding any of the meat from us," Kren said. "We will go where we please and with whatever forces we deem necessary to ensure compliance."

The corner of Hale's lips tugged into a sneer. He imagined thousands of Toth warriors on the streets of Phoenix, rounding up every human being they could find and sending them to "inspection," a loophole so big the Toth could fly a starship through it.

"Would you adjust the text to reflect that?" Hale asked with a smile.

A low growl came from the tank's speakers. The inspection clause rewrote itself, making it perfectly clear that the Toth would have the run of every inch of the solar system.

A slight vibration went through Hale's gauntlet. He glanced down at the data screen, which showed a failed delivery message.

"Got something from the ship," Elias said through the IR and into Hale's earpiece.

"Me too, looks like a glitch," Kallen said.

"You have your amendment," the Toth said. "Now sign."

"I'm terribly sorry," Hale said. "But this text isn't what I'm authorized to agree to." Hale rolled the pen back to Kren. "I'll need to have the whole thing reapproved, in its entirety, by Earth." He looked at his forearm screen and frowned. "It's the middle of the night cycle in Phoenix. We'll have to adjourn for at least another twelve hours."

A mechanical claw clamped down on the table edge and gouged out a hunk of metal.

"I'm frustrated too," Hale stood up, "just a bit more of a delay." *And maybe enough time for me to convince Earth what you're really after,* he thought.

A brief tremor rumbled through the dome.

"*Ice quake?*" Kallen asked. "*Not unusual for Europa.*"

"*Felt like artillery,*" Elias said.

Hale reached for his helmet.

A hiss rose from the warrior bodyguards. Kren scuttled away from the table.

"Iron Hearts," Hale said, "I think the negotiations are over."

A panel flipped open beneath Kren's tank. The feeder arm shot out like a striking cobra toward Hale's face.

Hale threw himself back as monofilament

wires from the bloody spike brushed over his face. He hit the ground and rolled to his back, drawing his pistol.

The feeder arm bashed against the solid table, unable to reach him. Hale fired two rounds at Kren, but the magnetically accelerated rounds ricocheted off the tank, leaving spider-webbed cracks against the glass. The Toth retreated, its tendrils flailing madly against the inside of the tank.

The feeder arm swung to the side and sent Hale's helmet flying across the room. Hale knew he wouldn't get very far outside the airlock without it.

"Elias?" Hale turned around and saw the two armor soldiers wrestling with Toth warriors in crystalline armor. He looked back at Kren; the overlord and his two bodyguards were stuffed into the airlock at the opposite side of the dome. Where had more warriors come from?

Hale saw his helmet half-hidden by a column. He rolled to his feet and ran toward it.

The air wavered between him and his helmet. Hale skidded to a halt and raised his pistol as a ghost materialized from thin air. Hale fired his pistol and the gauss bullet crumpled against the apparition. A Toth warrior snapped into life, covered from snout to tail tip in crystal armor. It was eight feet tall and held a halberd in its double-thumbed hands.

Hale gave his pistol a worried glance and started shooting.

The Toth roared at Hale and charged, unfazed by Hale's shots.

On the third pull of the trigger, the warrior blew apart with a crack of thunder. Hale's ears lit up with a screeching whine. He looked back at Elias and saw a single smoking barrel on his forearm cannons, a dead warrior at his feet.

"If you weren't so delicate, we'd be out of here by now, crunchy," Elias said, the words barely making it over the mosquito buzz in Hale's ears. Elias motioned to Hale's helmet with his cannons and Hale stepped around the steaming remains of the Toth that had charged him.

"You think there are more?" Kallen asked as

Hale popped his helmet over his head.

"Backs to the wall. Just in case," Elias said.

"Anything from the *Breitenfeld*?" Hale shouted, running toward the airlock.

"Don't have to yell, jarhead, and no," Kallen said.

"What?" Hale asked.

"You blew his eardrums out with the concussion from your cannons," Kallen said. She waved her own cannons across the empty dome as the airlock opened and the three moved inside.

"His peashooter wasn't cutting it," Elias said. "What was I supposed to do?"

The outer airlock doors opened and Elias rushed out first. He swung his torso around on his waist actuators and his cannons flashed in the near vacuum, sending gauss rounds the size of Hale's fist over his head.

Hale saw a pair of Toth warriors tumbling through the sky above his head. Yellow blood froze into snow as their ruined bodies went end over end. The gauss cannons packed enough of a punch to send the warriors on a ballistic trajectory like a kicked football back on Earth.

Hale opened the emergency radio frequency. "*Breitenfeld*, this is Hale. We've got a code red on the surface. Need immediate extraction." Hale forced his jaw open and tried to pop his ears. The ringing seemed like it had gotten stronger since he put his helmet on. "*Breitenfeld?* Do you read me?"

Even if they answered him, Hale wasn't sure he could hear it.

"Can either of you…what're you looking at?" Hale asked the armor soldiers. Both of them stared over Europa's stunted horizon.

A starship rose beyond the pale-blue plain of ice, a pointed mass of jagged corral flat and wide like a broadsword, ugly nodules of engine banks for a hilt. The hull shifted through hues of red and brown, like it was covered in old blood. It was the largest spaceship Hale had ever seen, dwarfing the *Breitenfeld* and almost as large as Titan Station.

"I think we're in trouble," Kallen said.

A silver shuttle blasted from the surface,

escorted by four Toth dagger fighters. Kren, retreating toward the Toth battleship.

"Where's our shuttle?" Hale asked.

Points of light grew on the battleship, then blossomed into blasts of energy. Ragged bolts of white energy streaked toward Hale and the soldiers and tore overhead, leaving ionized trails of plasma in Europa's scant atmosphere.

"Definitely in trouble," Kallen said.

"There!" Hale pointed off to the side of the dome where sunlight glinted from a pair of ships speeding toward them.

"Not ours," Elias said. "Draw them in, bouncing Betty when they're close enough. Your turn to babysit."

"Least he doesn't complain nonstop like MacDougall," Kallen said as she scooped Hale up with an arm and bounded across the ice. Hale squirmed uselessly before recognizing the wisdom of trying to hold on to Kallen for dear life.

Energy blasts smashed into the ice yards away, shooting geysers of steam and shards of dirty ice into the sky. A streak of energy blazed over Elias' shoulder. Chunks of ice exploded from the impact of the near miss, and a lump the size of Hale's hand crashed into his right knee.

Even with his armor, the blow turned the joint into a white-hot epicenter of pain. He grunted in agony and tried to reach his knee, Kallen held him fast. The display on his visor showed the armor plates and graphene-mail layer damaged, but his suit wasn't compromised.

"Sorry," Kallen said. "Damn crunchies always trying to get hurt around me."

"Get ready." Elias' helm swiveled around to see the pair of Toth fighters on their heels. The helm snapped back around.

"Boost!"

The two soldiers fired their jet packs and soared into the sky. Hale's vision grayed out as the sudden acceleration sent his blood rushing out of his head.

Elias and Kallen spun around and aimed their gauss cannons ahead of the approaching Toth fighters. Both soldiers fired on full auto, muzzle flashes so close together it almost looked like they'd fired lasers instead of a hail of gauss shells.

The armor sent out a curtain of fire for the Toth to fly through. A Toth fighter took a shell to the fuselage, spinning it out of control. It plowed into Europa's ice, hull fragments blending into the surface. The second banked out of its attack run, accelerating away from Kallen's gauss rounds that missed their target by mere feet.

The Toth fighter's engines flared as it sped away. It looped over and came back for the humans falling back to Europa. The Toth jinked from side to side.

"I'm low on ammo," Elias said.

"I've got three seconds on full cyclic left," Kallen said.

"I'll draw him off," Elias said. "You get the crunchy back to the—never mind."

A pair of Eagle fighters came over the horizon. The lead Eagle destroyed the Toth fighter with a single burst of fire.

"Hale, this is Gall. We've got a Mule right behind us to get you home," Durand said. "Why are you three—*bordel de merde*…that ship is big."

"Gall, this is Iron Heart One," Elias said, "ready for pick up."

****

Valdar and Utrecht leaned over the tactical plot where solid blue icons showed Hale's transport and escort ships hovering over Europa's surface. Red triangles marked the known Toth positions and an alien cruiser mirrored the *Breitenfeld* opposite the mining dome.

"The cruiser dumped garbage again," Utrecht said. "They stick to a decent schedule, voiding about every eleven hours or so. There were bodies…again." The gunnery officer tapped the plot and a picture of unsuited menials floating in space next to the Toth ship popped up next to the large red icon.

"Only ever the little ones?" Valdar asked.

"That's right. The high-res pics we got of the bodies show…bite marks," Utrecht said, his face blanched. "I don't know how Garret thinks we can have some sort of relationship with these things. No respect for their dead, cannibalism, then there's what the leaders eat."

"We aren't negotiating a cultural exchange," Valdar said. "Hale should have an agreement worked out soon, and the Toth will be long gone." *Along with the proccies,* he thought.

"Captain," said Lieutenant Erdahl, the ship's communication's officer, as she twisted around in his seat, "we've got a priority transmission from Earth."

"I'll read it in my ready room," Valdar said.

"It's coded vermillion, sir," Erdahl said. A hush fell over the bridge. Vermillion cyphers used the most complex encryption the Atlantic Union had and were only ever used when high command thought all-out war was imminent.

Valdar went to Erdahl's chair and pulled a glove off. One of the screens had a deep red border with a warning that a message was for Valdar's eyes only. The captain pressed his palm against a small plate and lines of text filled the screen.

Valdar frowned.

"You know what a lepton pulse is?" he asked Erdahl.

"No, but the fact that we've only got five minutes to get ready for it doesn't make me feel very confident," Erdahl said. "If only vermillion cyphers could hold more than two hundred characters."

"Send a warning to Hale and his escort. Tell them…be alert, but don't spook the Toth," Valdar said, walking to his command chair slowly and deliberately. Any sign of unease or panic would provoke an exponentially worse reaction from his bridge crew.

He sat in his command chair and flipped open a clear panel. He pressed the READY ALERT button and amber light flooded the bridge. Crewmen on the bridge and across the ship donned void helmets.

Valdar waited until the last person on the bridge had her helmet on, then he took his armored

234

helmet from beneath his chair and snapped it over his head. The void suit beneath his overalls pressurized with a slight click in his ears.

"Gunnery," Valdar said. "I want you to ready a main-gun firing solution for the Toth cruiser, but do not slew the guns or prime the rails, understand?"

"Aye-aye, Captain, but it'll slow us down if we do have to fight," Utrecht said.

"We charge the guns and point them at the Toth and we *will* have a fight," Valdar said. "Let's not ruin all Hale's hard work through an abundance of caution." Valdar pressed a key on the side of his arm rest. "Engineering, what will a lepton pulse do to the jump engines?"

"Can't say for sure, sir. I'm an engineer not a theoretical physicist. The only instruction Lafayette gave me for the jump drive when he left was 'Don't touch it.' Want me to stoke the fires?" Levin asked.

"Prep for a jump back to Earth," Valdar said. He didn't miss having the long-winded

Karigole around until this moment.

"Lepton pulse wave in T minus thirty seconds," Erdahl said.

"I wonder what it'll do," Geller said over the bridge's open IR comms, "send the ship to dimension X or turn us all into purple tentacle monsters?"

"Hot mike…ensign," Valdar said through grit teeth. The young officer did his best to sink into his chair and away from the rest of the bridge's gaze.

But he does have a point, Valdar thought. *Those engines surprised us on more than one occasion.*

"Three…two…one," Erdahl said.

Valdar gripped his armrests tightly…and the lepton pulse came and went without any obvious effects.

"Shall we stand down, Captain?" the XO asked.

"No, wait and see if the Toth react," Valdar said. A tinge of anxiety crept into Valdar's mind.

Did Garret and Ibarra know he'd sabotaged the negotiations? Every report he'd sent back to Earth showed that Hale was following their instructions to stall; there was nothing to suspect. Erdahl controlled the only IR transmitter that could reach Earth and no one else on his ship knew the real truth...except Hale, but Hale trusted him.

He'll understand, Valdar thought. *When it's all over, he'll understand.*

"Toth ship...no change," Utrecht said.

"What's that?" Lieutenant Neely pointed toward the front reinforced-glass windows. A swath of space beyond Europa undulated, smearing starlight from left to right.

"Gunnery," Valdar said as an icy pit of fear formed in his chest, "charge up the main guns. Now!"

The anomaly grew brighter until it burned bright enough that the auto-filters on the windows darkened. The light died away, leaving behind a gigantic starship that looked like a miles-long hunk of coral reef had been sent into space. Massive crystalline weapon emplacements studded across the hull spoke of the ship's purpose: war.

"Toth cruiser powering weapons!" Ericsson announced.

"Battle stations!" Red lights whirled to life across the bridge and the *Breitenfeld*. "Helm, bring us about," Valdar ordered. "I want Europa between us and that battleship two minutes ago. XO, get Hale and his team back aboard. We're jumping for Earth the second they're recovered."

The Toth battleship began a slow turn toward the *Breitenfeld*. Shadows crept across its immense hull, cast by coarse towers of corral-like material.

They were playing us, Valdar thought. *Stalling to get that thing closer to Earth.* Valdar's face flushed and hot anger gripped his heart. He'd been a fool, he realized, to think the Toth could ever have been trusted.

"Rounds loaded. Main guns ready to fire in thirty seconds," Utrecht said.

"Any word from—"

"Cruiser firing! All hands brace for impact," Ericsson's warning went to the whole ship. Valdar braced himself against his command chair.

A bolt of blue-white energy snapped over the forward rail-gun battery. Light from a second bolt grew against the port side. The impact punched against the *Breitenfeld,* canting it to the side and twisting the ship on its axis. Valdar slammed against his restraints hard enough for his arms to fly out in front of him.

"Hull breach on decks nine through thirteen," Ericsson said. "Forward flack batteries are offline."

"Guns?" Valdar asked.

"Lost our firing solution," Utrecht said. "Right the ship and I can put the big guns to work."

"Already on it," Geller said. Valdar felt the ship tremble as thrusters across the bottom of the vessel roared to life. "Coming back to our original bearing in three...two...one."

"Fire!" Valdar commanded.

Lightning arced over the rail-gun vanes.

Rounds the size of a small car catapulted through magnetic fields and ripped toward the Toth cruiser.

Ericsson looked up from her scope, "Hit!" She looked back in her scope and twisted a dial on the base, cycling through camera feeds. "She's venting atmosphere…still under power. Toth cruiser is setting course right for us."

"Gunnery, fire at will with the main guns. Kill that ship before it can get any closer," Valdar said.

"Aye-aye, Skipper. Next volley in twenty seconds. What about the battleship?" Utrecht asked.

"We're better off bringing a warning back to Earth than trying to scratch the paint on that thing," Valdar said.

"Engine room," Valdar said, "how long until we can jump back to Earth?"

"Get us another four thousand kilometers out of the gravity well and I can open the gate right on top of us," the chief engineer said. "Every damn thing orbiting around Jupiter throws off the—"

"Incoming! Three shots from the cruiser!"

Ericsson announced.

"*Gott mit uns*," Valdar said quietly.

****

Durand inverted her fighter and looked "up" at the Mule idling on Europa's ice, steam billowing up from beneath its engines.

"Mule, you got them?" Durand asked.

"Have to strap the big boys down," Jorgen answered her. "I've got a feeling it won't be a smooth trip back to the *Breit*."

"What about Hale? How bad is he?"

"Crew chief had to hit him with painkillers," Jorgen said. "We've got him strapped in and drooling."

"I've got eyes on four bandits," Manfred said. "Make that six. Coming in fast and low."

Red triangles appeared on Durand's canopy courtesy of her fighter's computers. If the Toth had any electronic warfare capability, they hadn't used it to try to degrade her shipboard systems…yet.

"Mule?" Durand asked.

"I need two more minutes," Jorgen said.

"Lothar, Manfred, you stay with the Mule and escort it back to the ship," Durand said. "Sparks, with me." She banked her Eagle toward the Toth fighters and waited for Landas to form up on her wing.

"Gall, that's suicide," Manfred said. "The four of us—"

"Thank you, Manfred, this is my call. Turn and burn for the ship. We'll catch up," Durand said.

Manfred muttered in Dotok and went off the IR.

"Sparks, link your targeting computers with mine," Durand said. "Let's give them a surprise when we make our pass."

"We're linked," Landas said. "So used to doing this the hard way since we started fighting Xaros." Green diamond targeting reticules appeared over each hostile icon. A bar appeared next to each, decreasing slowly as the enemy approached.

"Don't get used to it," Durand said.

The half-dozen Toth fighters climbed up from Europa's ice. Three sped ahead of the rest, their serrated edges glinting in the sunlight.

"We split on the pass. You go high. Keep the guns on them," Durand said. The Gatling cannon slung beneath her fighter could put out fifty rounds per second, none of which were of any use if she couldn't keep line of sight from her weapon to the target. "I'm going low."

"Watch that ice, Gall. It doesn't look too soft," Landas said.

The bar counting down the outer edge of their engagement envelope shrank. The leading Toth fighters loosed bolts of energy, so Durand pushed her Eagle aside with a nudge from maneuver thrusters, keeping plenty of space between her and the potshots.

The targeting reticules flashed red. Durand squeezed the trigger on her control stick, her Eagle gyrating as the cannon fired. Her fighter's computers sent out bursts of rounds at each target, automatically compensating for the Toth's wild maneuvers as they broke formation and Durand rolled the Eagle over and dove it toward the ice. She saw a Toth fighter explode into a cloud of shrapnel before Europa filled her canopy.

"Splash two!" Landas said. "Think we nicked a third."

Durand's flight suit pressed against her thighs and stomach, fighting to keep blood in her brain and out of her feet. "Turn in and reacquire," she managed with a grunt.

A pair of energy bolts snapped past her canopy and exploded against the ice.

"I've got one on me," Durand said.

"I've got two!" Landas cried.

They sacrificed the first three just so the rest could get the jump on us, she thought. She glanced over her shoulder and saw Landas dodging fire high above.

"Dive toward me. I'll meet you halfway," Durand said. She skirted dangerously close to the ice, her engines kicking up twin trails of steam in her wake. A bolt passed over her canopy close enough that she ducked out of instinct. She glanced over her shoulder and saw the fighter closing in on her fast enough that she could almost make out the warrior behind the controls.

Durand put a hand on the throttle and yanked the control stick back. Maneuver jets pushed her nose away from the ice and brought her Eagle perpendicular to Europa. She gunned the thrusters as white-hot plasma burnt into the ice and shot her into the skies.

The supercharged particles lanced through the ice and burnt out a pocket of steam, steam that expanded so fast that it looked like a bomb had gone off. The Toth fighter flew through the wave of ice boulders and smashed into scrap.

Durand looked back at her handiwork and chuckled.

"Gall, little help here," Landas said. The Toth fighter on his tail fired several times, bracketing his Eagle.

"Dive, now!"

Landas banked over and flew straight toward Durand. The targeting reticule on the pursuing Toth went red. Durand put her trust in the computer and tapped the trigger. Two gauss rounds snapped past either side of Landas' cockpit and perforated the Toth fighter.

"That was some hot shit right there—"

A bolt of energy from the last Toth fighter impacted Landas' starboard engine. His Eagle went into a flat spin.

The Toth fighter's afterburners flared to life and it shot past Landas' stricken Eagle and Durand. There were red stripes behind the Toth cockpit.

"Ejecting!" Landas shouted. His canopy blew away with a pop of explosive bolts and his cockpit spat away from the fighter. Landas spun in the sky on a slow trajectory away from the moon.

Durand saw the Toth ace fly low across the ice, heading toward the distant battleship. Durand cut her speed and flew toward Landas. He waved to her as she neared.

"I'm OK," Landas said. "Not to rush you, but I can feel the radiation shrinking my nuts down to raisins."

"Mule, this is Durand. Got a fallen angel.

Can you make pick up?"

"Come back?" Jorgen asked. "Have we got clear skies?"

"Roger, last bogie is running with its tail between—"

"Gall? Gall! It's coming back!" Landas' arms waved frantically, trying to point toward the ice as he spun end over end.

Durand got her head around in time to see the Toth ace hurtling toward them, faster than her Eagle could have ever managed. She cycled power to her engines, certain that she was a sitting duck for the Toth.

The Toth fired a single blast, the blue-white light missing Durand by more than double her wingspan. The Toth fighter passed beneath Durand and vanished over the horizon.

"What the hell?" Durand shook her head in confusion, then looked around for Landas. His emergency beacon wasn't transmitting anymore.

"Sparks? Sparks?"

A dark object passed between her and the

Milky Way's band of stars. Durand tapped her maneuver thrusters to get closer.

"No…no, no, no," Durand said.

The burnt mass of what had been Landas hung in space. His flight suit was seared black. His charred skull leaned back on his shoulder, frozen in a scream.

"Gall, I'm not reading a distress beacon," Jorgen said.

"Disregard," Durand said. "He's dead. I'm en route back to the *Breitenfeld*. Gall out."

Bastard Toth came back just for him, she thought. The emptiness inside Durand began to thaw, and the warm certainty of hatred filled her heart.

****

Hale felt the Mule's landing skids hit the deck, bounce off, then land with a hard shake. He fumbled with his restraints, his mind foggy with painkillers.

"Stay put," Elias said, his armor folded against itself into an almost rectangle. "It's a mess on the flight deck."

"How bad is it?" Hale asked.

"We're listening to the flight deck's IR," Kallen said. "Forward section had a structural collapse. *Breit* nailed that Toth cruiser, but it got a couple licks in."

"Stand by for jump," thundered over the flight deck and into the Mule. "T minus six minutes and counting."

The ramp lowered with a pneumatic whine, Europa's bright face visible through the rear flight portal, shrinking as the *Breitenfeld* moved away. Armored doors ground toward each other, shutting away the moon. A pair of Marines climbed over the still-opening ramp and ran toward Hale, one carrying a medic bag.

"No, I'm fine," Hale said, holding a hand up to stop the two.

"Heard you were injured. Again," Yarrow said. He knelt next to Hale and ran a wire from his gauntlet into a plug on Hale's shoulder. Hale's vital signs came up on Yarrow's forearm screen.

"How bad is it this time?" Cortaro asked.

"It's just a bruise. For Christ's sake let me get to the bridge and talk to the captain," said Hale as he undid his restraints and tried to stand up. Cortaro's firm hand pushed him back down.

"Let the medic check you out, sir. Won't hurt," Cortaro said.

"His suit held integrity," Yarrow said. "His histamines receptors are going off the charts. Bet his immune system isn't fully recovered from that bug he got on Takeni."

"So I'm fine," Hale said.

"What happened?" Cortaro pointed at the mangled armor on Hale's right knee.

"He forgot to duck," Kallen said from her spot next to Elias.

"*Someone* decided to use me as a shield," Hale said.

"That's not…OK, that is what happened, technically, but not what I meant to do," Kallen said.

"Let's get that off you." Yarrow tapped a

command on his forearm screen and the armor on Hale's right leg decoupled from the rest of his suit. Yarrow cut away the pseudo-muscle layer and peeled it back from Hale's right knee.

His skin was a mess of dark bruises ringed with yellow. Hale's knee cap was twisted ninety degrees the wrong way.

"Huh," Hale said. He reached a finger toward the battered joint.

Yarrow slapped his hand away.

"You know, sir," Cortaro said, "if you come back from a mission in one piece, no one will complain."

"Look who's talking, Gunney." Hale cocked his head aside and glared at Cortaro's prosthetic leg.

"I've got bad news, sir. I need to null your painkillers right now. You're about to go into anaphylactic shock," Yarrow said. He took a small hypo-spray from his belt and twisted a dial. He pressed it against a port on Hale's neck armor and the lieutenant felt like Yarrow had injected him with ice-cold water.

"How long does it take to kick—" Hale screeched and bent over and grabbed his thigh.

"I'll get a stretcher over here soon as we've jumped. Dr. Accorso will give you the good stuff once we're in sick bay," Yarrow said.

Hale inhaled sharply through grit teeth. He looked at Yarrow, a man he knew was a proccie, and saw only a good Marine. Hale grabbed Yarrow by the shoulder.

"I wasn't...I wasn't going to let them take you," Hale said.

"Thank you, sir," Yarrow cracked a half smile. "Good to know someone thinks I really am somebody."

****

Kren scuttled up a ramp into the armored command bridge of the *Naga*. He shut the heavy doorway the instant his tank was safe within the miniature fortress. Menial crew slunk away from him and tried to hide behind their workstations. His chief warrior bowed to him.

"Lord Stix wishes to speak to you," the

warrior said.

"I thought he would be here," Kren said. "Put him on."

The perfect hologram of Stix snapped onto the bridge.

"What have you done?" Stix demanded.

"The humans must have had help from the Alliance. *I* certainly didn't give away this ship's existence," Kren said. "What of the thief ship? Is it destroyed?" Truly, he only cared that Hale was dead. Failing to kill the *baelor* himself would shame him for centuries. So long as the human had perished, Stix could be bribed to pass off any story Kren desired.

"It escaped," Stix said, "and with it any chance of us acquiring their technology without significant cost. You already lost one cruiser. Our return-on-investment ration suffers for your stupidity."

"This ship will be enough to subdue the humans. Make for their planet at best speed. us what we want."

Stix shifted from side to side in his tank.

"That is foolish," he said. "We should arrive with our entire fleet at once—ensure we have overwhelming force against their fleet."

"But my dear Stix…if we include Olux and the ships under his command, he'll claim a larger percentage of the acquisition." Kren's nerve endings twisted together. "You'd give up that much wealth for a negligible tactical advantage?"

"We can beat him to Earth orbit by several hours," Stix said. "These humans better be worth the risk. It's your life on the bond, not mine."

"Hurry, Stix. Get us moving. We won't get any richer just sitting here."

CHAPTER 11

Ibarra watched a holo panel on the gently curved ceiling of the command center. Live video feed of the Crucible's interior showed the shimmering field of an open wormhole.

The gigantic interlocking thorns of the Crucible shifted and twisted against each other. An angular shadow darkened the center.

Stacey, her hands flitting from control panel to control panel, took quick glances at the screen.

"The *Breitenfeld* is here. What're you waiting for?" Ibarra asked.

"The quantum field keeps fluctuating," Stacey snapped. "I change one variable and three more go out of variance. I try to close the gate now, I'll smear the ship all over the solar system."

"You're trying to solve this problem like a regular human. Stop it," Ibarra said. "You're much better than that. Connect to the Crucible directly and balance the equation."

"I did that once before—once—Grandpa. You and the probe did all the work." Stacey wiped a hand across her forehead and spun around to a blinking red control panel.

The *Breitenfeld's* shadow grew fainter.

"We're losing her," Ibarra said.

"Why aren't you helping?" Stacey's fists balled in anger as two more panels went red.

"I'm an interactive memory file, nothing more. The probe thought I might break something by accident if I could do more than menial tasks and make smart ass comments," Ibarra said.

"Not helping!"

"Use the neural interface, Stacey. If the ship goes back to Europa, it won't stand a chance against that battleship," Ibarra said.

All the control screens flashed red in time with each other. Stacey's shoulders slumped.

"Where is it?"

Ibarra waved a hand through the air. A square of basalt-like material on the floor squeezed into a lumpy mass as tiny grains of sand swirled over the surface and the lump rearranged itself into a high-backed chair. A silver halo attached to a bar stuck up from the headrest.

"Take a seat," Ibarra said.

"That looks…," Stacey backed away from the chair, pointing to it with a trembling finger, "that looks like the thing in the chamber beneath Euskal Tower. Where I found your body. What's it going to do to me?"

"The *Breitenfeld* is dying," Ibarra said.

"I swear, if this thing kills me, I will haunt you forever." Stacey sat in the chair and squeezed her eyes shut. The halo lowered around her forehead. She gasped and her body froze stiff.

"Stacey?"

"This isn't…that bad." She opened her eyes. They were transformed, now white fields churning with pale-blue haze.

"Your body was engineered, Stacey. Synthetic DNA was woven into your makeup so you could transmit massive amounts of data to and

257

from Bastion. A nice benefit is that you can tap into what makes you more than human, turn your mind into a supercomputer. So, gold stars all around. Now would you mind bringing the *Breitenfeld* home?" Ibarra asked.

The control panels switched from red to green. The wormhole within the Crucible collapsed, sucked into the center point. The *Breitenfeld* hung motionless in space. Scorch trails marred its hull and debris floated from a gaping exit wound through its starboard engines.

"Got it," Stacey whispered. Her eyes returned to normal and she pushed the halo off her head.

"I don't," her words slurred, "feel too hot."

Stacey's chin fell against her chest and she lolled forward.

Ibarra lunged toward her, his arms reaching out to stop her fall…but she fell right through his grasp. She thumped against the deck and rolled onto her back, her breathing quick and shallow.

"My little girl." Ibarra sank to his knees and

tried to stroke her hair with his holographic hand, his fingers passing through Stacey's dark curls. "You never asked for this…and look what I've done to you."

****

Lights flickered across the *Breitenfeld's* bridge. Valdar saw the great crown of thorns that was the Crucible and slapped the emergency release on his restraints. He swung around his chair and went to the XO's station.

Commander Ericsson shook her head at a wire diagram of the ship, red damage reports staining the ship like it was bleeding.

"We've still got a fire on decks three through six from the direct hit on the foundry," she said to Valdar. "Damage control parties have it sealed off, but I can't open the compartments to vacuum. Vents are fused or blown to hell."

"What about the engines?" Valdar asked.

"Numbers two and seven are wrecked—the engine room's trying to cut the batteries," she said.

"Bridge, this is Landis. We've got a

feedback cascade building in the main capacitor banks," the chief engineer's voice came through the ship's IR. "Recommend we slag the batteries before they discharge and fry the whole ship."

"So much for that idea," Ericsson said as she updated the damage control display.

"Landis, we slag the batteries and this ship becomes nothing but a still lump of metal in space dock," Valdar said. "The fleet needs our ship on the line. Can you save the engines?"

"I'll have to send crewmen into the stacks with—"

"Do it."

"Aye-aye, Captain," the chief engineer said, his voice betraying his disagreement.

"Sir, fleet command is hailing us," Erdahl said.

"Put them through," Valdar said.

"*Breitenfeld*, this is Admiral Makarov on the *Midway*. I'm sending ship tenders and the hospital ship *Mercy* to you right now. Looks like you had quite a scrap on Europa," the admiral said with a slight Russian accent.

"This is *Breitenfeld* actual," Valdar said. "Who am I speaking with?"

"Admiral Makarov, I don't believe we've met in person. Transmit your damage reports. The repair bots can get me a better time estimate once they have it," Makarov said.

Valdar muted his line with the admiral and looked back at Ericsson.

"Makarov?" Valdar asked. Ericsson shrugged her shoulders. Utrecht did the same when Valdar looked to him. The Atlantic Union space navy numbered in the hundreds of void ships before the Xaros invasion, but there were only ever a few dozen admirals. Those that commanded a fleet or smaller strike force became known across the fleet for their command style and record quickly and easily.

In all his years in the navy, Valdar had never heard of the woman offering to aid his ship.

"Anyone heard of an Admiral Makarov?" he asked. No one answered.

"*Breitenfeld*, respond," Makarov said. Valdar reopened the line.

"We're transmitting data now." Valdar pointed a finger at Ericsson. She threw her hands up in confusion before carrying out the captain's order.

"Sir," Erdahl said with a sigh of relief, "Admiral Garret is hailing us." Valdar nodded his head and she opened the channel.

"Admiral Garret," Valdar said, "the Toth have a dreadnought-sized vessel in orbit around Europa. They fired on us and tried to kill our ambassador as soon as it de-cloaked."

"They were playing us for time," Garret said. "Of course, we were doing the same thing. Can't trust anyone these days. The battleship is on its way straight to Earth, and it's moving damn fast for something that big. Get your ship back online, more to follow."

"Sir." Valdar felt a knot rise in his throat along with the urge to confess everything he'd done to sabotage the negotiations, his collusion with Fournier. All his plans had fallen apart the second the Toth treachery was revealed. There was no point in keeping things hidden any longer. "Sir, I must report that—"

The ship listed to the side, throwing him against his command chair.

"Engine six just malfunctioned!" Ericsson shouted.

"Fire engine nine. Balance us out and get us clear of the Crucible." Valdar pulled himself back into his chair and strapped in.

"Engine nine's not responding," Geller said.

"Valdar, you've got bigger problems than me right now, Garret out."

Valdar felt a vibration grow through his ship, rattling him against his restraints. It died away a moment later.

"Captain," Landis said, appearing on a screen inside Valdar's helmet. The chief engineer held up a blackened mass of wires connected to a stack of corroded plates. "I overloaded engine nine. We're going to need a couple more voltage sumps...and a new engine nine."

****

Valdar and Hale walked through a busy passageway, and crewmen moved aside or put their backs against the bulkhead when they glimpsed Valdar's rank insignia. Naval ships had narrow corridors, and every sailor—enlisted or officer— learned early in their career to make way for anyone that outranked them, the assumption being that the higher the rank, the more important their purpose and destination. Those with lower rank would suffer the inconvenience.

Hale followed in Valdar's wake, eyeing the sailors they passed by. The crew of the *Midway* was the exact mix of younger and older men and women he'd come to know on the *Breitenfeld* and every other spaceship he'd set foot on. Their uniforms were all crisp and new, but their faces were worn with exhaustion and stress.

Valdar led Hale into a wider passageway that ran along the spine of the carrier. Motorized carts carrying crates and sailors traveled up and down the center of the passage, separated from those on foot by a yellow and black railing.

"Flag conference room is another four minutes that way." Valdar pointed ahead. "Assuming they didn't move it. I served on the ship's electronic warfare division for almost a year back when I was lieutenant commander. Everything else seems to be in the same place."

"Sir," Hale said—he reserved "Uncle Isaac" for when they were in private— "this ship was crashed into a mountain outside Phoenix a few months ago. How'd they get it back in service? And the crew…"

Valdar spun around and held up a finger.

"Don't," he said.

"They're all proccies," Hale said with a loud whisper. "They have to be. I thought it was just a few here and there, but this…" Hale shook his head.

Valdar put his hand on Hale's shoulder. "Admiral Garret ordered us to come to this meeting. He also ordered us not to breathe a word about *them* to anyone. So keep your theories to yourself and don't mention any of the terms you were sent to negotiate with the Toth, even if Admiral Makarov asks you point-blank, understand?"

Hale raised his hands in mock surrender.

Two guards flanked the entrance to the conference room, both enormous soldiers covered from fingertip to toe tip in armor with enclosed helmets. Hale lagged behind Valdar. As the captain slipped into the conference room, Hale stopped in front of one of the soldiers. He couldn't see the soldier's skin beneath the armor and darkened helmet visor, but he had a suspicion these two were just like the one he'd encountered with his brother in Phoenix.

"What's your name?" Hale asked.

"Sir, Cobalt 928, sir," the soldier rumbled.

"How old are you?"

The doughboy cocked its head to the side. "Sir, I don't understand."

"You don't know the day you were born?" The doughboy didn't answer. "What're you doing here?"

"Protect the principal. Protect Garret from

not humans," Cobalt 928 said.

"Hale!" Valdar snapped at the lieutenant. Hale hurried over to the open door and followed Valdar inside.

The conference room was packed with officers who far outranked Hale. He had a sudden desire to find a corner to stand in, as he had little to offer any of the many captains—most of whom had wreathed ship-command stars pinned to their chests.

Valdar grabbed Hale by the arm and pointed to a small paper placard with Hale's name on it set on a long wooden table in front of an empty chair.

"Stand behind that chair and don't say a word to anyone," Valdar whispered to Hale. Hale did as instructed and glanced over the rest of the name placards, all for commanders and captains. Two large chairs were at the far end of the table.

"Room! Attention!" came from a senior master chief petty officer at a small side door. The room went silent as those assembled clicked their heels together and looked straight ahead.

"Be seated," Admiral Garret said as he

walked into the room. A stout woman with deep-brown hair and an admiral's stars on her shoulder followed behind him.

That must be the Makarov everyone's talking about, Hale thought.

Hale took his seat and reached down to touch his right knee. The robot doctor aboard the *Breitenfeld* had reconstructed his knee in less than a half hour and cleared away the contusions. It itched, which was a marked improvement from the searing agony he'd felt until a nurse had pumped him full of a synthetic opiate before his surgery.

"We have an update on the Toth battleship analogue, which we're designating as the *Naga*," Garret said. A hologram appeared on the middle of the table, the chaotic structure of the coral and crystal Toth ship rotating slowly. A mockup of the *Midway*, the largest ship ever constructed by the Atlantic Union, appeared next to the battleship, barely a third the size of the Toth vessel.

"She's big," Garret said. "She's ugly, and she's fast." The hologram switched to a model of the solar system, and the battleship shrank into an icon between Jupiter's orbit and the asteroid belt. "Our working hypothesis is that it came in with the rest of the Toth fleet, cloaked, and started moving toward Earth immediately. Now that it doesn't have to hide from us, she's accelerating. Computer models put it in Earth orbit in seventy-two hours."

Ship captains grumbled and shook their heads.

"The rest of the Toth fleet," on Garret's cue the solar system hologram expanded, a swarm of enemy icons within the orbit of Uranus, "is also on their way here. Math puts them at ninety-one hours away."

"Where are we going to engage?" a captain asked.

"We aren't, not right away," Garret said. "We have graviton bombs hidden through the asteroid belt that will disrupt the battleship's drives, force it to slow down. We've got a surprise waiting for it. If Task Force Odin can destroy or damage the battleship, we stand a better chance against the rest

269

of the Toth in a fleet-to-fleet engagement."

"There's been only one communication from the Toth since the *Breitenfeld*'s return," Makarov said. "They demand we surrender immediately and unconditionally. I responded and told them to go fuck their own mothers, if they have any."

"Lieutenant Hale," said Admiral Garret as he leaned back and cast his Argus gaze at the Marine, "you were the tip of the spear for the negotiations. Do you think the Toth can be reasoned with before this gets any uglier?"

Hale stood up to address the admiral. "Sir, they want…" His eyes darted over the dozens of proccies looking at him. "They want us all. Every last man woman and child is a prize to their whole, twisted way of life. I say kill them all."

Rumbles of agreement spread through the room. Makarov cracked a smile and nodded at Hale.

"Young buck stole my thunder," Garret said. "I was just getting to that part."

"Will there be any reinforcements from the

Alliance?" a captain asked.

The hologram shifted to Ibarra's head and shoulders.

"Ladies and gentlemen of Eighth Fleet, Marc Ibarra here." Ibarra rotated slowly. He looked right at Hale and winked. "We've a slight situation with the Crucible. The Toth slipped a Trojan horse into our friendly probe and we're keeping it offline until we can reboot it safely. The probe, and only the probe, knows the quantum gate signature to allied systems that could send reinforcements. We're on our own for a week...or three."

"Can we still use the Crucible?" Makarov asked.

"It's possible," Ibarra said.

Garret leaned over to Makarov and the two shared a quick side-bar conversation.

"Eighth Fleet," Garret said, "will hold high anchor over Luna. The rest of the fleet, everything that can still fight after we took the Crucible from the Xaros, will form a shield over Phoenix. I'm not going to recall the rest of Strike Force Odin until

271

they've had a chance to nail the *Naga*."

Hale leaned over to Valdar and whispered, "What about the Crucible?"

Valdar raised a hand slightly and shook his head.

"As for the *Breitenfeld*," Garret said, "I know she's earned some new scars, but I'm assigning her to Eighth Fleet."

Valdar's face went white.

"We'll have our next strategy session after the *Naga* hits the asteroid belt." Garret stood up. Every serviceman and woman in the conference room rose to attention and remained silent as Garret left the room, a small coterie of aides and normal human bodyguards followed him.

"Mighty Eighth," Makarov said, "if the *Naga* makes it to Earth, it falls on us to stop it. We don't know what it's capable of yet, but the Toth don't seem to have any qualms with sending it right for us."

"We've trained to take down larger Xaros constructs," a captain said. A streak of albino white hair hung loose over the left side of her face while the rest of her blond hair was held back in a regulation bun.

"We're not going to fight the Toth like they're Xaros," Makarov said. "I want all of you back to your ships ASAP. We'll run simulated fleet actions based off what the *Breitenfeld* brought back."

Makarov stood. "Captain Valdar, my ready room." The admiral left the room, without the same fanfare as Garret.

****

Valdar stood next to the door of Makarov's ready room, his eyes glancing between the few furnishings and decorations as he waited for the admiral to finish a one-sided conversation with her fleet's quartermaster. The walls held a single framed diploma from the Atlantic Union's naval academy in Rota, Spain. The highly textured paper and raised seals attesting to Makarov's graduation were pristine, a recreation of something Makarov thought she'd actually earned.

A small shelf held a large steel urn shaped like a bulb with ornate handles, intricate designs in the metal brought Valdar's mind to the shifting surface of a Xaros drone. A spout stuck out from the bottom of the urn, a tea pot rested on top of the device's flat top. Steam seeped up around the kettle from beneath the device. Two tea cups resting in saucers shared the shelf with the urn.

Admiral Garret's instructions to him had been blisteringly clear: don't let the Eighth Fleet suspect their true origins. How a large group of proccies, particularly those in uniform and with access to weapons, would react to the truth wasn't something Garret wanted to discover while the Toth were still a threat. The fleet was on a commo blackout to Earth and the rest of the navy. They were ignorant, and Garret meant to keep it that way.

Being on a ship full of proccies kept Valdar on edge. Fear scratched at the edge of his consciousness, a deep-seated suspicion that they were nothing but slaves to Ibarra's plans, ready to turn on the true born as soon as that hologram and his probe sent the word.

The inherent wrongness of their being made him sick to his stomach. Valdar had served around the globe, mingled with many different cultures and nations, never judging a person by anything but the quality of their character and their actions. The proccies…they evoked an almost atavistic fear of the Other from him.

Makarov gave the quartermaster a slap on the shoulder and he left the room.

"Sorry, Captain," Makarov motioned to a seat across from her.

Valdar sat down stiffly, his muscles tense.

"The lead engineer on the *Eisen*, the tender working over your ship, says he can have you back on the line in three days. I gave him twenty hours and two more dry-dock robots from Titan Station. He should make his new deadline," Makarov said.

"Thank you, Admiral," Valdar said. Calling her by a rank she'd never earned made his stomach churn.

"I know you by reputation," she said. "You

came up with the assault plan for the Battle of the Crucible, held the fleet together when the *America* and Admiral Garret went down. I have a tactical puzzle that I think you—and the *Breitenfeld*—can help me solve."

"Happy to help." Valdar's lips tugged at a sneer, which he masked with a scratch to his face.

"Are you all right, Captain?" Makarov looked at him with genuine concern.

She stood up and went to the urn. She took up the kettle by the handle and poured dark tea into the cups. She held a partially full cup beneath the spigot and twisted the handle, releasing steaming hot water into the cup. She prepared the second cup and placed one in front of Valdar, keeping the other for herself.

The smell promised a bitter taste. Valdar wouldn't have minded a few ice cubes and sugar to make the drink proper to his Virginia upbringing.

"I lost my original samovar," she said. "My family carried it out of Soviet Russia to Ukraine when the regime fell. My great-grandfather knew a little too much about the KGB—where they buried the bodies, kept all the money, that sort of thing. He decided to take a little culture, and some of the money, with him and the family. I had it in stored in Kiev, but the Xaros…This is a reconstruction from photos, not as good as the real thing."

No you didn't, Valdar thought. *Everything you are was a computer simulation. Fake.*

"Your ship's jump engines, we could use them to our advantage in the coming fight." She slid a data slate across the table. "What do you think?"

Valdar skimmed over the operation's order. His lips pressed together in concentration as he grasped the sheer audacity of what Makarov had planned.

"The missiles…if the Toth have better point defense systems than us, this won't work," Valdar said.

"Graviton seekers," she said, "no electronics to hack or jam. We were going to use these to overwhelm the Xaros' point defense, but with a little modification…"

"You came up with this?"

"The concept, my staff worked out the details. What? You think I found these stars in a cereal box?" Makarov gave Valdar a sly smile.

Valdar bit his lip.

CHAPTER 12

Captain Bakshi strapped himself into the command chair of the *Javelin*. He swiped the Sikh turban off his head and shoved it into a compartment beneath his chair. God would forgive the affront. He still had his *kirpan* knife on his person and an iron bracelet on his wrist.

Bakshi snapped his armored helmet on and attached it to air lines running from his headrest.

"XO, set battle stations for the task force, cleared for zero atmosphere conditions." A ship full of air risked fires and decompression damage during void combat. Fighting in largely self-contained and lightly armored suits increased the chances of surviving. Any injury that could pierce the suit would likely prove fatal, a risk every good void sailor understood.

"Condensers on full," his XO said, "we'll be zero atmo in five minutes."

Bakshi had commanded the *Rorke*, a much larger vessel than the *Javelin*. Moving lower on the tonnage scale from command to command normally meant career suicide for a naval career, but when Admiral Garret had explained the need and the reasoning behind this assignment, he'd accepted it willingly.

Sitting in a ship barely the size of a destroyer and anchored against an asteroid for months got old quick, but he and the crew adapted. They'd waited and trained for this moment; now the lancer concept would have its trial by fire.

"Spotters show the *Naga* on approach," his XO said. "It will enter range of the graviton mine in three minutes."

"Let's hope that thing works as advertised," Bakshi said, "or we're not going to be able to do much more than wave as it goes by."

"*Spear, Broadhead* and *Pike* report battle ready," the communications ensign reported.

"Arm the mine. Set gravity-well trigger to one million kilo mass trigger," Bakshi said.

Alcubierre drives warped space-time around a ship to propel it forward; the "flatter" the space-time, the faster a ship could travel. A sufficiently deep gravity well would disrupt the drives and slow the *Naga* down to a crawl.

"Mine is armed," the XO said.

Bakshi opened a tight beam IR channel to the other ships. "Task Force Odin, this is Bakshi. Engage attack pattern alpha once we clear the asteroid. Good hunting."

The *Javelin* lurched to starboard as the graviton mine activated. Bakshi slid against the right side of the command chair, then the ship jerked to a halt.

"Tether engaged successfully," XO said. "Rest of the squadron are green."

"Ready the release. Conn, keep us orientated on the target as we clear," Bakshi said.

The pull from the graviton mine lessened, and the *Javelin* groaned as the stress on its hull faded away.

"Detach cable," Bakshi said. The asteroid

slid across the view screen as the *Javelin* cut loose and drifted away. "Guns, charge the vanes." Electricity arced and sparked just below the view of the screen as the four rail-cannon launchers came to life.

"Two minutes until we clear the rock," the conn officer said.

"Too long. We're not going to give them a chance to get their drives back up. Conn, fire dorsal thrusters. Give us a push," Bakshi said.

"Aye-aye, burning."

The ship shuddered and the asteroid sped across the view screen. The *Naga* hung in the void, canted away from the *Javelin*. The *Naga's* engines flared to life with a blossom of white light.

"Christ, that thing's big," the conn officer said.

"All ships! Target center mass, clear all vanes on my mark…"

"Firing solution locked. All vanes ready," the gunnery officer said.

"Fire!"

The rail cannon mounted on the *Javelin's* ventral hull sent a shell hurtling through the twinned vanes' magnetic vortex, accelerating it to a velocity nearly six miles a second. The cannons mounted on the port, starboard and dorsal hull fired in succession seconds after the first round.

The lancer ships were single-purpose vessels designed to pack the punch of a much larger ship, at the expense of almost everything else that mattered to a void ship—range, crew comfort, speed and survivability. The concept behind their design held promise in a fleet action against a larger Xaros construct…in theory. The same theory held when using lancers as an assassin's mace against a single ship.

Sixteen rail-cannon shells cut through space, all converging against the center of the *Naga*.

"Ten seconds to impact," gunnery said.

"Reload and recharge. Squadron, get some space between us and fire at will. Wide spread," Bakshi said.

Bakshi leaned forward, his eyes locked on

the view screen. A ripple of light spread across the *Naga*, wrapping into a cocoon around the ship. More waves of light spread over the ship, like a faucet dripping onto a pool of water. The cocoon around the *Naga* faded away.

"No effect," the gunnery officer said.

"It's shielded," the XO said, her voice trembling with fear.

"Keep firing!" Bakshi ordered. "Commo, send an update back to Titan right this second. Keep our feed open no matter what happens." The ensign gave him a thumbs-up and frantically tapped at his keyboard.

"Incoming!" XO shouted.

"Conn, get space between us and—"

A searing bolt of energy streaked out of the *Naga*, retracing the squadron's rail-cannon shells. The white light overwhelmed the screen and Bakshi brought his hands over his face.

The light faded away. Chunks of debris floated through space around the *Javelin.*

"*Spear* is gone!" the XO said.

"Guns, why aren't we firing?" Bakshi asked.

"Vanes almost ready, sir." Three new bolts emerged from the *Naga.* "Firing!"

Bakshi watched as four more shells leaped toward the *Naga.* "Titan, this is Captain Bakshi with Task Force Odin. The *Naga* is shielded. I repeat, the *Naga* is shielded." An incoming bolt flared as it annihilated the first round from the *Javelin.* "Rail cannons are ineffective." The bolt diminished as the next two rounds passed through it and burst into fragments. "I'm sending back every bit of telemetry data we've got. *Spear* lost with all hands."

The bolt burnt through the last rail-cannon shell and smashed into the *Javelin.* Shattered vanes spun into space as the forward half of the ship crumpled under the impact. The bridge and engineering compartments went tumbling through the void, like they'd been swatted aside by a giant hand.

Bakshi tossed against his restraints. The XO's chair broke loose from its moorings and slammed her against the bulkhead with a sickening crunch. Bakshi's world went black seconds later.

****

Stacey, Ibarra and Rochambeau watched a grainy video feed. Broken work pods and smeared blood filled the *Javelin's* wrecked bridge. A gloved hand dangled in front of the camera.

"Ugh…report," Bakshi said. The hand lifted off screen. "Anyone?"

The blast door to the bridge bent inward with a screech of metal.

A Toth ululation screamed from the speakers.

The door fell off its hinges with the next blow. Toth menials filled the door, hissing at Bakshi. A gauss pistol snapped, killing the nearest menial with a screech of pain as more menials rushed into the room.

Bakshi screamed. A gauss pistol fell in front of the camera, still gripped by a bloody hand dismembered at the wrist.

The menials dragged Bakshi off the bridge, and his screams faded away.

Stacey turned off the recording.

"There's nothing after that," she said.

"What did he know?" Rochambeau asked, running the claw tips on his fingers through his goatee. "They took him to the overlord."

Admiral Garret's hologram appeared. "The rest of Task Force Odin's positions in the asteroid belt, graviton mines emplacements. The legacy fleet strength, but not the current number of hulls and crews."

"Nothing about Eighth Fleet or the shipyards within Ceres?" Ibarra asked.

"No, we kept him and the rest of Odin in the dark…for precisely this reason," Garret said.

"Their shields." Rochambeau rewound the footage. "There are several species in the Alliance with similar energy-screen technology. The Vishrakath, Caar Imperium, Tikari Collective, relics of the wars before the Xaros threat."

"Why didn't the probe give this to us?" Garret asked. "We could've incorporated this into our new ships."

Rochambeau clicked his tongue. "The Tikari thought energy shields would protect them from the Xaros disintegration beams, but the drones cracked the resonant frequencies and stripped the shields away. The probe didn't give you the tech because it would have been useless against the drones."

"How'd it work out for the Tikari?" Garret asked.

"They're extinct."

"So, how do we figure out the resonance freqs on the *Naga*?" Stacey asked.

"The probe could do it." Ibarra pointed to the empty plinth in the center of the command center. "But it's still compromised."

"At their current speeds, the *Naga* will be here in twenty-eight hours," Stacey said. "The rest of the Toth fleet twelve hours later. I don't understand why the big ugly isn't waiting for the rest, mass their forces as one."

"There's more than one elite," Rochambeau said. "One on the *Naga*. At least one more with the rest of the fleet. Whichever claims Earth gains a greater share of the profits."

"Thank God for small favors," Stacey said.

Garret tapped his knuckles against a table. "Focus, people. If we can't get past the Toth shields, then this is all over but the screaming. I need options from you big-brain types before I send my fleets face-first into an oncoming train."

"You're wrong to look at this like a military problem, Admiral," Ibarra said. "The Toth aren't here to beat us down and plant a flag. They're here for profit. And, as a veteran businessman, let me tell you that controlling costs is essential for a wider profit margin. That's why they were willing to talk with us on Europa."

"Nothing about what you just said solved the problem of the *Naga's* shields," Garret said.

"Those shields are running off a dark-energy battery, just like the one the *Breitenfeld* has for its jump drive," Ibarra said. "We disable that battery and the ship is vulnerable."

"Oh, that's all there is to it? Well, why didn't you just say you've got a magic wand hidden somewhere on the Crucible," Garret said with a chiding voice. "Push the damn 'We Win' button already or do you have something more practical in mind?"

"Subtlety and misdirection, Admiral," Ibarra said. "Hear me out."

****

"You'll do it?" Ibarra asked Rochambeau.

"Why me?" The Karigole crossed his arms across his chest.

"The list of humans I'd trust with something this vital is pretty damn short. I don't have to worry about any true-born or proccie sympathies with you," Ibarra said.

"The doughboys won't accept me, ghost," Rochambeau said.

"Only if they think you're not human," Ibarra said. "We cover that ugly mug of yours and you could pass. We just have to imprint enough of them with your vocal signature and they won't know the difference. Just so you know…this is almost certainly a one-way trip."

"If this is my final battle, then it will be worth it," Rochambeau said. "I agree to your task." He bowed slightly and left the command center.

"And you?" he asked Stacey.

Stacey looked at the chair with the halo and rubbed her hands together.

"It's not as simple as you make is sound. If the timing is off by a few seconds, then it will be a disaster," she said.

"Then get the timing right. You're a smart girl. I've seen you do harder math."

"There's more, Grandpa. The Qa'Resh sent me back with a gift, and if I foul this up, we may never get the chance to use it." Stacey went to a console and tapped on the control panel. A blue-green world with oceans and wide continents appeared in the holo projector.

"This is…the Qa'Resh just have a location, not a name. Let's call it Terra Nova. Earth-like down to the gravity and atmosphere content. Geologically stable, local space is clear of threatening comets and asteroids for a million years.

Life on the planet similar to our Miocene epoch—large mammals, oceans full of life and no intelligent natives. Couldn't ask for a better place for humans to colonize," she said.

"Pretty, but irrelevant when the Xaros overrun the galaxy," Ibarra said.

"That's just the thing. Terra Nova isn't inside the Milky Way. It's in Canis Major, a star cluster beyond the fringe of the Milky Way. The Qa'Resh think the Xaros will stop at the edge of the galaxy. If they do keep going, it'll take the drones almost ten thousand years to reach Terra Nova. The Qa'Resh gave me the gate settings to reach Terra Nova. We pack the *Canticle of Reason* and some of our civilian ships full of colonists, the omnium reactor and a couple fabrication units and we've got a chance to save our species."

"What about the Dotok?"

"You care? I'm surprised. There's room for them."

"Why are the Qa'Resh doing this? Don't tell me they found out about Terra Nova last week.

Every species in the Alliance would kill for a chance to escape the Xaros," Ibarra said.

"The one I talked to, she said the Qa'Resh feel guilty for what they've put us through. What'll happen if the Toth win this fight? Terra Nova is their chance at a cleaner conscience, but if I'm using the Crucible for this crazy plan of yours, I may not have the chance to get a colony ship through in the middle of a battle."

"A world safe from the Xaros." Ibarra raised his fingertips to the holographic globe. "But you won't be able to go. You have to keep the gate open."

"I'll stay behind, help reboot Earth with new proccies that fit more in line with what the Alliance wants from us," Stacey said, turning her face away from Ibarra.

"You agreed to that?"

"Don't get all high and mighty with me. You've cut worse deals with them. That was the agreement: Terra Nova in exchange for my help if the Toth take the planet," she said.

"None of these options are easy," Ibarra said. "Save part of the population and probably doom the rest to being slaves to the Toth, or fight to win with the risk of losing everything."

"Hedge our bets?"

"I'll get a small civilian ship loaded quietly, stop a run on the space port. If the plan falls on its face, we'll get something through to Terra Nova." Ibarra turned to a screen and scrolled through a ship registry.

"What about the Dotok?"

"Well, we can't always get what we want. You want to save them? You'd better start thinking with portals."

****

Standish slapped a fresh battery into his gauss rifle and attached it to the magnetic locks on his back. His squad mates snapped their armor on, glancing at a ticking clock above their lockers.

"I win again," Standish said. He brushed imaginary dust from his gauntlets.

"You don't win a damn thing until you pass

Gunney's inspection," Orozco said.

"It's fifty push-ups—in armor and with your pseudo disabled—for a gig. I learned my lesson after the third time he got me," Standish said.

A chest piece clattered to the ground and spun across the deck. Yarrow cursed and chased after it.

Orozco gave Standish a stern look then nodded his head toward Yarrow.

Standish scooped up the armor piece and smiled at Yarrow, who had sweat beading against his brow and flushed cheeks.

"Settle down, new guy," Standish said. He pressed the armor against the medic's chest and activated the fasteners. "You nervous all the sudden? What for?"

"You've been to the Crucible before, right?" Yarrow asked. "I don't know what's waiting there for me. That probe thing going to decide to vivisect me? Ibarra decides he wants a new body and I'm the prime candidate?"

"Hey, I'm the one that comes up with the

295

crazy ideas around here," Standish said. He grabbed Yarrow by the shoulders and turned him around. Standish attached Yarrow's back plate, then his air and battery packs. "Don't be so paranoid."

"I think I've got every right to be paranoid," Yarrow said. "The last couple months—literally my entire life—has been nothing but weird…stuff."

"Told you this would happen if you kept running your mouth with your conspiracy bull dust," Bailey said. She set a bag on a bench and laid out her sniper rifle.

"Kid's had a rough time," Orozco said.

"Life's been shit for everyone since the invasion," Bailey said. "Don't hear me bellyaching about it. Course, I drink heavily."

"We're not going to the Crucible, Yarrow." Orozco slammed his fists against his chest and stomped his feet against the deck. Ritual complete, he rolled his shoulders back, then pulled his Gustav heavy cannon from a separate locker. "We're going to Ceres. 'Strategic reserve.' Should be lots of sitting on our ass doing nothing. Let the navy finally win a battle."

"Is this knitting circle done jaw jacking?" Cortaro banged an armored fist against a locker next to the doorway. "The L-T is waiting for us on the flight deck and you know I hate it when the L-T has to wait on us for anything."

"Gunney, the warning order said we just need our standard kit," Bailey said. "Any idea how long we'll be away from the *Breit*?"

"Command wants warm bodies on Ceres," Cortaro said. "Anything else we need will be waiting for us."

"Anyone else suddenly think we're not going to be sitting around on Ceres for very long?" Standish asked.

"Shut up, Standish," Cortaro said. "Everyone to the armory for ammo draw then double time it down to the flight deck."

CHAPTER 13

Hale watched as Destrier transports passed through the force field at the stern of the ship's enclosed flight deck. Tiny puffs of air vented around the high-hulled ships and into the void. Hale didn't care to understand the engineering behind the force field, but it didn't seem perfect to him.

A nudge to his back got his attention. Durand, clad in her flight suit and carrying her helmet under the crook of her arm, nodded to him.

"Marie," Hale said, "there are two Eagles left on the flight deck. Where's the squadron?"

"Hawaii," Durand said with a roll of her eyes. "Titan routed orders through. My whole squadron's going to run intercept on the Dotok camp and the R&R center. I've got more Toth kills than any other fighter jockey and they want me flying holes in the sky over an empty hotel. Such *connerie*. You?"

"All my Marines and the armor to Ceres. We'll get more details when we arrive." Hale watched as the cargo ramp on a Destrier lowered; a large metal box was tied down at the end of the cargo runners. "What's with the heavies? The *Breitenfeld's* a strike carrier, not a cargo ship."

"The captain didn't say." Durand shrugged. "He didn't seem too upset the last time we spoke. Bit distracted. He OK?"

"He's been acting all kinds of weird since we got back from Takeni," Hale said. "I don't know if it's stress or something else."

A crewman in a power-lifter suit lumbered over to the open Destrier.

"Looks heavy," Hale mused.

"Time to go," Durand said. "Kill some Toth for me." She walked off without a second glance.

"You...too," Hale said as he watched her leave. She wasn't the same woman he had known. What joy she'd once had inside her from before the war had calcified, leaving her with a heart of stone.

****

Kren's tank sat nestled in a mound of elaborately embroidered pillows, an affectation from his days when he still had his body. Useless, but a nice reminder of just how far he'd improved his own station in life.

Menials worked around him in the armored vault that served as the *Naga's* bridge, its bulkhead's angles jutting outward like they were in the center of a gigantic gemstone.

Kren felt an itch deep within; the urge to feed was growing. The spike beneath his tank scratched at the housing, begging to come out. He let the urge pass. Soon he'd gorge himself on the humans, and the hungrier he was, the better the high.

Besides, all the menials on the bridge were highly trained and difficult to replace.

"Lord Olux grovels for your attention," a menial said, not daring to look directly at Kren.

"Does he? Make him wait," Kren said. He was the one in control of the *Naga*. He was the one who'd found this new resource. He was the one who was going to become richer than any Toth, second only to Mentiq's glory. Olux must be reminded of his low station compared to Kren.

"Olux…" the menial slunk away from Kren, "dares threaten to remotely disable your life-support functions if he is not addressed very quickly."

"Put him through," Kren said.

A perfect hologram of Olux appeared on the bridge.

"Kren, you will slow your ship and wait for the rest of the fleet to reach you," Olux said, his nerves twisting with anger. "The humans will surrender when they face our full might."

"But then you'd earn a larger share of the profits," Kren said. "The *Naga* has already beaten the humans. They know they can't win. I see no reason to diminish my return on investment for your sake. Don't you agree, Stix?"

A second hologram appeared—Stix, his tank adorned with gold and platinum armor plates. "I drank from the human captain. The humans are weak. I will not split my share for your concerns."

"Your obstinacy is noted and will be reported to Dr. Mentiq!" Olux shouted.

"I'm sure the good doctor won't care, not when he has a never-ending supply of human meat." Kren tapped a claw arm against the deck twice and the menial cut Olux's transmission.

"It is unwise to anger him," Stix said. "He is one of Mentiq's favorites."

"Mentiq values those who make him richer, not those that polish his claws," Kren said. "How much of a lead do we have on that leech?"

"Substantial. We can decimate their fleet and have the humans begging for mercy before Olux arrives. I've no contact through the Alliance probe. They must have discovered the implant and shut it down."

"The virus was still worth the price we paid. The star gate will play no part in this fight." Kren tucked pillows against his side, an old habit. "Let's agitate the humans a bit more. I do love meat that's been stressed for days. It adds a subtle texture."

A claw tapped in the direction of the communication's menial.

"Open a frequency, audio and visual, all known human channels," Kren said. The menial slapped its tail against the deck once the order was obeyed.

"Meat," Kren said the word slowly, "you will surrender the procedurally generated humans and their methods of creation. Your pathetic military will surrender and you will submit to us. Any resistance will be met with overwhelming force. Accept this mercy now. You will not get a second chance."

Kren tapped a claw and the menial closed the channel.

"Put that on repeat," Kren said.

"I thought the plan was for a complete harvest of the planet," Stix said.

"It is, but if they give up the procedurals, it'll save us trouble, less worry about breaking anything valuable," Kren said. "Will you join me in the bridge?"

"No. This ship's warriors are competent, but little more. I will fight the ship from the weapons deck. That is why chairman Ranik sent me on this expedition. I will earn my share."

"Do be careful, corporate brother. It would be a shame if you were to perish and I inherit your share."

"The same to you," Stix's hologram vanished.

****

Hale tromped down the long ramp of the Destrier transport. They'd landed inside an enormous cavern of smoothed-out gray regolith. When Hale'd learned that he and his Marines were going to Ceres, he'd assumed the Crucible—not inside Earth's newest moon.

Two soldiers waited for him at the bottom of the ramp in gray-scale armor, a captain with close-cropped blond hair and a first sergeant with a perpetual scowl across his face. Hale saluted the captain.

"Lieutenant Hale, *Breitenfeld* Strike Marine

detachment," he said. He jabbed a thumb over his shoulder at Steuben who'd followed behind him. "Steuben, with the Karigole, if you couldn't tell."

Gunney Cortaro led the Marines away with the first sergeant.

"Captain Hunter, Alpha Company 95th Ranger Regiment," the soldier said. "Rochambeau was with us for a couple weeks. I didn't think there was much more about shipboard operations we could learn, but he taught us a few new tricks. Glad to have you here with us."

"I didn't even know this," Hale said, looking around the cavern as transport craft and cargo loaders moved about in a hangar larger than the *Breitenfeld's,* "was here."

"Xaros made this cavern and the others," Hunter said. "They converted Ceres' mass into the Crucible, hollowed out some pretty impressive voids in the process. Don't know why they didn't just take it off the surface. Maybe aesthetics? History aside, did Command tell you what you're here for?"

"'Strategic reserve,'" Hale said.

"Ha. That's one way to put it," Hunter said. "Follow me." He pointed to a set of blast doors on the far side of the hangar and started walking.

Hale fell in to Hunter's left.

"Lieutenant Bartlett, he was one of mine," Hunter said. The young officer had led a team of Rangers on Anthalas; all were captured and killed by the Toth. "Shame to lose him and the rest of his team on Anthalas. Good soldiers, all of them."

"How…long was he with you?" Hale asked.

"Almost a year. Picked him up right out of Ranger School," Hunter said.

Hale nodded slightly. *Hunter must be a proccie,* he thought.

The joined metal plates on the blast door slid aside as they approached. Hale came to a stop, his jaw slack at what lay beyond the doors.

A massive cavern held four *Breitenfeld*-class strike carriers side by side, each resting in a massive scaffolding. Construction bots and workers moved over the hulls, installing hull plates and engines to the ships. The far end was nearly grayed out by a mist of wispy clouds.

"Woah," Hale managed.

"Yeah, it's a sight," Hunter said. "They've got a supercarrier almost done in cavern epsilon. Crews are coming in daily from the R&R facility on Hawaii. Damn squids get a nice break while their shiny new ships are getting built. My soldiers have been stuck in here for months running sims, but there's no better welfare for soldiers than first-class training. Come on."

Hunter walked toward a set of stairs inside a metal scaffold running up the cavern wall.

"How're they going to get these ships out?" Hale asked.

"They built the doors first." Hunter glanced up at metal hinges dug into the rock across from the ships. "Amazing what Ibarra's construction bots can manage since the invasion. Him and that probe were sitting on tech improvements that put us forward another fifty years. Makes you wonder what could've been if he opened up the floodgates the day that probe got here."

Hale followed the captain up the stairs two at a time to keep pace.

"You saw the video of the Xaros attack," Hale said. "There were billions of drones. You think it would have ended any different with better tech?"

"Several species with larger populations and superior technology have fallen to the Xaros," Steuben said. "Yours was one of the few successes the Alliance has ever had against the enemy."

"No arguments there, but playing Monday-morning quarterback takes my mind off the fact that my hometown and everyone I ever knew were erased off the planet," Hunter said. He stopped three flights up, next to a hover sled. The craft had a flat top and a small booth for the pilot. A dozen armed Marines could stand on it with ease.

"Ceres has a couple hundred of these," Hunter said. "Standard cargo lifters for the shipyards. Fabricators are putting armor plates and rocket-assist pods on units in cavern delta right now."

"For what, exactly?" Hale asked.

"The Toth ship, the *Naga*, our fleet can't touch her with rail weapons," Hunter said. "Ibarra thinks he can get the shields down long enough to land boarders—my Rangers and your Marines. We get in there…disable the ship anyway we can. You and Steuben have been on a Toth ship. I need you to help me figure out where to go once we're inside."

"We were on a Toth cruiser, not the same thing as the *Naga*," Hale said.

"The Toth follow a singular design—protect the elite," Steuben said. "The ship's master will be well protected deep within the ship. We kill the elite and the entire ship will falter."

"Hard imagining my company and a couple Strike Marines able to take on the whole ship if they're that dedicated to keeping one Toth alive," Hunter said.

"Then we feint," Hale said. "Put pressure on the elite and draw off defenders from the engines, computer core."

"And who's going to draw that fire?" Hunter

asked.

"Me. I'm *baelor*. The Toth have a vendetta against me," Hale said. "If Steuben is on the headhunter mission—"

"I will kill every overlord I see," Steuben said with certainty.

"The Toth know he means business," Hale said. "It could work. How're we going to get onto the *Naga* with these things?"

"Yeah," Hunter said, "that's where things get a little weird."

CHAPTER 14

Shannon elbowed away the woman pressed against her side. The Mule was designed to hold no more than a dozen armed Marines, not the thirty true born crammed into its cargo bay. She would've had space to stretch her arms, but the tarp-covered case tied down in the center of the bay was more important to the mission than any of the commando's comfort.

"We've got enough air for this, right?" someone mumbled.

"Only if you keep your damn mouth shut," Shannon hissed. Amateurs. There were enough former military and more than one deserter in the group to keep discipline at an acceptable level, but a couple overly excited pure civilians with more élan than training were in the group.

She understood why Fournier brought them

along; they were expendable.

"We've got docking clearance," Fournier said over the intercom. "Our woman on the inside has a red undershirt. Don't hurt her."

A volunteer, the same fool that insisted on speaking, fumbled with a magazine on his chest harness. Shannon snaked a hand between bodies and grabbed the man's wrist. She shook her head from side to side. He was more likely to accidentally shoot a true born before they ever got to the *Lehi*.

The whine of gauss carbines came from the stern of the cargo bay. Four former Marines in full armor, wearing the true-born patch of the Earth held by a pair of hands painted over the globe and the anchor Marine Corps emblem, readied themselves.

"Secure the bridge and lock down the rest of the ship. Remember, everyone on this ship is either a proccie or one of Ibarra's collaborators," Fournier said. "No mercy."

Shannon chewed on her bottom lip. She'd told Ibarra about Fournier's plans and asked him for permission to liquidate the true-born leader and his lieutenants before they carried out the boldest move in the group's history. Instead, Ibarra instructed her to make sure the assault went off without a hitch, and to build them the device in the center of the cargo bay.

She'd worked for Ibarra for almost half a century, always trusting that he meant to build a bigger, better world than the governments she'd abandoned. He'd always given her an out from any assignment, and the codes in her pocket to override the *Lehi*'s lifeboats were the sole comfort she had on this mission.

But something about this gnawed at her. Why did Ibarra want the true born on the *Lehi*? There were easier ways to get rid of them, and without risk to the priceless procedural tanks on the ship.

The Mule landed hard, and the press of bodies swayed against each other.

The ramp lowered quickly and the four Marines squirmed over the edge as soon as they could. She heard shouts and more than one shot from a gauss carbine. The mass of the true born rushed off the Mule, shouting at the top of their lungs and brandishing their weapons in the air.

Shannon had no choice but to move ahead with the scrum.

The *Lehi*'s cargo bay was barely big enough for two Mules. A dead woman in a dark gray jumpsuit lay on the deck, her bloody arms wrapped around her stomach, an empty pistol holster on her thigh.

Shannon knelt beside her and brushed deep red strands of hair away from the dead woman's face, as her pale blue eyes stared into nothing. She recognized the woman from somewhere, but she couldn't place it.

"Sir, what do we do with them?" someone called out.

Shannon looked up and saw three rows of doughboys standing at parade ground attention near the far bulkhead. All wore armor, their faces covered by dark enclosed helmets. Each held a bulky rifle that looked too heavy for Shannon to even lift. None showed the slightest awareness of what was going on around them.

"Leave them alone," Fournier said from behind Shannon. "They'll make a nice gift." He stomped down the ramp, a giant smile on his face.

"Don't bother with the traitors, my dear," he said to Shannon. "I need you to move our insurance policy to the center of this hell pit."

A true born led a hand-bound and gagged Lawrence from inside the Mule to the top of the ramp and slammed the butt of a gauss carbine into his kidneys. Lawrence groaned through the rag tied through his mouth and fell to his knees. The guard put a boot against his shoulder and kicked him down the ramp.

Lawrence rolled to a stop next to Shannon, bleeding from a gash across his forehead and his nose. Shannon fought to keep her anger in check. She'd found a place for more enhanced interrogation methods during her long career in espionage, but never outright sadism.

"Put him with the rest of the crew," Fournier said. "Now, where's our camera man?"

****

The tanks sent a chill down Shannon's spine. Each held a procedural human being floating in clear liquid, tubes and wires running from their heads and mouths into buzzing machinery at the top of the tank. Thick cables ran from each tank into a massive computer bank attached to the ceiling.

The procedurals were of differing races. Most looked to be in their twenties and thirties, but a few tanks on the edges held men and women that looked like they were on the edge of elderly, while others were barely teenagers.

What the hell is Ibarra doing with them? Shannon asked herself.

She turned her attention back to the large case that two men had lugged into the tank room for her. She unsnapped the latches and flipped the lid over. The bomb was crude by her standards, blocks of mining explosives attached to a detonator with wires. It had to be obvious—those were her orders from Fournier—make it so no one doubts what it is.

What wasn't obvious were the blocks of denethrite beneath the more mundane explosives. The Ibarra Corporation used denethrite charges to crack asteroids. They were the second-most explosive material mankind possessed, after nuclear weapons. Fournier asked her to build a bomb that would destroy the tanks; Ibarra told her the bomb must take out the entire ship.

"Activate it," Fournier said. Shannon keyed in a five-digit code that brought the detonator to life; she picked up a hand trigger and gave it to Fournier.

"Flip the cover and press the button three times," she said. "Hold the last press. Range is good beyond five kilometers."

Fournier stuffed the trigger into his jacket and tapped his forearm screen.

"Jenkins, break anchor. Take us to the Toth ship as fast as this thing will go. Dump the Mule and the life pods," Fournier said.

"Sir, wait…" Shannon felt panic grip her

heart. This wasn't the plan. "What're you doing?"

"Showing Ibarra and the Toth our resolve," Fournier said.

The *Lehi* shook beneath Shannon's feet as the engines powered up. The people in the tanks swayed back and forth, tugging against the tubes and wires attached to their skulls.

"Give me a tight-band IR transmission to Titan," Fournier said. "Let's get to the Toth ship without any further issues."

The cameraman touched his earpiece then counted down from five with his fingers.

"My name is Cebile Fournier. True-born forces have seized the *Lehi*, the ship where Ibarra and his traitors manufacture their abominations. Their proccies. We are taking this ship, Ibarra's only source of these things, to the Toth. We will deliver the technology to the aliens to bargain for our planet's safety and to rid humanity of the cancer spreading from this ship."

Fournier stepped to the side and held a hand toward the bomb.

"Any attempt to stop us and we will detonate this device. The production tubes and the computer used to create the proccie minds are our only bargaining chip with the Toth. Don't force me to destroy it." He nodded slightly and the camera turned away.

"It's sent," the cameraman said.

"Good." Fournier turned to Shannon. "Round up the prisoners and bring them to the cargo bay. I'll cut another video for the Toth. Tell them we come in peace and bearing gifts. We can deactivate the device once we're beyond Ibarra's reach."

You keep thinking that, Shannon thought.

"Let me check over the device first," she said. "Make sure Ibarra and his probe aren't trying to tamper with it." She waited until Fournier and his hangers-on left the gestation room.

Shannon cracked her tooth.

"I saw," Ibarra said. *"Make this fast. You're moving out of range."*

"This has gone too far, Marc. Way too far.

319

Let me put an end to this. All I have to do is free a few prisoners and kill the true born on the bridge," Shannon whispered.

"You have to let this play out, darling. There's a way out coming—just wait for it. Do you trust me?"

"You've asked me that question for fifty years. Of course I do."

"Then stay with it. And no matter what happens, don't let the Toth get ahold of that ship," Ibarra said. "Want you—" static overrode his voice "Eric…and sister to me. Don't—" There was a slick click against her eardrum as the connection ended.

Shannon opened a hidden compartment beneath the bomb and fished out another remote detonator. She slid it into a pocket inside her jacket.

"You've never let me down before, Marc," she muttered. "Sure hope this plan of yours is a doozey."

****

Lieutenant Jared Hale jumped off the back of a truck onto a dusty road. Doughboys followed his lead, rocking the drone vehicle on its axle with their bulk. The doughboys formed into even ranks on the road shoulder, without a word shared between them. They stood at a modified parade rest, one hand on the small of their back, the other holding a shovel or pick axe.

Bulldozers in the distance crushed through thick vegetation. Robot arms gathered the fallen trees and plants and fed them into industrial processors, turning them into planks of wood or packed blocks of cellulose. All around Jared and his charges, automated machines destroyed a once pristine nature preserve.

Even with the efficiency of twenty-first-century construction techniques, they were moving far too slowly.

Jared raised his forearm screen in front of his face, looked "through" his arm and saw the red overlay where his detail was supposed to be working.

"Indigo," Jared said, pointing to small red flags in a line through disturbed earth. "Dig a trench. Same depth and width as we did in the last place, you remember?"

"Sir, yes, sir," The doughboy snapped his oversized shovel into his hands like it was a rifle and jogged toward the flags. The rest of the doughboys followed after him. A truck rumbled past as Jared sent an update to Loa headquarters. The duracrete layers would arrive in two hours, and he'd get an earful from Major Robbins if he was behind schedule.

Mauna Loa, the tallest volcano on Earth, rose through the clouds, a column of steam snaking up from the summit. The R&R center spread from the base of the mountain—where massive steel doors sealed off whatever the Ibarra Corporation had buried within—toward the surrounding Pacific. The center had rows of prefabricated buildings with an attached landing pad boasting twelve new Eagle fighters from the *Breitenfeld*. He made a mental note to seek out Durand and get more from her about what the *Breitenfeld* and his brother had been up to these past months.

He might get an hour's reprieve from the never-ending construction assignments once the trench lines around Loa were complete. He thought the doughboy reassignment to Hawaii would mean more field time with them, not manual labor.

"Jared!" another lieutenant named Douglas called to him from the back of a truck. The young officer jumped off and waved. "You believe this? I just relocated all the Dotok from the Milolli camp to the bunkers and now my bubbas and I are digging ditches out here with you."

"They don't complain," Jared said, nodding his chin at the newly arrived truck.

"I sure as hell will," Douglas said to Jared. The army officer shouted instructions to the doughboys in the back of the truck and put his hands on his hips. "I thought command shipped us out here to do field tests on the doughboys, see if they can fight. Don't tell me Ibarra went through all the trouble of building them just to turn them into glorified field hands."

"Weren't you here for R&R awhile back?"

Jared asked.

"Yeah, just slept a lot and went to the beach," Douglas said with a shrug. "Nice break from space. Why?"

"Seem odd to you that we're going all out to harden an R&R spot from the Toth?"

"Could you imagine the blow to morale if we lost our only vacation spot?" Douglas chuckled. "But ours is not to reason why. Ours is to do or die. Maybe Robbins—hey! Agate 229! Don't throw dirt on Onyx 37!" Douglas shook his head at Jared. "And I thought eleven bang-bangs, regular army infantry, were a bunch of knuckle draggers."

A truck's breaks squeaked as it stopped next to the work area. A robot arm dropped pallets of armored plates on the side of the road.

Jared shook his head. This was going to be a long day.

CHAPTER 15

"To the Toth, we come in peace, and we come bearing gifts," Fournier's broadcast cut to video of a camera going from empty escape-pod bay to empty escape-pod bay.

"Sir, the *Lehi* will be within range of our gauss emplacements in minutes," Utrecht said. "It's a civilian ship. One hit from the rail guns will turn them into dust, but our point-defense guns could put a couple holes in them. Take out their engines."

The *Breitenfeld* anchored a few dozen kilometers away from the Crucible, far from the rest of Eighth Fleet in orbit around Luna, and not far from the course the *Lehi* was on to the Toth battleship.

Valdar rubbed his thumb against his fingers, debating. Disabling the *Lehi* would be easy, but doing so would destroy the procedural lines and a fight with the Toth would be assured. If he did nothing, the Toth might leave the system with the proccies and never darken Earth's doorstep again. If he ordered the ship destroyed, with Fournier on it, he could cover up his involvement with the man and his group.

A few days ago, this decision would have been simple. Now, with the Toth betrayal on Europa and his ship scarred by battle, he couldn't make up his mind.

"Sir? What should I do?" Utrecht asked.

Valdar slammed a fist against his armrest.

"Guns, I want you to—"

"Captain, priority message from Admiral Makarov," Erdahl said. "She's ordering us to stand down."

Saving her own kind, Valdar thought.

"You heard her," Valdar said. "Orient our gauss and rail emplacements away from the *Lehi*. Don't want anyone getting nervous and doing something stupid."

"Toth vessel is reducing speed and vectoring

away from Earth," Ericsson said. "*Naga* and the *Lehi* are on an intercept course."

"Looks like the Toth are interested in Fournier's offer," Valdar said.

The *Lehi* skirted through the *Breitenfeld's* range.

Obeying Makarov's order was the right thing to do, the only thing to do without an apparent mutiny, but deep inside his heart he felt like he'd make a terrible mistake.

****

Shannon stood in the cargo bay with Fournier and the leaders of the assault. Dozens of the *Lehi*'s crew and workers were on their knees at the edge of the cargo bay, hands bound behind their backs and hoods over their heads. Some whimpered in fear; others begged their captors, pleading that they were "just following orders" or that Ibarra somehow forced them to work the proccie lines. Shannon didn't hate them as their loyalty wavered; denouncing Ibarra might save them. Silent stoicism offered them no chance of living to see another day.

The doughboys were still in the cargo bay, now pressed into a corner and under command of a single armed true born. Even without their weapons, the hulking constructs looked formidable.

The view of the star-studded void lurched to the side.

"Toth tractor beam has us," came over the loudspeakers.

One of the traitor Marines activated his gauss carbine.

"No need for that," Fournier said. "Put your weapons away, all of them. We will welcome the Toth aboard, show our good faith."

Shannon tugged at her jacket and covered the pistol on her hip.

The star field vanished as the *Lehi* entered the uneven hull of the *Naga*, and blood-colored shoals came down around the ship like a curtain. Panicked whispers darted around the cargo bay as the true born grasped just how big the *Naga* had to be if it could fit a cargo ship like the *Lehi* inside it.

"Maybe this wasn't a good idea," someone

said.

Fournier snapped his head to the side, searching for the offender.

Light grew beyond the upper edge of the open cargo bay. An open section of the Toth hull slid into view, and Shannon saw clawed feet milling around as the *Lehi* rose higher. Toth warriors and menials, all armed with weapons that looked like metallic vines twisted into the shape of rifles, let loose sibilant warnings as the two open bays came level with each other.

Shannon's heart leapt into her throat as she came face-to-face with the Toth. The warriors were almost half again as tall as her, a feral intelligence gleaming from their eyes as they looked over the humans. All of them took quick breaths through their snouts, trying to get the human's scent. Their three pairs of limbs looked nearly identical to each other, as if the rear and mid-arms could carry a weapon as easily as the upper arms. Metallic bolts and screws attached skull caps to the warriors, and wires ran directly into flattened ears and ridged

329

bones around deep-set eyes.

The four armed menials scurried around the Toth deck, ducking between the warrior's legs and scuttling over their hindquarters without notice from the larger species.

The *Lehi* jerked to a halt, nearly flush with the Toth cargo bay.

"Weapons," a warrior croaked, "surrender or die."

"We will comply," Fournier said loudly, placing his hands over his head. The rest of the true born followed suit and looked up at a camera blister on the ceiling. The force field on the *Lehi* dissipated.

Toth menials scuttled aboard, their claws scraping against the deck. A menial made straight for Shannon. She stepped back, her atavistic fear of reptiles and snakes overwhelming her composure. The menial snapped its jaws at her and plucked the pistol away.

"Enemy?" a low voice said from behind her. She turned around and saw a doughboy with his

330

fists balled in front of his chest.

"No! Shut up, you idiot." The minder took a truncheon from his belt and rapped the doughboy across the knuckle. The doughboy growled, then lowered his hands.

Menials, their arms loaded with human weapons, walked back to the *Naga* on their hind legs. A smaller menial with smoother scales grabbed the edge of a captive's hood and lifted it up, giving the woman under the hood a face-to-face look at the creature. She cried out in horror.

The menial gave off a *tss-tss-tss* sound like laughter. It never saw the warrior that stomped on it from behind, crushing its spine with an audible pop. The warrior grasped the menial with the same limb that crushed it. The small creature's arms flailed wildly, its legs hanging limply as the warrior held it over the gap between the two ships and let it go.

The menial bounced between the two hulls like a pinball as it fell away.

Ibarra, I could really use that exit right about now, she thought.

A warrior with gold pins embedded into its chest scales stomped against the deck twice.

"Thoth na Stix!"

The menials faced the large doors leading into the Toth cargo bay and prostrated themselves.

The doors opened, and an elite with crystalline plates arrayed against its tank like armor strode into the cargo bay. Warriors averted their gaze and cleared a path from the elite to the edge of the cargo bay.

As it strode toward Shannon, the disembodied nervous system in a gilded tank filled her with dread. Shannon suddenly wished Ibarra had told her about the probe decades ago so that she could have told him to get rid of it so that humanity might never have had to come face-to-face with monsters like this.

"Which of you is Fournier?" the elite asked, its voice frightfully perfect.

"I am." Fournier raised a hand from behind his head. "And who do I have the honor of addressing?"

"Stix of Tellani Corporation," the elite said.

"You're not the same Toth we've seen before," Fournier said. He lowered his hands to his side. "I hope we can reach an agreement with you."

Stix floated in his tank, nerves loose and dangling.

"What is the meaning of this?" a claw arm pointed at the kneeling prisoners.

"Most are procedurals and yours to take," Fournier said. He unhooded one man, Lawrence. The administrator tucked his chin against his chest, refusing to look at the elite. "This one is involved with the production. He will answer your questions."

"Everything for their production is on this ship?" Stix asked.

"And nowhere else," Fournier said.

Stix's feeder arm snaked out of the housing beneath his tank, its tip caked in red blood. When the spike tip popped open, Shannon backed away, her eyes glued to the writhing dendrites.

The arm rose into the air and stabbed into

the skull of a hooded prisoner. Her shrill screams ended within seconds. The corpse slid from the tendrils that had invaded her skull and fell to the floor.

"Yes…" Stix said. "Yes, these are exquisite. A false mind in a weed body. Their taste is different but sublime." Stix bobbed up and down in the tank, the light within darkening to a deep purple.

"These are the only ones that know how to operate the equipment. I'm sure they can have more for you in a few—"

The feeder arm slammed into Lawrence's skull and pulled him into the air. He twisted around, his eyes rolling back in their sockets, mouth agape. His hands quivered madly before his entire body went slack.

Stix tossed the corpse aside like it was a piece of garbage.

"Stix," Fournier raised his hands in front of him and tried to back away, "pace yourself. There are plenty more where they came from."

"Ha-wai-eee," Stix said. A claw arm

clamped down on Fournier's shoulder and pulled him toward Stix. "What of the facility on Hawaii? There are more tubes there. Many, many tubes."

"No," Fournier went pale, "he swore that this ship was the only place they make the proccies. I promise!"

The feeder arm rose in front of Fournier's face as dendrites flecked in blood danced over the true born's face.

"Many more on Hawaii. A better prize than this ship…and Dotok? New meat for the market. Why did you lie to me?" Stix asked.

"No! No! Never!" Fournier's crotch darkened as he lost bladder control.

"I like the fear," said Stix as his feeder arm pounced on Fournier's skull. The human leader didn't even scream as the Toth drained him to nothing.

Shannon turned and ran, shoving stunned true born aside as she rushed toward the doughboys and the ladder leading below decks next to them. She heard terse Toth commands behind her and screams from the unarmed true born as they realized that they were next on the menu.

A doughboy—one that moved with confidence and had only four fingers on his hands—pushed his way out of the pack.

Rochambeau pulled his helmet off and pointed at Stix.

"Soldiers! Attack!"

A doughboy knocked the true-born minder aside and charged toward the Toth. Their heavy footfalls rattled the deck.

Rochambeau reached beneath his back plate and drew the short sword he'd kept hidden. The heirloom Karigole blade flashed in the air. A thrill went up Rochambeau's spine as Stix, the Toth that led the betrayal of the Karigole, rocked back on his claw arms in surprise.

The doughboy at the front of the charge took a blast from a Toth rifle in the chest. The soldier staggered backwards, then charged forward again. Toth warriors closed shoulder to shoulder around the elite and leveled their rifles at the doughboys.

Three shots tore an arm off a doughboy and knocked him on his back.

The constructs leaped over the gap between the two ships. One landed on top of a hissing minion, trampling it without effort. More went down to the warrior's rifles as they herded Stix toward the exit.

A doughboy grabbed a Toth rifle, struggling with the warrior until it shot the soldier in the gut. The doughboy groaned and fell to his knees, his hands locked on the rifle. A doughboy smashed a meaty fist into the warrior's snout, caving its skull in with a shower of sparks from the skull cap.

Rochambeau jumped over the chasm. He reached under his breastplate and pulled out a metal cylinder attached to a long handle.

An energy blast hit the doughboy in front of him, turning its head into a smoking wreck. The fire lessened as the doughboys made it through the fusillade to grapple with the warriors.

The Karigole despised the idea of using the doughboys as little more than meat shields, but their sacrifice would not be in vain. Rochambeau slashed his sword through the brainstem of a warrior and impaled the blade through the rank pins of another. He grasped the cylinder with his free hand and twisted it hard.

A snap told Rochambeau that the shaped charge grenade was set for impact detonation.

Stix broke away from his bodyguard and made for the door as fast as its bulk and claw arms could take it.

Rochambeau took three long steps toward the Toth elite and leapt into the air. He slammed against the tank and dug his claws into its armor plates.

The brain inside the tank lashed at him against the glass.

"I could not ask for a better way," Rochambeau said. *"Ghul'Thul'Ghul!"*

Rochambeau slammed the grenade against the tank. A small explosive charge morphed a tungsten disk into a molten lance of plasma. The superheated metal sliced through Stix's tank like it wasn't even there and flash boiled the brain within. The tank exploded, sending hunks of jagged shrapnel into the warriors and doughboys battling around it.

Rochambeau rolled across the deck, his body aflame with pain. He stopped on his back, staring into the ceiling. His limbs wouldn't move. The taste of blood was thick in his mouth. The sound of the melee around him faded quickly.

Rochambeau greeted death with pride. The architect of the Karigole xenocide—Stix—found death at his hands. A deafening darkness closed around him. His final thought went to his brothers, hoping they could also find a worthy death.

****

Admiral Makarov waved her hand through a holo tank. The senior staff officers and Kosciusko watched as the space around Earth materialized, with icons displaying over the legacy fleet over Phoenix, and her Eighth Fleet burning toward the pulsing red *Naga* beyond the orbit of the moon. The Crucible lay far beyond the battle lines, where the

Breitenfeld waited, still surrounded by tenders and repair vessels. The *Breitenfeld* looked helpless and broken, just like Makarov wanted.

She and her staff would control the battle from the Combat Information Center, located directly behind the ship's bridge, while the *Midway's* captain handled the ship. Makarov had enough to worry about without trying to steer the supercarrier. All wore the shipboard armor and enclosed helmets, ready for combat.

"The strike force from the Crucible reports they've breached the *Naga*," a staff officer said.

Makarov tapped the *Naga* and her fleet. A dashed line appeared between the two along with a timer.

"Forty-five minutes until we're in their engagement envelope," Makarov said, "maybe fifty before our rail cannons can touch it."

"If we cut our speed, it'll give the strike teams more time. This will be a short fight if their shields are still up when we get in range," an aide said.

"No," Makarov shook her head. "We give the *Naga* any more time and it'll make range on Titan Station and Phoenix. Neither of which can take a punch."

"Admiral, we've got new sensor contacts," an officer in the forward section of the bridge called back.

"Send it to my tank," Makarov said.

A swarm of tiny icons emerged from the *Naga* and lines traced their projected course toward Earth.

"Are they abandoning ship?" Makarov asked.

"No," Kosciusko said, "there are a few lifeboats aboard any Toth vessel, and they are only for the overlords. Those are fighters and troop transports."

"This doesn't make any sense." Makarov watched as the smaller Toth craft pulled away from the *Naga*. Their course put them on track to break atmosphere over Hawaii. "They're not coming to intercept our fleet? There's nothing of strategic value on Hawaii but the Dotok camps and the R&R centers."

"Their fighters don't have the range to make it to Phoenix if they're flying through atmo from Hawaii," an aide said.

"What could they possibly want?" Makarov trailed off as she made the connection. The Toth were only there for the proccies. They took a risk to bring in the *Lehi*, the only proccie production facility there was. If the Toth were moving on Hawaii, then that meant...

Makarov's muscles tensed into knots as the realization hit her. There was another facility, hidden from her. She and her fleet had just finished their R&R. The truth became self-evident. She knew what she was.

Makarov turned her gaze to Kosciusko. The Karigole nodded slowly.

"I want..." Makarov cleared her throat. This was no time for introspection. She pointed a finger at the aerospace wing commander. "Cavanaugh, I want a full interdiction launch prepped and in the void. Throw everything we've got at the Toth fighters. You understand?"

Cavanaugh tilted his head to the side. "Everything? Should we maintain—"

"Everything! I want hedgehog shells launched into that mess of Toth as soon as we have firing solutions ready. What do we have on Hawaii?"

"One squadron of Eagles from the *Breitenfeld*," a Marine officer said. "A few companies of doughboys relocated from Phoenix."

"Tell them they're going to have company," Makarov said. *Damn Ibarra for keeping this secret from us,* she thought. *We can't afford to lose what he's got hidden down there.*

"I'll join the Dotok squadron," Kosciusko said.

Makarov dismissed him with a wave of her hand.

"Admiral, new contacts—"

"Thank you, Commander. I see them," Makarov said.

"No, ma'am, it's the rest of the Toth fleet!"

Dozens of Toth warships decelerated at the edge of the Earth's gravity well. They wouldn't be in range for another hour, barely enough time for her to take out the *Naga* before she'd have to deal with the combined might of the entire Toth fleet.

"This just got complicated," Makarov said. "Get me Captain Valdar on the IR."

****

Ibarra reached his hand into a holo tank and rotated the image of the *Naga*. Shields distorted light around the massive ship's hull as tiny motes of light swarmed from multiple points across the ship. Icons popped over the motes, marking them as dagger fighters and larger transport craft.

"They're going for it," Ibarra said.

Stacey, bound against the halo chair, sucked in a sharp breath. Tendrils of solid light arced from her skull to the halo like electricity travelling up a Jacob's ladder.

"I can't...I can't feel the space within the shields. The dark-energy signature is throwing everything off," she said.

"Don't strain. I have someone on the inside who'll take down the shields. Soon. Any second now." Ibarra put a fist next to the *Naga* and mimicked an explosion. When none came, he tucked his hands against his arms. "Come on, Shannon."

"Shannon? Aunt Shannon is on that ship?" Stacey asked.

"I couldn't give this mission to just anyone. She'll pull through. She always does."

"We're going to lose her…" Half her face jumped with a painful tick.

Not for long, Ibarra thought. "Shannon" had died twice before, once to the Xaros invasion and again after her flawed re-creation uncovered the truth about her existence. The profile he'd used to approximate his old head of security was the most detailed program he'd ever devised. He'd have her back, with a few parts of her memory adjusted for her own sake.

"Does she have a beacon?" Stacey asked.

"Maybe I could get her out."

"No. She's a big girl, darling. She volunteered for this. Knew the risks going in," Ibarra lied.

"She and Uncle Eric were always so nice to me," Stacy said as a tear slid down her face. "I would have liked to see her again."

The swarm of Toth craft veered toward Earth. Ibarra didn't need the computers to tell him they were heading straight for Hawaii.

****

Shannon sprinted down a narrow passageway, the slam of her feet against the metal grates ringing through the air. The Toth had gone mad since the Karigole killed the elite, ripping the ship apart and dragging away every human they could find.

A high-pitched ululation rang through the air. She didn't bother looking over her shoulder at the pack of menials hunting her down. She heard their claws skittering over the deck, snarling at each other.

She saw a door slightly open ahead of her and bashed it open with her shoulder. She slammed the door behind her and activated the pressure seals. She was in a crew cabin—double bunks with a mess of clothes and data slates.

Claws raked against the outside of the door, rattling it against its hinges as the menials tried to force their way in. The pressure seals were meant to keep the cabin safe if the ship suffered a sudden decompression, not serve as a panic room. The view through the single small porthole was of the enormous Toth hangar.

I'm backed into a corner, she thought.

Shannon jabbed a knuckle against her false tooth.

"Marc, can you hear me? Everything's gone straight to hell. The Toth are all over the *Lehi* and I'm…" The banging intensified against the door. The guttural command of a Toth warrior sounded through the door.

"I'm not going to make it out of here." Shannon took the detonator from her coat pocket, then waited for a response. None came.

She flipped the safety latch off with her thumb. A pale-green light blinked from the detonator switch, signaling it was in range and in contact with the bomb.

Toth claws punctured the door, and metal screeched as the warrior scratched a triple gash across the door. A yellow eye glared at Shannon.

"Had to happen sometime," she said. "Here we go…" She pressed her thumb against the detonator once, twice, then held it down.

The bomb deep inside the *Lehi* exploded, sending a torrent of fire and white-hot hull fragments into the *Naga*. A wave of fire incinerated decks and thousands of Toth before blasting through the outer hull. Atmosphere vented from the exit wound until emergency airlocks slammed shut throughout the ship.

The *Naga's* engines sputtered, and the energy shields protecting the ship vanished.

CHAPTER 16

A cheer went through dozens of Marines and soldiers as they watched a plume of fire erupt from its hull. The ship listed to the side.

"Buckle up—that's our cue," Hale said. His Marines knelt next to the armor plates welded to the side of the grav sleds and connected anchor lines from their belts to magnetic plates. The navy boatswain's mate in the control compartment looked at Hale and gave him a thumbs-up.

Dozens more grav sleds floated level with his, all loaded down with strike teams. Three sleds held the Iron Hearts.

"Hale, we're good to go," Hunter said through his helm IR.

"Roger, sir. Good hunting," Hale said. He switched off his transmitter. "Marines, the *Lehi* got us a way in. It's up to us to rip the *Naga's* heart out

349

and finish the job."

Steuben's hand closed over his sword hilt.

"Every Toth life is forfeit, but the elites are mine," he said.

"Can I stand *behind* him when we get on board?" Standish asked.

A point of white light coalesced in front of the grav sleds and then expanded into a white circle almost fifty yards in diameter.

"Here we go," Hale said. "*Gott mit uns!*"

The sled hummed and accelerated forward. Hale gripped a handrail and watched as the portal neared.

A wave of white light engulfed the sled, and Hale had a brief sensation of floating.

Reality snapped back. The sled was in the void, Luna hung low below the sled, and the *Naga* was just ahead. Small segments of the crusted hull broke away around the damaged docking bay in the middle of the ship. Plumes of fire burst forth and were quickly snuffed by airless space.

"Hang on," the boatswain's mate said.

Rocket pods flared and Hale felt a tug against his magnetic locks against the sled.

"All those shuttles that hit atmo," Yarrow said, "that should mean fewer Toth on board, right?"

"Yes, but the elite's personal bodyguard will never leave their master's side," Steuben said. "Most bodyguard contingents are several thousand strong."

"You're just full of all kinds of good news, aren't you, big guy?" Standish said.

The rockets died down. Hale's sled broke off with five others, flying toward the base of a massive weapon crystal.

"We're not here to fight every Toth we meet," Hale said. "We're here to get the Toth's attention, pull them away from the Ranger's targets."

"So the biggest, meanest Toth will come looking for us. Lovely," Standish said.

The sled dove past the weapon's crystal the size of a city bus and angled itself parallel to the hull. The anti-grav thrusters fired, slowing it as it descended next to the uneven hull that reminded Hale of the broken lava rock fields on Hawaii. The sled came to a halt.

Hale uncoupled himself and grabbed the upper edge of the armor plating. He swung himself over the edge and keyed his grav boots to pull him toward the *Naga*. The hull was barren. Irregular weapons pylons and small plumes of gas vented from punctures and broke up the expanse.

Sleds streaked overhead as the Ranger teams broke away to the individual objectives. Small groups would hit the Toth in many locations at once. If everything went as planned, they'd plant their explosives and signal for extraction before the Toth could mount an effective resistance.

Cortaro bounded toward the joint between the crystal cannon arm and the hull, Orozco and Bailey behind him. Marines dismounted off two other assault sleds. The Iron Hearts didn't wait for their sleds to touch down; they leapt from the still-moving craft and used their jet packs to maneuver to the hull. They landed hard, their backs to each other.

The sleds rose from the surface and sped away.

"Good luck, Marines," his boatswain sent.

"Thanks for the lift. Sure hope you can find Titan Station," Hale said.

"Setting charges," Cortaro said.

Orozco took a spool of wire from his belt and tossed a weighted end to Bailey. She slapped the end against the hull as Orozco drew out the line. Cortaro grabbed the wire and brought a few feet taut against Bailey's hold. He held the wire against the hull and pressed a wide-barreled tool over the wire. The tool jolted as it fixed a large staple, connecting the wire to the hull. The trio repeated the task, forming an imperfect octagon of wire against the hull.

"Sure hope that's big enough for us," Elias said. "We didn't get all dressed up for the view."

Cortaro slapped a power pack to the wire. The Marines stepped aside and put their backs to the cannon arm.

"Going hot," Cortaro said. "Watch for decompression."

Hale took loping strides over the hull and stopped next to Cortaro. The gunnery sergeant tapped on his forearm screen and looked away from the wire.

Blaze wire burned hot enough to rival the surface temperature of the sun, focused along a few millimeters beneath it. The blaze wire glowed ruby red and started sinking into the hull.

"You think they're still pressurized in there?" Cortaro asked.

"Find out in a second," Hale said.

The cut hull section exploded away from the hull like a popped cork. A gale of breathable air roared into space, ambient moisture freezing into snow. Menials rode out on the blast of air, flailing for several seconds before hard vacuum ended their lives.

"And that, boys and girls," Standish said, "is why we don't fight in atmo."

The air from the *Naga* abated. Hale glanced over the lip of the breach and saw a corridor lit by flashing blue lights lying a few yards within an open slice of armor.

"The command bridge should be directly beneath us," Steuben said.

"Let's go knock on the door," Hale said.

"Excuse us." Elias barged in front of Hale, with Kallen and Bodel behind him. The Iron Hearts crawled one by one into the breach. As the third soldier entered, Lafayette jumped from its back, a light spacesuit over his head and torso.

"I believe you humans call this crashing the party," Lafayette said.

"You were supposed to remain on the Crucible," Steuben said. "Let some part of us survive."

"And what? Sit on my shiny metal ass while you three kill Toth?" Lafayette detached a gauss carbine from his back. "I think not."

"Breach is clear," Elias said.

"The more the merrier. Follow me,

Marines," said Hale and jumped into the *Naga*.

****

Twin blasts from an air horn jolted Durand from sleep. She'd mastered the military art of grabbing a catnap whenever and wherever possible years before; waking fully alert came hand in hand with nodding off instantly.

She snatched her flight helmet from a hook on the wall and ran out of the small office. Her pilots were in the ready room, card games and reading slates tossed aside as they sealed up their flight suits. All looked to her for the reason behind the alert siren.

The door to the ready room burst open, and one of the mechanics stuck his head in and said, "Holy shit! You got to see this!"

"Make a hole!" Durand shouted as she ran for the door. Pilots stepped aside, one grabbing Lothar—who'd stood still looking at his brother in confusion—and pulling him out of the squadron commander's way.

Durand got outside. The mechanic pointed

into the pure blue sky, where distant explosions blossomed and faded away. Streaks of white contrails formed behind high-speed craft dogfighting in the upper atmosphere.

She glanced at the screen on her forearm: nothing but an error message.

"What gives, ma'am? I thought the Toth would attack Phoenix before they ever came here. All we've got is Dotok civvies and empty barracks," the mechanic said.

"Our luck is shit," Durand said. She looked to the adjacent landing pad where her Eagles were prepped and waiting. She knew a fight was coming to Earth and had put every one of her fighters on ready alert as a precaution.

Her pilots crowded against each other to get out of the glorified shack they'd been waiting in.

"Mount up!" Durand shouted. She ran for her waiting Eagle and slapped on her helmet. She shimmied up the ladder leading to her cockpit and jumped inside. Her crew chief attached air lines and data wires to the back of her helmet as she ran through the preflight checklist.

"Gall? This is Major Robbins in the Loa R&R defense center. Can you hear me?" came through her helmet.

"This is Gall. I've got you on IR and nothing else," she said.

"The Toth are jamming everything. We got a partial transmission from Eighth Fleet. They said we've got fighters and landers inbound."

"No kidding. Does fleet command know that my squadron is the only thing this island has that can fly and shoot?"

"I'll be sure to tell them if I can get a line open to them again. The Eighth launched fighters. Aren't they going to help?"

Durand swiped at a data screen and looked at the last known position of the Eighth Fleet in Earth orbit and did some quick calculations in her head. Her jaw clenched as her situation on Hawaii became clear.

"I doubt they can do much more than they already are," Durand said. "At that range, any Eagle that hits atmo won't be able to make orbit again without recharging their engines. That fleet's air boss won't sacrifice his fighter cover for whatever's down here. And whatever air support we've got in Phoenix can't get here for two hours. We're on our own from the edge of space to the Pacific Ocean."

The crew chief slapped her twice on the shoulder; she was hooked in. He got out of the way and the canopy lowered around Durand.

"Fleet say why the Toth are moving on us? Do they want the Dotok?" she asked.

"Uh...that's need-to-know," Robbins said.

"You think I don't *need* to know? I'm trying to figure out how to run an interdiction mission and I need to know what I'm trying to interdict! Where are you sitting? I will come over there and—"

"There is a research facility buried into the side of Mauna Loa. We believe that's their target."

"The R&R center? Why?" Durand cycled power to her retro-thrusters. Icons for the rest of her squadron flashed green, ready for takeoff.

"That's classified," Robbins said curtly.

Durand slammed a fist against her canopy and mumbled a curse.

"103rd, this is Gall," she said over the squadron channel. "The Toth are coming in force. *We* are the fight between earth and sky. We…" she hesitated against telling the half truth she'd got from Robbins, "we saved the Dotok once before. We need to do it again."

She cycled power into the engines and lifted off from the landing pad.

"Take off in sequence. Whoever scores the fewest kills buys the drinks," she said.

She nosed her fighter upwards and blasted into the sky. She felt the urge to fly straight for the flash of the dogfight above the atmosphere. Good men and women were dying and it wasn't in her nature to shirk from battle.

She leveled her Eagle and flew north.

"103rd, come to fifty thousand feet and stagger by flights. I want eyes peeled and heads on a swivel. Nothing's going to sneak up on us," she said.

"We're not going to attack?" Filly asked.

"We take out whatever gets through that fur ball up top. Keep them away from the facility near Loa," she said.

"What about the Dotok camps?" Manfred asked. "We've got soldiers armed with rifles and little else to defend everyone that made it off Takeni."

"That too," Durand said. She gnawed on her lip as a hard decision reared its ugly head.

"So what's the priority?" Glue asked. "The Dotok or that facility?"

"If we have to choose, that means enough Toth bandits made it through that the only thing we've got to worry about is not dying. So don't worry about it," Durand said.

A dozen red diamonds appeared on her canopy, all on approach to Loa. Images of the serrated-blade fighters and bulbous transports blew up next to the icons. Durand adjusted course toward the hostiles and gained elevation.

"Blue flight with me up top," Durand said.

"White and Red, I want you to go in swinging hard. Peel off as many fighters as you can so Blue and I can pick off transports. Everyone understand?"

Eleven pilots replied in sequence.

"Remember," Durand said, "these are Toth, not Xaros. If these lizards don't kill you, they will eat you."

Somebody chuckled over the IR, but only one somebody.

"Nag, open your targeting computer," Durand said. She hit a switch and a progress bar popped up on the canopy. It froze and flashed red almost immediately. "Figures," Durand muttered. "Everyone, we've got a hostile malcode environment. Stick to eyeballs and good shooting."

She glanced down and saw the blue square icons of White and Red flights on her visor. The eight craft sped ahead. The Eagle's glass cockpit, tech almost a hundred years old, hadn't been compromised by the Toth electronic warfare…yet.

"Manfred, Lothar, I know your families are down there, but this is where your fight is, understand?" Durand asked. The two Dotok pilots flew as a pair next to Durand and Nag.

The brothers spoke in Dotok briefly before Lothar said, "We've been studying your sacred texts. Our warrior creed shares much with the 'star spangled' hymn about standing 'between a loved home and war's desolation.' You know it, yes?"

"Do I sound American to you?" Durand snapped, doing nothing to conceal her French accent.

"Do...you?" Manfred asked sheepishly.

"Bandits entering rail-cannon range," Glue said. "Permission to engage."

"One shot each," Durand said. "Don't drain your batteries if you don't have to. Let's show these bastards who they're messing with." Durand activated her fighter's rail cannon, and a pair of vane tips emerged from the fuselage.

Thunderclaps broke from the rail cannons of White and Red flights as their slugs shattered the sound barrier. Durand watched the rounds streak toward the Toth formation. Two slugs connected, annihilating a transport and a fighter, the hypervelocity rounds nearly pulling the transport inside out as it tore clean through its gleaming white hull.

A yellow exclamation mark flashed on her canopy; her gauss cannon was ready.

The Toth fighters fired afterburners and came straight for the Eagles while the transports flew low over the ocean, spreading a wake across the surface.

Durand pressed a trigger on her control stick and her Eagle bucked like it had been hit. The fighter undulated through the turbulence the rail cannon left behind. Firing the rail cannons wasn't a joy in the void, firing them on a lower power setting in atmo wasn't high on her list of fun things to do either.

"Splash two more," Manfred said.

"Blue, we skip the fight with the fighters. Get the transports," she said.

Gauss cannons pelted the oncoming fighters. The *brrrrt* of Gatling fire made it to Durand over the noise of her engines and the wind howling across her cockpit. The corner of her mouth pulled into a smile—how she loved that sound.

As the rest of her squadron crossed lances with the Toth fighters, the air below her turned into a swirling mass of planes and gauss bullets crisscrossing with burning bolts of energy. She craned her head over her shoulder, watching to see if any Toth fighters broke away to pursue her, but nothing followed.

"The transports are slowing down," Nag said.

"What?" Durand watched as the wake behind the low-flying transports lessened. "Easy targets," she said. "Smoke them and get back to the rest of the squadron."

The transports came to a complete halt. Durand fired off a long-range shot, the fan of bullets splashing around the idling transports. One round struck home, canting the transport to the side and spinning it around.

Additional, heavier splashes erupted from

the water. Durand's head snapped from side to side. No one else had fired.

"I see Toth warriors are jumping from the transports," Lothar said.

Durand closed within effective range with her gauss cannons and let off a long burst, joined by the rest of the squadron. Bullets blew the transports full of holes. One exploded in midair, and the rest crashed into the ocean, trailing smoke and fire.

Durand flipped her Eagle over and slowed as she passed over the burning wreckage. She saw a flash beneath the surface, like a fish retreating into the depths.

"Can Toth swim?" Nag asked.

"More bandits inbound," Lothar said. "Fighters and at least…twenty more transports."

"Back to White and Red," Durand said. She looked to the sky. Descending contrails of more and more Toth breaking through the upper atmosphere appeared beneath the wild melee in space.

This is going to be a long day, she thought.

****

Hale ducked behind a bulkhead and banged a fist against it twice. There was a squeal of metal and a hurricane rush of air past him. Bits of trash and dying menials tumbled down the corridor.

The interior of the Toth ship was close to the last alien vessel he'd been on. Hexagonal passageways of metal grates over thick pipes, the metal was spaced just far enough to give the Toth menials handholds on any surface. There was plenty of overhead space to accommodate the overlords, which left room for the three armor soldiers leading the way through the ship.

"Clear," Elias announced.

"Pressure's equalizing, sir," Cortaro said, reading from his forearm screen. "Looks like they're getting their act together."

Their boarding action had been easy up to this point: the armor soldiers pried open airlocks, exposing compartments to vacuum. The unsuited menials they'd encountered were too busy dying of decompression to put up a fight.

The sounds of banging doors and Toth

language rose as the air thickened.

"Keep moving," Hale said. "We wait around too long and they'll—"

A blaster bolt sliced through the air and struck the deck next to Hale's feet. A torch of fire burst to life at the point of impact, sparks shooting out from damaged cables.

The armor's gauss cannons cracked like sudden thunder. Hale peeked around the bulkhead and saw an open turbo lift at the end of the passageway, the pulped remains of a team of armed menials dripping down the walls.

"Can we take that lift to the command deck?" Hale asked Steuben.

"We're three decks above the overlord, but the lifts are death…" Steuben lifted the edge of his visor and took a deep breath though his nose. "I smell ozone." The Karigole looked up at the ceiling.

Metal tubes glowed red. He felt heat coming through his helmet as the red lightened to a blazing white. The ceiling exploded, pelting the Marines with metal fragments and a wave of flame.

Hale managed to get his arms up around his head before the blast of overpressure shoved him against the bulkhead. His head bounced against the wall and sent stars swimming through his vision.

"Contact!" someone shouted.

A flood of menials poured through the jagged hole in the ceiling, right in the center of the Marine's formation. Hale switched his gauss rifle to SHOT and swung the barrel toward a hissing pack of Toth running right for him.

He hesitated. Cortaro was in his line of fire, grappling with a Toth that had wrapped its limbs around the Marine. His Marines were well armored, carrying gauss weapons that could knock out a Xaros probe. Engaging in hand-to-hand combat with the Toth was not how they wanted to fight this battle.

Hale swung the butt of his rifle into a menial's snout as it leaped at him. The impact snapped the creature's neck and deflected it into the bulkhead. His reverse swing caught another Toth in the torso, snapping bones and earning a squeal of pain.

He leveled his rifle and sent a blast of tungsten-coated cobalt pellets into a mass of menials. Yellow blood burst into the air as the shotgun blast ripped through four aliens.

A warrior thumped to the deck in front of Hale. Crystalline armor plates refracted the fire's light, making it look like an inferno raged across the warrior's body. It howled an ululation that triggered Hale's audio dampers. The warrior raised a six-clawed hand over its shoulder.

Hale backpedaled and snapped off a blast from his rifle. Pellets careened off the crystal armor, leaving hairline fractures across the surface.

The warrior looked away from Hale and hissed.

An armored fist slammed into the warrior's helmet, shattering it into pieces. Elias snatched the warrior by its exposed throat, lifted it off the deck and slammed it face-first into the bulkhead next to Hale with a sickening crunch.

Elias tossed the jerking body aside and

pointed a bloody yellow finger at Hale.

"Next time I tell you to—"

A shadow moved behind Elias in the smoking ruin between decks. A blast of energy hit Elias in the back, sending him staggering toward Hale. Elias hunched over, his massive shoulder striking the bulkhead inches above Hale's head. Hale looked up at Elias' helm and saw a lighting-strike crack through the visor over his suit's sensors.

Enormous claws wrapped over his shoulder and yanked Elias away.

A warrior wrestled Elias to the deck and pulled a jagged blade as long as Hale's arm from its back.

Hale switched his rifle to HIGH power and raised the barrel toward the warrior.

High-power shots were supposed to be done from a firm firing stance as they expended almost a quarter of the weapon's battery and accelerated the round to the highest velocity the barrel could withstand before blowing apart. The recoil kicked the weapon against Hale's injured knee and sent it flying from his hands.

The round cut through the warrior's flank and wrecked the bulkhead on the other side. Its head reared up, then the entire warrior fell limp atop Elias. Elias shoved it aside and fired his forearm-mounted cannons through the hole in the ceiling.

Bodel and Kallen stomped past Elias, smashing menials to death and crushing the skulls of any still fighting with the Marines.

Hale pushed off the bulkhead. His Marines were smeared with Toth blood, but they were on their feet.

"Sir, you dropped this." Cortaro handed Hale back his gauss rifle. "I believe this is yours too." He held up the gauntlet with the forearm screen. It was cracked and smoking around where a shot pellet had embedded in the center of the screen.

"Sorry," Hale said. "Elias was—"

"If I can get over Steuben blowing my damn leg off I'm not going to complain about a little nothing like a cracked screen," Cortaro said.

A dead Toth warrior slid through the breach and fell against the deck with a whump.

Elias rolled onto his hands and knees, a shallow crater smoking against his back armor.

"You hurt?" Hale asked.

"There's a dent on my interior tank. Nothing serious." Elias got to his feet slowly.

Steuben, his bloody sword in hand, stepped around Elias and made for the elevator.

"Steuben, wait," Hale said.

"There is nothing to wait for, Hale. The longer we tarry, the more time the Toth have to find us again," Steuben said. He knocked the flat of his blade against his thigh, sending yellow droplets spraying against the deck.

Hale looked at the hole in the ceiling and down to the floor.

"I've got an idea," Hale said.

"Now we're in trouble," Standish said.

"How many more breach kits do we have?" Hale asked.

****

Jared ducked beneath the trench line as a Toth fighter screamed overhead, an Eagle in hot pursuit. The Eagle's Gatling cannons lit up and the Toth fighter lost control. It twisted into a corkscrew spiral and slammed into the mountainside with a burst of fire.

"Sir, enemies!" Indigo poked at Jared hard enough to almost knock him from the firing stoop.

"I know, Indigo, but I told you we're not shooting at the fast movers," Jared said.

"Not sky. Water." The doughboy pointed a meaty finger to the waves breaking against the beach. Jared scanned over the white-topped waves, looking for landing craft. Nothing.

Streaks of fire tore red scars across the horizon. The Eagles had been in one hell of a dogfight for almost half an hour, and Jared couldn't tell which dying ships were human or Toth.

"I don't see anything," Jared said. He'd never encountered a lying doughboy, but they were easily confused.

"In the water, sir," Indigo said.

Doughboys pointed at the ocean, grunting and pointing their rifles through breaks in the parapet. His doughboys wore little more than simple composite chest armor and open-faced helmets, archaic compared to his Marine power armor.

A doughboy hefting a thick tubed grenade launcher shifted from foot to foot at the bottom of the trench.

"Boom boom, sir?" it asked.

"Not yet, Magenta. I'll tell you when," Jared said. The only thing the doughboys ever got anxious over was fighting and eating. The platoon's grenadier was a little more eager than most of the others.

"Sir, enemy!" Indigo slapped at the parapet.

"I'm telling you," Jared said, looking back at the ocean, "there's nothing there." A shadow emerged from a cresting wave. *Was that a shark?* he thought.

"Black Six, this is Gold Six," he said to Douglas over the local IR net. "My guys say they saw hostiles on the beach. You got anything?"

A bolt of energy snapped from between crashing waves and struck the lip of the trench a foot from Jared. Sand and pulverized duracrete exploded next to his head. Jared slipped off the firing stoop and fell into the muddy trench.

A doughboy picked him up and tapped at the side of Jared's helmet.

"Sir, OK? Sir?" The doughboy shook him roughly enough that Jared's head bobbled.

The Marine knocked the doughboy's hands away.

"I'm fine, Slate. Let go of me." Jared looked at the trench line and saw every doughboy staring right at him. "If you see the enemy, shoot it!"

Indigo's rifle snapped. The doughboys' rifles were sturdier than Jared's gauss rifle, both to withstand more high-powered shots to wreck Xaros drones, and to keep the doughboys from breaking them.

"Boom boom?" Magenta asked.

"Put airbursts over the waterline!" Jared shouted over the growing cacophony of doughboy rifles. "Save ten rounds for final protective fire on engagement line delta."

Magenta looked at Jared and grunted in confusion.

"Yes, boom boom!" Jared pointed toward the ocean.

"Boom boom!" Magenta angled the mortar launcher into the air and braced it against his hip. The recoil of the 60mm shell staggered Magenta back a step. It had enough force to shatter a normal human's hip and femur.

They might not have been built smart, but Jared was thankful that the doughboys were built tough. He climbed back onto the firing stoop and looked over the parapet.

Toth warriors came ashore with the waves. Dozens of the six-limbed terrors charged toward the trenches, firing their energy weapons from the hip. Doughboy shots stopped the warriors dead in their tracks, striking with enough force to send shattered armor spinning through the air.

Jared glimpsed beyond the breaking waves

and saw a tide of Toth warriors coming in. He slid his rifle over the sandbags and fired. A wave pushed a dead warrior ashore, yellow blood streaking through the salt water back into the ocean.

He ducked down and opened every commo channel his suit could access.

"All units, all units. We've got a massive Toth assault in sector thirty-seven. Requesting air, armor and orbital support." A blast of energy exploded through the armored plates set up against the trench wall. A doughboy bounced against the ground, a smoking crater in his chest. Pyrite 221, the first doughboy that ever called Jared anything but "sir."

Jared felt a spike of anger-driven adrenaline flow through his limbs.

"This is Gold 6 in sector thirty-seven. Does anyone read me?" Jared stood up and fired back at the Toth.

****

A Toth menial clutched an energy rifle close to its chest. It twisted one of its chameleon-like eyes at the great gemstone command bridge in the center of the chamber where its immortal master was safe, protected by tons of impervious armor and the brave efforts of the menial, its spawn-kin, and the hated warrior cadre who took all the credit for the menials' hard work.

The command bridge nested against great metal rails. Massive treads connected the rails to the bridge, ready to take it through the ship and eject it into space if the threat to the overlord proved too great.

Of course, the menial knew it would die if the armored doors beneath the bridge opened to vacuum, but what was his sacrifice compared to the safety of the true immortals? It would continue its duty in the ancillary control section: monitoring wastewater production and treatment. The human assault teams had severed waterlines to several sections of the ship, secondary damage as they cut power lines running from the ship's reactors. A forked tongue snapped out and licked dust away from its left eye.

Nothing of worth happened in the ancillary area. Menials kept to their stations, keeping minor systems up and running to keep the overlord content. Whatever was going on in the main bridge where Immortal Kren remained safe during the battle was far more important than the menial's concerns.

Five different menial bodies had been tossed from the main bridge since the humans attacked. Whatever was going on in there, Kren was not pleased.

The smell of burning ozone and melted fiber-optic cables tickled the menial's snout—not unusual, as parts of the ship were still on fire and the cyclers had spread the smoke throughout the ship. What bothered the menial was how strong the smell was.

It looked up with one eye. A burning circle glowed in the ceiling, growing steadily brighter.

The menial turned both eyes to the unusual happening. It clicked its tongue twice to alert the nearest warrior.

The warrior stomped over and gave the menial a customary blow to the back of its head. The blow landed hard enough to sting, expressing favor. The menial bared his throat to the warrior and pointed to the ceiling.

There was a pop in the air. A white-hot cord fell to the deck beside the menial. It jumped back and cowered behind the warrior.

A massive *thump* came from the dark circle in the ceiling. A second *thump* and a cut section of the hull fell toward the menial. The last things it saw were Elias crouched atop a cutout of the bulkhead between decks, and the soldier's boot stomping down on its head.

Elias fired both barrels from his cannons into the warrior's chest, and pulped organs and yellow blood exploded through exit wounds in its back. Bodel and Kallen fell through the hole in the ceiling and landed beside Elias as he mowed down the Toth warriors and menials surrounding the armored command bridge.

Command consoles exploded as gauss

rounds ripped through them, the bullets embedding in the bulkheads, puncturing holes the size of a man's thumb.

Hale fell through the ceiling, using his anti-grav linings to soften the impact as he landed between the Iron Hearts. The rest of the Marines followed him one by one.

"Secure the doors!" Hale pointed to a set of large sliding airlocks on the far side of the room.

Lafayette landed hard next to Hale, his cyborg legs and feet ringing against the deck.

"The overlord has to be in there," Lafayette said. "Leave him to Steuben and I once we crack the shell."

"Want me to knock?" Bodel asked. He kicked a dead warrior aside and walked up to the giant flattened gem-shaped command bridge.

"Wait." Lafayette picked up a Toth rifle and tossed it at the bridge. An electric field embraced the weapon and burnt it to dust.

"I thought us being here would bring every swinging-tail lizard down on us," Standish said. He looked around the control room full of dead Toth and wrecked equipment, then shrugged.

"Maybe he thinks we're not a threat to him while he's in that thing," Bailey said.

"I'm insulted." Elias grabbed a dead Toth by the arm and tossed it at the command bridge. It disintegrated just like the weapon.

"Any word from the other teams?" Cortaro asked Hale.

"I've got absolutely nothing on IR or radio," Hale said, glancing at the beacon on his belt.

"They should've made their assault objectives by now," Cortaro said. "What if we're the only ones where they're supposed to be?"

A holo emitter came to life on one of the pylons connected to the command bridge. Kren's tank appeared, floating in the air above the humans.

"Ah, my *baelor*," Kren said. "You came right for me. You have a flair for the dramatic. Impressive."

"Surrender," Hale said. "If I have to smoke you out, this won't end well."

"I think now," Kren said, "my best troops are cleaning up the last of your kind as we speak. I will offer you this mercy: I will stop jamming your primitive communications long enough for you to demand that your last holdouts throw down their weapons. This is your last chance to leave this ship alive."

Hale's rifle snapped up to his shoulder and blew the holo emitter to dust with a single shot.

"He's panicking," Hale said. "Toth never negotiate when they have the upper hand."

"The other teams must be close," Steuben said.

Kren appeared again. "You insolent little maggot! I will—"

Standish shot the new emitter.

"Not that this isn't fun," Standish said, "but at some point more angry Toth will come looking for us."

"I can hit it with my rail gun," Elias said, "but in this confined space the blast would kill everyone who's not in armor."

"The overlords only fear death," Steuben said. "If the Rangers succeed in disabling the ship, he'll bolt." His gaze went up and down the rails that lead into an interlocked portal beneath the bridge.

"So we trap him here," Hale said. He picked up a shattered screen from the floor and tossed it at the nearest rail. It bounced off. "Gunney, wrap a blaze wire around that and slag it."

"Yarrow, give me your breach kit," Cortaro said.

"Sorry, Gunney," the medic said, pointing to the hole in the ceiling, "I used mine three floors up."

"Orozco?"

"Negative, used it."

"Who still has a breach kit?" Cortaro asked. The Marines looked to each other, but no one said anything.

"Only thing worse than a crunchy is a jarhead crunchy," Elias said. He held up a hand. It sunk into the forearm, to be replaced by a cutting torch. "Move."

Elias fired up the torch. Hale had to avert his eyes from the blazing wedge of fire as Elias pressed it against the rail. A shower of sparks burst from the contact point. Kallen stomped over next to Elias and added her torch to the job.

"It's slow," Elias said.

"How long?" Hale asked.

Lafayette, his cybernetic eyes needing no protection, glanced over the Iron Heart's arms at the rail.

"Maybe twenty minutes before they're through," he said.

A warrior ululation came though the walls.

"I don't think we've got that much time," Hale said.

A deep roll of thunder shook the deck plating. The groan of tortured metal filled the air and the *Naga* lurched to the side. Hale bumped against Bodel's armored leg and grabbed on to keep from falling.

Marines locked their boots to the deck, swaying, as their inner ear and their eyes gave them very confused indications of what was "up" anymore. As lights flickered out, pale yellow strip lights activated across the ceiling and at the wall joins.

The only one unfazed by the change was Lafayette.

"The ship has lost main power," the cyborg said. "Internal gravity is offline."

"Then why do I feel like I'm about to slide off the floor?" Cortaro asked.

"I do believe we're in Luna's gravity well," Lafayette said.

"Rangers blew the reactors," Hale said. "We're going to crash into the moon." The beacon on his belt vibrated. A lit button pulsed red.

Hale grabbed the beacon. "Time to go," he said.

"No!" Steuben pointed at the command bridge. "The overlord is still in there. We can't leave until he's dead."

"He'll die in the crash," Hale said. He flicked the safety catch off the button.

Steuben grabbed Hale by the wrist. The Karigole bent slightly at the waist and locked eyes with Hale.

"Take your men. Lafayette and I will stay until the end," Steuben said.

The treads powered up with a high-pitched whine. The iris beneath the command bridge opened slowly and it inched down the rails, slowly gaining speed.

Steuben let Hale go and ran next to the rail where Elias and Kallen still kept their torches burning. He drew his sword from the small of his back and jammed it between the rollers and the rail. The blade bent and squealed, but the roller and the rest of the command bridge ground to a halt.

The iris froze, barely open a foot in diameter. Air howled over the lip as it poured into the vacuum beyond the iris. The overlord's bridge would have a straight shot to the safety of open space once it opened.

"Sir," Cortaro grabbed Hale by the shoulder, "the overlord will be a sitting duck for our fleet. We need to leave."

Hale mashed his finger against the button. Nothing happened. He looked around the room, then pressed the button several more times.

"I thought the Crucible would open a portal for us as soon as you hit that," Bailey said.

"Ibarra sent us on a suicide mission, didn't he?" Orozco asked.

"Every other team on this bucket is probably asking for an extraction at the same time," Hale said, not entirely convinced by his own excuse. "We squat and hold until Ibarra gets the portal open for us."

Steuben's blade shattered and the command bridge began rolling toward the iris.

"Or until we're smeared across the moon," Standish said. "Everyone will look up at the wreck and think 'poor bastards never had a chance.'"

"Standish." Lafayette held a hand out to the Marine.

"Yes, I'll shut up."

"No, toss me a grenade," Lafayette said.

Standish removed a fragmentation grenade from his chest plate and chucked it through the air. Lafayette caught it and held it in front of Elias' face.

"You cup your hand over it and tamp it against the weakened metal," Lafayette said.

Elias nodded and offered his hand. Lafayette pulled the pin and set the grenade on the armored palm and released the spoon. It flew off with a *ching*.

"What the hell are you doing?" Hale yelled as he and the Marines ducked away from the explosive.

Elias lifted the cutting torch from the rail and slapped the grenade against the red hot metal, keeping his hand cupped over it. Kallen pressed her hand on top of it, servos whining in their shoulders as they mashed the grenade against the rail.

When the grenade exploded with a muffled *whump*, the heat-malleable rail proved weaker than the force of the armored hands. Explosive force follows the path of least resistance, much like water rolling down a hillside. The explosive force of the grenade reflected off the armor and went into the rail.

The rail buckled toward the still-opening iris. Elias shook his smoking hand and kicked the rail, buckling it further. The command bridge twisted against the rails and ground to a halt.

"And to think my parents wanted me to be an artist, not an engineer," Lafayette said.

A portal snapped into being twenty feet above Hale's head, its surface roiling like a stormy sea.

"Time to go!" Hale shouted. His Marines ran for him as he looked around the room, searching for a way to get up and through the portal.

"I don't think our boots can get us up there," Orozco said. "Not with the crazy—"

Bodel's massive hand grabbed Orozco by the waist and flung him toward the portal. Orozco vanished into the wavering disk with a ripple. Bodel snatched up Marines and sent them through the portal with little grace or patience.

Steuben and Lafayette stood next to the

damaged rail, watching the Marines depart.

Hale stumbled toward the Karigole as the deck shifted beneath his feet.

"What are you doing? We need to leave," Hale said.

"This is our fate, Hale. Leave us to it," Steuben said.

"The hell I will." Hale tried to grab Steuben by the arm, but the Karigole slapped his hand away.

"Elias," Lafayette nodded at Hale, "would you please?"

Elias wrapped an arm around Hale's waist and picked him off the deck.

"Steuben! Don't!" Hale squirmed uselessly against Elias' hold as the Iron Heart carried him toward the portal. "Elias, we can't let them die!"

"Let go of me!" Cortaro slammed a fist against Bodel's grip. The gunnery sergeant went flying into the portal.

"Elias, damn you!" Hale went limp and tried to slither away, but Elias tightened his hold into a vice. Hale jerked to the side…and fell to the deck.

A ramp extended from the far side of the command bridge, and Toth menials swarmed out of the opening and charged at the Karigole. Their gauss weapons cracked, slaughtering the menials without hesitation.

A Toth warrior swung his blaster barrel over the edge of the ramp and sprayed energy bolts, killing menials as the bolts stitched across the deck.

A blast caught Lafayette in the shoulder. The impact slammed him against the bent rail as his rifle went spinning through the air. It landed in front of Hale with Lafayette's arm still attached.

Lafayette sank to his knees and fell over.

Steuben leaped aside and rolled to his feet. He hit a Toth warrior with a burst from his rifle. Two rounds shattered the warrior's armor; the third blew through its chest and bounced off the back armor. The gauss round ricocheted through the warrior's armor, nearly liquefying the Toth.

Kren emerged and ran for the opening double doors at the far side of the chamber.

Elias aimed his cannons at the overlord's

tank, then shifted his aim to the side. He fired a single shot that sheered through half the tank's legs. Kren tipped over and fell off the ramp, onto a bed of dead menials. His remaining limbs grasped at the air like a crab turned onto its back.

Hale killed the last two menials with his rifle and got to his feet.

Steuben helped Lafayette up and put the cyborg Karigole's remaining arm over his shoulder. Steuben half dragged Lafayette toward Kren.

"*Baelor!* Save me!" Kren pleaded. "You'll need someone to negotiate with the rest of the Toth, please!"

With one hand, Steuben leveled his gauss rifle at Kren and shot the tank. The bullet cracked the glass. Two more shots smashed spider-web fractures into the tank.

Hale got two steps toward Kren before Elias' hand stopped him.

The Iron Heart shook his head.

"Please! I-I can make you all rich!" Kren's nerves pressed against the tank, as if trying to ward off the Karigole.

Steuben and Lafayette stood over the tank. Lafayette took his arm away from his battle brother's shoulder. He raised his fist over his head.

"I surrender! Yes, surrender!" Kren squealed.

Lafayette chopped his fist into the tank. Liquid seeped from the cracks. He struck again, and the glass shattered beneath his fist.

"Anything! I'll do anything!" Kren's voice was tinny.

Steuben reached into the tank and grabbed Kren by his tendrils.

"No!" Kren's scream trailed into distortion as Steuben pulled Kren out of the tank. His brain and nerve endings flailed madly.

Steuben slapped his hands into what remained of Kren's body and gripped the gray matter with both hands. He dug his fingers into the pulsing mass. The tendrils wrapped around his wrists and tugged weakly.

Yellow blood burst beneath Steuben's

fingers. A roar rose from his throat. He raised Kren over his head and ripped the overlord in half. Steuben looked at the bleeding mass in his hands, tossed them aside and shook blood from his hands.

"Now we can leave," he said.

Kallen ran over and picked up the two Karigole.

"Elias," Hale said, "I should be the last one ou—hey!" Elias grabbed Hale by the ankle and tossed him into the portal.

Hale's entire world became a white abyss. Tiny blue strands of electricity danced across his armor as he felt himself tumbling end over end.

He blinked and found himself floating in space. The great spikes of the Crucible surrounded him. The portal had dropped him in the center of the star gate's iris. He made out the *Breitenfeld*, surrounded by construction scaffolds and tenders attached to its hull like moray eels.

The *Naga* descended toward the moon, trailing smoke and venting atmosphere behind it like a comet's tail. The flash of exploding fighters and energy bolts sparkled over Hawaii.

"Hello?" Hale asked. "Gunney? Anyone?" He'd kept some momentum from Elias' throw, gentling spinning end over end.

A new portal engulfed him.

Hale felt the pull of gravity and fell. He glimpsed a dark pool of water and slapped into it. Water flooded over his visor. He thrashed his arms and legs around, desperately trying to swim, but void-rated combat armor was anything but buoyant.

Something yanked him out of the water. He wiped mud off his faceplate and found Cortaro and Bailey on either side of him, their armor caked with dark mud. They were in a swamp full of tall trees, and croaking frogs surrounded them. Hale's feet sunk into mud and water lapped over his knees as he looked around.

"Where is everyone? Where the hell are we?" Hale asked.

"Sir, you're a lieutenant. You're never supposed to say that second thing," Cortaro said.

"We've got everyone but the armor and the

Karigole," Bailey said.

A portal opened over the treetops, and Steuben and Lafayette fell with the snap of breaking branches.

"I'm not climbing another bloody tree, God as my witness," Bailey said.

"Lafayette is hurt," Hale said. He sloshed through the swamp to where he saw the Karigole land. He heard the Iron Hearts arrive behind him, hitting the water like cannonballs.

They found Lafayette draped over a branch, black fluid leaking from the stump attached to his shoulder. He slid back and grabbed the branch with his remaining hand, then dropped into Cortaro's waiting arms.

"That was a most unsettling experience," he said.

"Yarrow! Medic, get over here!" Cortaro yelled into the swamp.

"Don't be ridiculous," Lafayette said. "He's a doctor, not a mechanic." Lafayette rotated his stump around. A gout of dark fluid spat out and stained the water around their knees.

"You're not...dying?" Hale asked.

"The pain receptors sent my system into shock briefly, but my squishy parts are just fine," Lafayette said. He tore damaged tubes and wires from his stump and tossed them away. "Not the first time this has happened."

Hale removed his helmet and breathed in fresh, humid air.

"I think we're in Hawaii, sir," Bailey said.

"We were supposed to go back to Ceres," the lieutenant said. "Why did Ibarra drop us here?"

Steuben climbed down from the tree, his claws digging into the bark.

"You alright?" Hale asked as Steuben splashed into the swamp.

"Killing Toth will never bring my people back," Steuben said. "But ripping that overlord to pieces was quite satisfying."

The rest of his Marines emerged from the swamp.

"Where are we on ammo and batteries?"

Hale asked Cortaro.

"We've already cross-leveled everything, barely a magazine per Marine and we're low on juice and air."

"I can hear gauss fire to the southeast," Steuben said.

Hale cocked his ear to the sky and heard a distant *snap snap snap*. The sounds grew closer together as more and more rifles joined the chorus.

"We move to the sound of gunfire," Hale said. "Let's go."

CHAPTER 17

Jared glanced over the edge of the parapet and saw more Toth emerging from the surf. The beach was littered with dead warriors, buffeted by waves and sinking into the sand.

The single second he dared expose himself was enough to draw three shots from warriors charging up the beachhead. He ducked and jumped away from the trench wall before the blasts blew the sandbags on the parapet into gouts of dust and fused glass. The Toth picked him out as a leader early in their attack and had sharpshooters competing to be the first to blow his head off.

There were more warriors on the beach and swimming toward the shore, more than his soldiers could handle.

"This is Gold 6," he said into the IR net, "any Crimson elements read me?"

Energy blasts snapped overhead, tracing streaks of superheated air. The trench line had partially collapsed. A mound of dark soil and wrecked armor plating half filled the bottom of the trench. Doughboys ducked beneath the parapet and reloaded fresh batteries and gauss bolts into their oversized rifles.

Heavy gauss cannons opened up behind his position. White-hot tracers flashed overhead as the team of Marines and heavy gunner soldiers in a bunker one trench line back opened fire on the attacks. The heavy weapons had remained silent and hidden until there was enough Toth on the beach to risk announcing their presence. The havoc created by the heavy weapons up and down the beachhead might be enough to slow the Toth advance long enough for him to get his troops to safety.

"Fall back!" Jared tried shouting over the din of battle. The doughboys remained focused on shooting Toth.

Jared grabbed a doughboy by the belt and tried to pull him off the firing stoop.

"Fall back! Damn you!" Jared yelled. He flexed his pseudo-muscles and got the doughboy off the firing stoop. He pointed to the narrow communications trench leading back to the next defense line.

Indigo looked annoyed with Jared, then nodded as the Marine officer repeated the order.

"Everybody!" Indigo bellowed so loudly that Jared's sound dampeners engaged. "Move!"

Doughboys stepped back from the firing line and hustled past Indigo and Jared into the communications trench.

A war cry rose from the beach, a rumbling ululation that made the hairs on the back of Jared's neck stand up.

"More coming," Indigo said.

"Lots more." Jared watched the last doughboy enter the trench. He looked back and saw dead doughboys lying half-buried in the rubble. A single mottled hand stuck up from the dirt, bent at the wrist like it was reaching for something. One sat with his back to the wall, legs stuck out straight, his head lolled to the side, rifle still clutched in one hand. Blackened flesh marred the neck and shoulders of the dead soldiers. Jared took a step toward the doughboy, but Indigo's massive hand pressed against his chest.

"Go," he rumbled.

"What if he's not—"

Indigo shoved Jared out of the trench and prodded him toward the next defense line.

The report of heavy gauss cannons grew stronger. Jared knew that if the gunners would risk firing the weapons on full cyclic, and possibly overheating the barrels and shorting out the capacitors, then the Toth were making a serious push for the trenches.

A high-pitched whine filled the air. Jared looked up and saw Toth transports flying low toward the trenches. Hatches beneath the transports swung open and a thick crystal cannon arm popped out of the hatch. A focused blast of lightning struck out from the crystal and arced over Jared's head.

The heavy gauss cannon fire lessened.

Jared switched his rifle to HIGH and aimed at the crystal of the nearest drop ship. His first shot struck the ship's hull, rattling it from side to side.

"What doing?" Indigo poked at Jared's shoulder as he tried to get another shot on the drop ship.

"How about you try helping? Shoot the crystal!" Jared's next shot didn't even connect with the ship.

"Yes, sir." Indigo hefted his rifle and snapped off a shot. The crystal beneath the drop ship shattered. Stored energy ran up the gun arm and the drop ship exploded in midair, raining hull fragments all around them.

"Good shooting, Indigo. Keep doing that," Jared said.

Heavy thumps reverberated through the ground as the drop ships continued their bombardment. Jared turned and ran through the zigzagging trench, Indigo on his heels.

A blast struck the ground to his right, raining rocks and loose soil over his head. Another blast hit so close the concussion nearly knocked the air out of him. Lightning struck in the middle of the trench mere yards ahead of him. The explosion threw Jared hard against the trench wall. He bounced off and slammed into Indigo.

Jared lay in the mud, staring at a burning sky. He fought to breathe, but his lungs refused to work. He slammed a fist against his stomach, trying to shock his diaphragm back into gear. He managed a weak breath, then rolled onto his hands and knees. Something in his chest ached with each new breath. Broken ribs if he was lucky, a collapsed lung if he wasn't.

"Sir, OK?" Indigo asked, a jagged hunk of stone sticking out from his jawline, red blood dripping from the wound.

The doughboy pulled Jared to his feet and brushed dirt from the Marine's uniform.

Jared leaned against Indigo. He tried to shout a warning, but could barely manage a weak croak.

A Toth warrior leapt into the trench. A

clawed hand swiped across Jared's chest and sent him spinning.

Indigo hammered the butt of his rifle into the warrior's helm, cracking it open. The doughboy jammed the muzzle of his rifle against the warrior's shoulder and reached for the trigger to shoot it at point-blank range.

The warrior backhanded the rifle away from Indigo and whipped its tail over its shoulder. The spiked tip gouged a hole through the doughboy's armor, then slashed him across the face as the warrior twisted his body away from Indigo.

The doughboy pounded a fist into the cracked helm, breaking it apart with hammer blows. The Toth jabbed at Indigo's face. The soldier caught the Toth's hand by a clawed finger and wrenched a digit back against the wrist. The Toth's finger ripped off with a high-pitched scream of pain from the warrior.

Indigo tossed the finger aside and brought his palms against the side of the Toth's head with a thunderclap of slapping flesh and breaking armor.

Indigo held his grip on the warrior's head and pressed his hands together.

The Toth scraped bloody gouges across Indigo's forearms before it started thrashing from side to side like a hooked fish.

There was a creak of buckling armor. Indigo's hands came together, crushing the warrior's skull with a pop. The doughboy tossed the warrior aside like child with a broken toy, then scooped up his rifle.

"Sir? Sir, OK?" Indigo found Jared lying on his side, his hand pressed against his chest.

"I'm not sure, Indigo," Jared said. "Wait, don't—"

The doughboy pulled Jared's hand away and frowned at the chest plate. There were deep scratch marks across the armor, exposing ripped pectoral pseudo-muscles.

"Scratch," Indigo said. He reached up and plucked the rock fragment from his jaw and tossed it aside. Impact from Toth cannons shook the trench walls.

"We go." The doughboy tossed Jared over his shoulder and carried him away.

****

Durand kicked her Eagle over and dove toward the ocean. Her Gatling cannons ripped hypervelocity slugs after the Toth fighter she pursued. A single round clipped the Toth's wing and spun it into a wild barrel roll. The fighter plunged into the water and shattered into pieces.

She skimmed her Eagle over the surface, scanning the air around her. Burning Toth ships descended from orbit, casualties of the void fight far above. Red and black streaks cut across the sky like a slow-motion meteor shower.

"Gall! I've got one squeeze of the trigger before I'm out of ammo," Nag said over the IR.

"I can take out two more," Manfred said.

Durand glanced at her ammo counter: twenty rounds left. Barely a single burst.

"Lothar?" Durand asked.

"I've been empty for the last two minutes," the Dotok said. "Been scaring Toth off Manfred's tail and herding them in front of his guns."

"103rd," Durand said over the squadron's channel, "break contact and get to FARP sierra." The construction crews had cut several forward arming and refueling points in the dense jungle around the R&R center, all manned with small teams of robot pit crews that could swap out an Eagle's empty ammo canisters and drained batteries within a minute.

"That's north of Loa," Glue said. "We're giving them a straight shot to the beaches."

Durand tracked her squadron as they broke away from the Toth invaders and flew to the northeast. The Toth didn't give chase. She followed her pilots, down to ten Eagles. She glanced over her shoulder every few seconds. Silver glinted in the sunlight as more Toth landers and fighters entered the atmosphere whole and undamaged from space.

A half-dozen landers loitered off the coastline, dropping more Toth warriors into the sea.

"Feet dry!" Filly announced as her Eagle flew from over the ocean to over the beach. They were minutes away from the FARP.

"Red flight, you're first in the chute. Top off and get back in the air. White and Blue follows in sequence. We return to the fight as a whole," Durand said.

A pair of Eagles slowed to a hover over the jungle, then descended slowly. Turbofan engines blew through treetops, and branches and palm fronds ripped into the air.

"Brat and Kilo are wheels down," a pilot announced. "Got bots working us over, should be airborne in ninety seconds."

"Incoming!" Glue shouted.

Durand banked her Eagle into a roll out of reflex. Energy bolts snapped past her cockpit, scorching a thick streak of permanent smoke into her canopy. Three Toth fighters shot past her, one with red striations around the canopy.

The Toth ace had come for her.

Durand slammed a foot against a rudder bar and her tail swung to the side, pointing her fighter straight at the pair of Toth fighters making a beeline toward the FARP. She gunned her afterburners, feeling the press of acceleration against her body.

"I'm with you," Manfred said, his Eagle settling next to her wing.

"We've got more on the way," Glue said.

"Knock 'em down and get back to the beaches," Durand said. The ace was trying to pull her away from the refueling point, leaving it more vulnerable with each Eagle that followed the ace into the volcano's shadow. She understood, and she didn't care.

"I'll get the two on the left," Manfred said.

"How many pulls you have left?" Durand asked.

"Two. You?"

"Enough. They're yours."

A Toth fighter cut its engines. Tiny maneuver thrusters tipped its nose over and opposite to the momentum of the ship's direction. Energy blasts blossomed from the fighter in a wild arc over the jungle toward Durand and Manfred.

Durand snapped her fighter to the right and

rolled over an incoming blast. She overshot the attacking fighter as it fell away from the other two Toth. She glanced back to see Manfred flying straight for the fighter. The Dotok angled his engines as he cleared the Toth by a few feet and flared his afterburners.

The flames torched the Toth's cockpit and slapped the fighter into a dead spin. Durand turned away before it could crash into the jungle.

"I saw you do it on Europa," Manfred said, "thought I'd save the bullets."

The remaining Toth fighters banked around the far ridge of the volcano.

"Pat yourself on the back later," Durand said. "Cut over the peak and find them." She brought her fighter into an almost vertical climb and flew up the steep ridgeline extending north from the mouth of the ancient volcano.

Rays of sunlight struck over the ridge, diffusing through the clouds as they disintegrated over the windward slope. Durand squinted as the apex neared, trying not to look into the rising sun.

A Toth fighter roared across her nose. Her
Eagle shuddered as it passed through the fighter's
wake. Alarms blared through the cockpit as wake-
driven air swarmed around her ship and broke her
wings' lift. Her Eagle fell out of control and moved
through the air with the grace of a thrown rock.

Durand slammed her control stick from side
to side, trying to turn her fighter toward whatever
direction she was moving to regain some lift. She
felt a moment of weightlessness then her Eagle
arced toward the downward slope of the
mountainside.

Her wingtip dipped to the side and almost
cut into the mountainside before the controls
responded. She got her fighter level and opened the
throttle to gain air speed.

A bolt of energy snapped past her canopy,
striking her fuselage hard enough to send her
wobbling like a drunk through the air. She dove into
a deep canyon between spurs running down the side
of the mountain, vibrant green cliffs pressing
against her.

She banked away and flew just over the treetops, energy bolts chasing her.

Durand braced herself and fired the fore-mounted maneuver thrusters. Her head jerked forward and her chin bounced off her chest as she lost what little airspeed she'd gained. The Toth ace snapped past her.

Durand gunned her afterburners and lined up a shot on the ace's tail. She pulled the trigger and a red error message popped up on her canopy: a red X through the gauss cannon on a wire diagram of her ship.

"Ah, *merde*. Manfred, where are you?" Durand asked. She kept on the ace's tail, matching his maneuvers as he led them toward the ocean.

There was no answer from the Dotok.

The ace leveled out, practically taunting her to shoot.

He knows, she thought. She broke off her pursuit and crossed over a wide sandy beach, then traced the coastline back to the FARP where she'd left her squadron, flying as fast as her engines could manage. An amber-colored warning icon appeared on the canopy—her batteries were nearly empty.

She dodged over towering waves and glanced behind her. The ace's fighter glinted in the morning light. She let out a string of expletives that would have made Chief MacDougall blush.

A bolt cracked past her and blasted a fountain of water ahead of her. She corkscrewed over and around the plume and flew so close to the ocean's surface that her engines kicked up steam and sea spray behind her.

The ace matched her elevation, shooting half-aimed blasts around her.

Durand grabbed the override on her landing gear and pulled the handle. Three wheels extended from beneath her Eagle. She dipped her left wing to the ocean. The landing gear hit the water and ripped from its moorings.

The wheel careened across the surface and slammed into the ace's cockpit. The Toth fighter sank slowly, then slammed into the ocean. It skipped against the water like a stone and hit the water flat against the ship's belly. It skidded over the water and broke through a wave as it rumbled ashore. The dagger ship crashed into a thicket of palm trees. Smoke broke around the fighter as brush ignited into flame.

Durand breathed a sigh of relief and changed course to the FARP. She looked over the side of her ship at the wrecked ace, unsure if it was alive or dead.

****

Admiral Makarov watched the *Naga's* plot projection on her holo tank as the warship turned toward the moon.

"Admiral," an aide waved to her from the navigation station, "the *Naga*'s deep in Luna's gravity. There's no way it can recover, even if the engines come back online."

Excited chatter broke around the bridge as more and more sailors and Marines turned their heads to look out the front windows. The *Naga* angled toward the moon's surface like a slow-motion arrow in flight. The rough triangle point of the ship's prow glinted in sunlight, a ruddy column of smoke and debris tracing the ship's path through space.

"Any word from the assault elements?" Makarov asked.

Ibarra's hologram came to life next to the admiral.

"We've got some of them out," he said.

"Why only 'some'?"

"We opened portals for every beacon we had contact with. Four teams. The rest…" Ibarra shrugged.

A sailor raised a fist in the air and cheered as the *Naga*'s prow hit the moon's surface with an explosion of dust. The warship's keel snapped in half, and the fore crumpled, ejecting hunks of hull platting across the gray plains of dust. The back half hit flat against the moon, scouring a wide path behind it. Clouds of dust billowed around the wreck like a fog bank, hiding the devastation behind a ghostly blanket.

The bridge exploded in cheers as the first

real victory against the Toth played out across the moon's surface.

"Prep the *Breitenfeld*," Makarov said to Ibarra. "This isn't over yet."

"She's ready," Ibarra said and vanished.

Makarov slammed her fist against the side of her holo table.

"Status on the incoming fleet and the attack on Hawaii!" she shouted. The crew, suitably chastened, bent their heads back to their workstations.

"Enemy fleet is slowing near the Lagrange point past lunar orbit," a tactical officer said. "They're maneuvering into attack formation, heavy ships in a Namura cone." The Namura formation, named after the Japanese void admiral that managed a few victories against the Chinese before his country was conquered, put heavy ships at the apex of a cone, lighter ships toward the base. The tip of the cone would drive toward the center of her ship like the tip of a massive spear.

"Commo, open a channel to the Toth ship.

Let's see if they want to head home after the *Naga* bit the dust," Makarov said.

"They're actually hailing us," said the lieutenant in the commo work pod. "Wide frequency, the whole system's picking it up." Makarov pointed a knife blade hand at her gunnery and intelligence officers. They nodded emphatically and hunched over their work screens.

Makarov snapped her fingers and pointed at the holo tank.

Olux's tank hovered over the table.

"Meat," Olux said, "you will surrender. The cost of this acquisition is already too high. Give me the procedural technology and I will not burn your city to the ground. Surrender the procedurals in your Eighth Fleet—every single one of you—as tribute and I will leave you in peace, never to return."

Makarov felt a chill run down her spine. This conversation needed to end as soon as possible. She glanced at the intelligence officer, who shook his head.

"Toth," Makarov said, "let me make you an offer you can understand. Get. Out. You tuck your tails between your legs and leave our solar system and never return. Or I will break the rest of you over my knee just like we did to your little toy."

"Makarov," Olux said, a tremor going through his nerves, "you are procedural and will not be spared." A stunned silence fell across the bridge. "Garret is true born. He will order your surrender to preserve himself and Phoenix. Your fleet is procedural. You will surrender. For every procedural killed fighting my fleet, I will take five true born from your city. Choose. Now."

The officers around the tactical table looked at each other in confusion. Makarov saw the conflict playing through their minds as they considered the Toth overlord's claim.

She felt several quick vibrations from her forearm screen, an urgent message from Garret that read CRY HAVOC. NO SURRENDER. She was starting to like him.

"Are you the same Toth that negotiated the

arrangement on Europa?" Makarov asked. "You all look the same to me in your tanks."

"Irrelevant!" Olux bobbed in his tank. "Your forces above Ha-wai-eee will stand down immediately. Any damage to the facility there will be repaid to Phoenix tenfold."

The intelligence officer waved to Makarov and gave her a thumbs-up.

Makarov slashed her fingertips across her throat and Olux vanished. "Jam everything else coming out of the Toth fleet," she said.

"We've got him." The intelligence officer reached into the holo tank and touched a Toth battlecruiser halfway between the base and the apex of the Namura cone.

"All ships hold current formation and burn toward the Toth fleet with…" Makarov's hands danced through the holo tank and repositioned the Eighth Fleet, "angle of attack 328-mark 12. Can't have any missed shots from us or them bombarding the Earth."

"Ma'am," her chief tactician went pale, "that

many Toth ships will break our line, pick us apart in detail. We won't last long."

"Never interrupt your enemy when he's making a mistake," Makarov said. "Relay the orders and someone get me Kosciusko," Makarov said.

A small screen popped to life on her forearm. The Karigole sat in a fighter cockpit, blasts of energy and dashing fighters filling the space around him.

"Got a minute?" Makarov asked.

Kosciusko's video jittered as he let loose a burst from his Gatling cannons. "I am killing Toth. Make this quick."

"We traced the overlord's transmissions to a single battlecruiser. You were right. He's hidden himself away from the most dangerous place on the battlefield. If he's going to cut and run, I'm going to need my fighters back to chase him down," Makarov said.

Kosciusko grunted and craned his neck to the side, looking down at Earth.

"The landing force is substantial,"

Kosciusko said. "Let me cut away a squadron to defend the island. I'll bring what fighters I can back to the *Midway* and escort the bombers."

"Hurry." Makarov glanced at sensor readings for Olux's battlecruiser. "There's a dark-energy signature on his ship. He must have a jump engine. If he gets away and tells the rest of his kind what happened here, I bet they'll be back with an even bigger fleet."

"He'll run as soon as he starts to lose," Kosciusko said. "I'll return as soon as I can." His video cut away.

"Admiral, the fleet is in position and burning toward the enemy fleet. We'll enter weapons range in ten minutes," the tactical officer said. He looked nervous as he sipped from a water tube, his skin clammy beneath his visor. This wasn't like the officer she knew—or thought she knew. And it wasn't the coming battle that had disturbed him so.

"Fleet-wide address, now," Makarov said. An icon flashed on her visor, alerting her that she was live to her fleet.

"Dragon slayers, this is your admiral. What the Toth overlord said is true. We are...procedural. You, me, every one of our shipmates. I just learned this a few minutes ago...and it changes nothing! I am Admiral Dasha Valia Makarov of the Atlantic Union Navy. Earth is my home. Your home. No matter how we came to it. The Toth came here to take us away and enslave us. I don't care if I was molded from clay and touched by a fairy's wand. I will fight these alien bastards to the hilt. Save whatever doubts you have until after the battle. The only thing that matters right now is victory. Makarov out."

The broadcast icon on her visor vanished. She tapped a command and captain Valdar, armored and hooked into his command chair, popped up on her forearm screen.

"Ma'am, the *Breitenfeld* is ready," Valdar said.

"Time to shine, Captain. *Gott mit uns.*"

****

Hale stopped next to a burning building,

exhausted and breathing hard from running several miles through rough terrain. He saw the trench lines surrounding the Loa facility. The forward lines were overrun, swarming with Toth warriors as they advanced on the base built into the side of the mountain. Only a trickle of warriors advanced from the sea.

A dozen enemy landers loitered over the battlefield, pounding the defenders with their cannons. Burning lander wrecks littered the battlefield and inside the facility's perimeter. An explosion overhead caused Hale to look up. Eagles danced in the sky with Toth dagger fighters.

He'd left the Iron Hearts to deal with the breach in the lines where they'd found their way into the R&R center's perimeter.

"Sir, let me hit 'em with Bloke," Bailey said, tapping the bag slung over her shoulder that held her sniper rifle.

"Do it." Hale pointed to a building with a singed hole in the roof, its windows blown out.

Bailey kicked the door open and vanished

inside.

"Hey, wait for us!" A group of sailors carrying gauss rifles and wearing nothing but fatigues ran up to Hale and his armored Marines. A petty officer stopped in front of Hale. "We got the armory open, didn't want to die cowering under our bunks. Which way to the fight?"

"Take your pick. It's everywhere," Hale said. "But I'm going that way." Hale pointed toward the embattled trench line. "Follow me!" He waved his hand over his shoulder and took off running.

Bailey's rail rifle fired with an earsplitting crack. One of the landers shunted to the side and lost power. It crashed into a mass of Toth soldiers and exploded.

Hale ran around shattered trees and jumped over the remnants of the once beautiful forest. Bailey's rifle boomed again.

He burst through a smoking bush and found himself at the edge of the trench lines. Toth warriors had overrun the first two defense lines. Gauss bullets and blaster shots crisscrossed between the

427

Toth-occupied trench and the final line held by Marines and doughboys. Hale saw a half-collapsed stairway leading into the trenches and ran for it.

A Toth lander exploded, launching flaming fragments and spinning hunks of shrapnel over the battlefield.

Hale got into the trenches and slapped each Marine and sailor on the shoulder as they came in behind him, counting. He admired the sailors' bravery. The flimsy coveralls were no protection against Toth weapons compared to the power armor he and his Marines wore.

Steuben was the last one in the trench. Hale tried to get around the Karigole as they worked their way forward.

"You think the warriors know the *Naga* was destroyed?" Hale asked. "Would that get them to surrender?"

"It won't matter. Toth warriors will not stop fighting until an overlord commands them," Steuben said. "We have no choice but to kill them all."

"Somehow I knew—"

A lander roared overhead toward the buildings beyond the shattered forest.

"Bailey?" Hale broadcast over radio and IR. "Bailey, they're coming for you. Displace!"

There was a distant explosion from the mountainside—and no answer from Bailey.

"Come on, Marines!" Cortaro's command pulled Hale back from worrying about his sniper.

Hale ran into the final defense line. Wounded Marines and Army soldiers lay crumpled against the trench wall, and more were being carried in. Marines, soldiers and doughboys snapped shots over the parapet, ducking back down before well-aimed blaster shots could find them.

"Yarrow," Hale said to the medic, "do what you can."

"Sir, with all due respect, if I don't lend my rifle to this fight, I don't think it'll matter if I treat the wounded or not," Yarrow said.

A blaster bolt blew through the lip of the trench and tossed a Marine from the wall. Hale caught the woman on her way down. Wisps of blond hair stuck out from her broken visor.

"You OK?" Hale asked.

"Sure, third time that's happened today," she said. She had a sergeant's stripes on her shoulder armor and her chest.

"Who's in charge?" Hale asked.

She looked at his rank and name stenciled on his chest and frowned. "I thought you were, Lieutenant Hale."

"What? I just got here," he said and pushed her to her feet.

A Toth ululation broke through the air.

"Here comes another charge," the sergeant said. She tapped at her waist then looked at Hale and his new arrivals. "If you've got grenades, now's the time!" She jumped onto the firing stoop and lifted her rifle over the edge of the trench to shoot.

Hale jumped up next to the sergeant, and his Marines found a piece of the wall without being asked. He looked over the edge and saw dozens of Toth warriors charging toward him like a pack of hungry wolves.

Hale grabbed a fragmentation grenade from his belt and hurled it at the enemy. He tossed his last two grenades with a little less force, catching the forward edge of the charging warriors. He brought his rifle to his shoulder and put a round in the center of a warrior's chest. It collapsed and rolled snout over tail, tripping up the warrior behind it.

The warriors stampeded toward him. They were fearless in the face of the massed rifle fire from the defenders and their dead were only an issue when they got in the way of the others. Hale watched as a Toth warrior lost its left fore- and mid-arms to gauss fire, stumbling as it bled out. A warrior smashed it to the ground and the wounded Toth was trampled by those coming from behind.

A low whine sent a tremor though the ground—a lander hovering high above the trench line. Hale snatched his last grenade, an anti-armor shaped charge, from his belt. He cranked the grenade twice and used his augmented strength to hurl the grenade into the air.

The radar-activated detonator picked up the Toth lander and exploded, the tungsten disk deforming into a bullet and carrying the explosive energy from the grenade into the lander. The explosively formed penetrator pierced the bottom of the lander and blew through the top. The lander swung from side to side, then stabilized. The crystal cannon glowed with power.

Before Hale could shout a warning, a bright lance skewered the lander and shot out the other side.

"Bailey?" Hale asked.

The lander nosed down and plummeted toward the trench. Hale yelled a warning at a dirt-caked Marine and a doughboy running toward him. The lander crashed near the edge of the trench and upended, slamming across the top of the trench and over the fleeing Marine and doughboy.

"Here we go!" Cortaro shouted. Hale swung around and saw a Toth slide into the trench, knocking the Marine sergeant off her feet. The warrior's tail swept across the trench and dented the armored walls right in front of Hale's face. The warrior lashed out at his Marines. One hand wrapped around Standish and lifted him into the air.

With the warrior between Hale and the rest of his Marines, any shots from their gauss rifles ran a significant risk of friendly fire. Hale snapped his rifle onto his back and slapped a hand against a catch on his right gauntlet. A Ka-Bar blade snapped out of the housing and over his hand.

Hale leaped onto the warrior's back and punched the blade into the Toth. The blade careened off the armor with a shower of sparks. Hale grabbed the edge of a crystalline plates just as the warrior tried to buck him off. He held on by the tips of his fingers and jammed the tip of his blade between the plates and rammed it home.

The warrior let off a bark of pain and tried to swing a fist at Hale, but the Marine had become a painful itch that the warrior couldn't scratch. The warrior launched itself against the trench wall, slamming Hale against the armored walls. His armor took the brunt of the blow and his blade stayed embedded in the warrior.

Hale twisted the knife and a spray of yellow spattered across his visor.

Cortaro, his own Ka-Bar unsheathed, ran up to the Toth and rammed his blade into the warrior's belly. A low moan came from the warrior. It lashed out at Cortaro and knocked him aside.

A doughboy leaped onto the warrior's upper shoulders and rained bare-knuckle punches against the Toth's helm. The Toth twisted aside and tried to climb out of the trench. Hale tried to yank his blade free, but it was stuck fast against the armor plates. The Toth got halfway over before the doughboy grabbed it by the arm and pulled it back into the trench. The dirt-covered Marine jammed a gauss pistol into the cracked helm and fired twice.

The warrior collapsed, its six limbs twitching.

Hale twisted his blade to the side and pulled it out with a wet slurp.

"Thanks for the assist," the dirty Marine

said. "Did you…Ken?"

"Jared?" Hale snapped the blade back into the sheath and finally recognized his brother.

"We've got to stop meeting like this," Jared said.

"Where's Standish?" Cortaro called out. Hale looked around the trench, but didn't see the Marine anywhere.

There. An armored glove stuck out from beneath the dead warrior, fingers grasping at dirt.

"Help me." Hale's hands slipped against the bloody body before finding a firm handhold. He got the corpse up a few inches, then it rose easily. Indigo, his lips broken and bloody, smiled at Hale. The doughboy was missing several teeth.

Cortaro and Orozco grabbed Standish by the arms and pulled him free from the Toth. The Marine's helmet had compressed slightly, popping a visor pane from its grooves.

"To hell with these things," Standish said. "They're worse than banshees!"

Yarrow grabbed Standish by the chin and

turned his head to look at him.

"Are you alright?" Yarrow asked.

"Do you know what that smelled like?" Standish asked, pointing an accusatory finger at the body. "Ugh, I think I got some of its blood in my mouth." He lifted his visor and spat into the dirt.

"He's fine," Yarrow said.

Jared grabbed a rifle from a dead Marine and jumped onto the firing stoop.

"There's still plenty more where that came from," Jared said. He looked over the top and did a double take. "They're retreating?"

The *boom boom boom* of gauss cannons echoed through the trench. The three Iron Hearts rolled up to the edge of the trench, their legs folded and treads extended. The double-barrel cannons on their forearms sent death into the fleeing warriors.

Overhead, dozens of Dotok fighter craft filled the air, strafing the Toth as they tried to retreat to the safety of the ocean.

Elias leaned to the side and transformed his treads back into legs. He glanced down at Hale.

"You just going to stand there or are you going to help me win this fight?" Elias asked. He stepped over the trench and charged the Toth, cannons blasting.

CHAPTER 18

Ibarra watched a holo tank showing the Toth and Eighth Fleets closing on each other, prow to prow. A few Toth fighters emerged from each ship, their course plots taking them straight to the *Midway.*

"Stacey, get ready," Ibarra said.

Stacey, strapped into the halo chair, groaned.

"It's hard…" she whispered. "So many mass shadows from the fleet." Her jaw clenched and Ibarra felt the great thorns of the Crucible shifting against each other. "I don't think I can do this." A drop of blood trickled down from her left ear.

"Focus on the equation. It's one equation with many parts, remember? The same way you taught yourself quantum mechanics when you were five, remember?" Ibarra asked.

"That didn't—nnng—hurt like this!" Stacey shouted.

The Toth's long-range guns opened fire on the Eighth Fleet, scoring direct hits against a strike carrier. The *Yorktown* lit up with damage reports and fell back from the wall of ships.

Ibarra sent a command through the station. On a separate monitor, repair ships bolted away from the *Breitenfeld*. Scaffolds spun away into the void, leaving the still-damaged ship bare.

"Now, my girl," Ibarra said. Two more ships of the Eighth Fleet blinked red in the holo tank. "Now, Stacey. People are dying."

Stacey squeezed her eyes shut. When she opened them again, they glowed white.

****

A jump portal spread from the center of the Crucible and swallowed the *Breitenfeld*. When reality snapped back into place, the ship found itself in the center of the Toth fleet, pearlescent vessels surrounding it in a giant cone.

"Flight deck," Captain Valdar said, "get the

missile pods in the void right this second."

"Shall I open fire?" Utrecht asked. "We can nail some of the smaller vessels without any risk to the Eighth."

"Hold," Valdar said. "We're here to break through the wall, not knock on the door. Engineering, ready the jump engines."

"Sir, the jump caused an overload in the dark-matter buffers." Levin's voice was reedy with panic. "I've got to purge them before we can go anywhere. It'll take time."

"The mission goes forward," Valdar said. "Everyone on this ship has the rest of their lives for you to fix the problem. Valdar out." He cut the channel and looked at Ensign Geller. "Tell me the moment the jump engines are back online."

"Aye-aye, Skipper," Geller said.

"Sir, flight deck reports the first pod is in the void," Ericcson said.

"Get us clear," Valdar said. "We don't want to be in the way."

****

Four cubes nearly the size of a Destrier transport floated behind the *Breitenfeld*. Each cube held sixty-four point-detonation missiles. The missiles were meant to fight the Xaros, who'd proved adept at jamming or coopting any kind of computer and guidance system, but the infrared communication system used by the human fleet remained intact. Unwilling to slap sailors into missiles and use them as kamikaze guidance systems, the engineers and planners working for Admiral Garret found a way to guide munitions to a target.

Starting in the 1940s, air forces had used TV guidance systems attached to bombs to create "smart" weapons. IR guidance systems connected to each missile in the cube linked back to the *Breitenfeld* and to several dozen sailors sitting in front of holo screens attached to a mouse and keyboard watching the camera feed from each missile.

Men and women serving in the Atlantic Union navy had played video games since before they could walk. Creating the software allowing the *Breitenfeld*'s sailors to steer missiles over IR had taken less than an hour.

Panels popped open on the cubes and missiles slid free. A sailor named Rouen moved his mouse and saw the star field shift as the missile responded to his commands. He turned the missile toward his designated target—a Toth cruiser at the apex of their formation—and hit a key to engage the missile's engines.

The game was simple: fly the torpedo into the Toth ship. Sixty-three other sailors played the same game as their missile came free of the pod.

Rouen steered the missile from side to side, confusing any point-defense system the Toth might have active. The Toth, though, seemed entirely preoccupied with firing on the Eighth, and not shunting any weapons power to the flanks exposed to the incoming missiles.

Rouen had zoned out while Chief MacDougall said something about how one of those Karigole he'd seen walking around the ship knew that the Toth didn't manage their power allocation very efficiently. All Rouen cared about was the extra shore-leave chit his section chief promised to whoever scored the most hits on the Toth. Killing the Toth and surviving the battle would be nice, but *actual* shore leave…Rouen smiled and licked his lips as the cruiser grew larger on his screen.

****

A rare smile spread across Makarov's face as missile tracks appeared from the pods.

"Execute maneuver Hornblower," Makarov said.

The first wave of missiles sped into the Toth ships at the tip of the cone. The denethrite explosives packed into the cones were considered a "safe" explosive, unlikely to explode if agitated by the normal bumps and hazards of asteroid mining, but when rammed against something at several hundred miles an hour, the explosives would detonate without the need for a fuse.

The ships of Eighth Fleet accelerated toward their enemy at full engine burn. Rail cannons crackled to life and bombarded the Toth ships just as the first missiles found their targets.

Confusion, the fog of war, "Murphy" was a constant factor in any battle. Makarov's plan was to bombard the sole decision maker in the Toth fleet, Olux, with key decisions that only he could make. Would he react to the attack from within his formation by the *Breitenfeld* and the IR-guided missiles, her Eighth Fleet accelerating into attack range and hitting him hard, or the sudden concentration of fire on his own vessel?

"*Breitenfeld* reports eighty percent missile detonation against their targets. They're launching the second wave now," her tactical officer said.

Toth ships blinked red, falling out of formation and bleeding atmosphere as missiles ripped through them. She didn't need the denethrite missiles to destroy the Toth outright, just knock them out of the fight long enough for her fleet to close the distance and finish the job.

The *Midway* lurched as her rail cannons joined the battle.

Makarov tapped Olux's flagship; it was pristine.

"Why aren't we scoring any hits on this ship?" she asked. Rail-cannon shells zipped toward Olux and vanished before they could strike.

"The ships around it massed their point-defense systems to protect it," the tactical officer said. "If we redirect frigate squadron epsilon it might—"

Makarov held up a hand. The two fleets were in a slugging match, and Toth ships were dying faster than hers. She was winning, but paying a terrible price in blood and ships for it.

"Have Epsilon make an attack run on the Toth flagship. Get Valdar and Kosciusko on the line," she said.

****

Kosciusko sent a ripple of fire into a Toth fighter, tearing it into a brief plume of fire and debris.

"67th Fighter Squadron, follow me back to the *Midway*. We have a new mission," the Karigole said. He pulled his Eagle, the cockpit expanded to accommodate his much larger frame, into a loop and skimmed across the surface of a Toth cruiser. He fired a burst of shots into a cannon crystal, shattering it into millions of pieces. He slalomed around point-defense turrets, passing close enough that he could see the menial crews crammed around the base of the energy weapons.

He pulled away from the ship and fired his afterburners, chased by dozens of bolts of blue-white energy. The flare of an incoming missile's burning engines blazed ahead of him, heading straight for the Toth ship. Kosciusko swung his fighter to the side, guiding the cruiser's point-defense turrets away from the incoming missile.

The missile streaked past in a blur.

He looked over his shoulder and saw the missile burst just within the cruiser's hull. The ship exploded like a star gone nova, sending flame and scorched hull plating in every direction. A small core of burning oxygen and wrecked energy banks remained at the center of what remained of the ship.

He found the *Midway* at the center of the Eighth Fleet and changed course to intercept.

"Jaws, the *Shiloh*'s getting pounded by Toth fighters," said an aerospace force pilot with the call sign Packer. "Why are we breaking off?"

Seven Eagles formed up around Kosciusko. The forward landing bay doors on the *Midway* opened like a great maw.

"There is only one Toth that matters in this fight," Kosciusko said, "and it is time for the killing blow."

"Bombers from the 663rd are coming out hot off the rails," Packer said. "Where's our objective?"

"A cruiser, I'm sending you the target location now," Kosciusko said. Condors zipped out of the *Midway* and angled toward a half-dozen Toth destroyers and battlecruisers bunched together, separated from the *Midway* by dozens of human and Toth ships locked in combat.

Kosciusko flew above the lead Condor bomber and matched his speed with it. The rest of the Eagles formed a cordon around the bombers. The Condors, three-person craft loaded with torpedoes against their wings and hulls, fired their afterburners and sped toward Olux's flagship.

Kosciusko found the *Breitenfeld*, a line of burning motes streaking from the missile pods toward Olux's ship. If everything went as planned, the missiles should arrive seconds before the bombers got within range.

Point-defense turrets on the ships surrounding Olux massed fire against incoming rail-cannon shells. A flash of distorted energy marked the death of each round as the Toth defenses proved nearly impenetrable.

"Target the picket ships around the flagship," Kosciusko said. "Strip away its defenses and clear a shot for the big guns."

The last Toth overlord was there, hiding deep within a battlecruiser and using its own kind as a shield against harm. Kosciusko's hand tightened around the control stick. If only he could get his hands on the overlord. The truest revenge was to see the fear in an enemy's eyes before they died, but blowing them out of space was a worthy satisfaction.

"What're they doing?" Packer asked. The Toth ships near Olux shifted places, forming a sphere of ships centered on the overlord's battlecruiser.

"They're trying to run," Kosciusko said. The pocket of ships broke out of formation and burned straight for the *Breitenfeld*. Bolts of energy struck out against the line of missiles snaking toward the flagship. "Bombers, when can you engage?"

"We're in range now, but their point defense—"

"Fire. The cordon will turn a blind eye to everything but a threat to the overlord," Kosciusko said.

"Fine by me. Rifle!" the bomber leader said. Missiles released from the bombers and launched toward the closest Toth cruiser.

"Bandits incoming," Packer said. Toth fighters spat away from the flagship and accelerated toward the attacking bombers.

"668th, there is no prize for returning to your ship with unspent missiles," Kosciusko said. "Shoot everything you've got. Eagles, with me." He fired his afterburners and flew toward the incoming fighters.

A pair of Toth fighters broke away from the pack and fired at the lead missile. The bombardier controlling it over IR used the missile's maneuver thrusters to jink it from side to side, like a hummingbird at a feeder. It evaded the fighter's energy blasts, but not the fighter itself when it crashed into the missile.

The second fighter suicided into the following missile.

"Send your next salvo into the uppermost cruiser," Kosciusko said. "We'll make this a bit more difficult for them."

His Gatling cannons threw out a barrage of fire, forming a cloud of high-velocity rounds directly in front of the Toth fighters as they angled up to intercept the next round of missiles. The

Eagles around him added to the fog of gauss shells. Void fighting held to Newton's First Law: the gauss rounds would continue on with their same speed and vector until they came into contact with something. At far enough distances, a spray of shells would dissipate to the point where hitting anything would be a miracle, but when the enemy target was close and speeding straight into the fire, the odds of an intersection were much higher.

The Toth fighters split away from each other. One clipped the outer edge of the gauss rounds and exploded.

Kosciusko picked out a target and hit it with a snap shot. He rolled away from the oncoming mass of the shattered fighter and looped over. The Toth fighters hadn't slowed or turned around to dogfight. Half broke for the missiles in space; the other half made straight for the bombers.

A Toth fighter exposed its belly to the Karigole's guns as it banked over toward the bombers. Kosciusko blew it apart with ease and spat through the brief ball of fire the dagger ship left behind. A missile streaked just beneath the Toth fighter and accelerated hard down a clear path to its target.

Three missiles blew past Kosciusko's nose, a Toth fighter in a futile pursuit. The Toth dagger fighters were fast, but there was still a biological pilot in the cockpit that could take only so much acceleration. The missiles had no such limitation.

A missile hit home, blowing a burning crater out of the cruiser. The ship cracked on its keel, spilling crew and hunks of metal into space.

"Help! It's—"

The transmission ended when a Toth fighter collided with a Condor.

"Lost connection with my missile!"

"Coming right at us!"

The comms channel descended into chaos as the Toth fighters reached the Condors and the nimble craft pounced onto the hulking bombers.

"Kosciusko!" Admiral Makarov flashed onto his screen.

"Busy!" He fell onto a dagger ship's tail and

wasted several shots failing to shoot it down.

"The flagship's powered up its jump drives," Makarov said. "It's breaking clear of the escort. Have the bombers target it now!"

"Not possible!" A Condor blew apart under a barrage of energy blasts in front of Kosciusko.

"This is the *Breitenfeld*." Captain Valdar appeared on the screen. "We can make the shot."

"How? You're showing your guns and maneuver engines are offline," Makarov asked.

"Lafayette stitched together a few power systems when we were over Takeni. Should get a salvo off with my ventral turrets without blowing my ship up in the process," Valdar said. "Probably."

Olux's flagship slid out of the sphere of escorts and away from the battle. A small pool of light came into being on the flagship's path, an opening jump gate.

Bursts of light erupted from the *Breitenfeld* batteries. Point-defense turrets on the flagship came to life, their fire crisscrossing into an apex that sank toward the flagship. A cannon shell died, but the defensive fire kept blasting away until the guns couldn't track any closer to the flagship without hitting it.

The flagship's guns went silent. The ship canted to the side and rolled slightly, a plume of fire blazing from a massive hole in its side.

Kosciusko turned his fighter toward the stricken ship and fired his afterburners. This wasn't over yet.

"Jaws, what're you doing? We got it!" Packer said.

A section of the flagship blew out, and another armored bridge shaped like a flattened gem emerged. It floated in space then sped toward the still-open wormhole. Overlord protection chambers were incredibly durable; only a direct hit from the *Breitenfeld*'s main guns could have killed Olux while he was inside it. Kosciusko pushed his engines past their red lines, his fighter blaring warnings at him.

"Admiral Makarov," Kosciusko said, "tell my brothers…no, they'll understand.

Ghul'Thul'Ghul."

Kosciusko's Eagle bucked beneath him as he closed on Olux. He felt at peace when his Eagle slammed into the command bridge. The impact cracked the outer shell of the bridge and sent it spinning end over end. It angled away from the open portal, trailing air and crystal fragments. Electricity arced over the surface. More and more crooked fingers of light gripped the gem as a glow burned from within.

The overlord's command bridge exploded, annihilating Olux so completely that not even ashes remained.

CHAPTER 19

A Mule landed on the *Breitenfeld*'s command deck. Teams of medics rushed to the lowering ramp and got on board before the ramp edge had touched the deck.

Valdar watched from the sidelines as the medics carried a sailor away on a stretcher. They'd been on recovery duty for hours, tracking down emergency beacons from sailors trapped within dead spaceships or from escape pods. A few were rescued from the void between ships, but not many.

The Toth fleet had descended into chaos with the death of the last overlord. The Toth warriors in charge of the ships had refused to surrender. Every last one of their ships and fighters was chased down and destroyed by the Eighth Fleet.

As the rescue mission after the battle wound down, the fleet would begin recovery.

A line of body bags stretched out alongside

the flight line, all picked up by a search and rescue team he'd sent to the *Ticonderoga*. His tiny morgue had filled up hours ago. The crew was making room in the cargo bay for these bodies, and the many more to come.

Admiral Makarov walked up to Valdar. Her face was gaunt, lined from the constant stress of command during the battle and the chaos that followed.

"You knew," she said. "You knew what I was when we first met, didn't you?"

"That you are procedural? Yes," he said.

"Did it bother you? Following orders from someone like me?"

"It did. It was hard to accept you as an admiral, not…"

"Some tube-grown *thing*? I understand your hesitation. So why? Why did you go along with my plan? You could have refused, taken your ship full of true born and sided with the Toth," she said.

Valdar felt a sting of fear. Did she know what he'd done with Fournier?

"Your plan was…brilliant," Valdar said. "I couldn't have come up with anything better. And I never had to question your loyalty. You cared about Phoenix. Your sailors. I don't think you would have done anything different if you were true born."

"Look at them," Makarov said, staring at the body bags. "Can you tell which are proccie, and which are true born?"

"No, ma'am."

"Neither can I. I couldn't tell them apart before the battle. I can't do it now. Maybe the rest of the fleet and any of Fournier's surviving believers will see it that way too. Circumstances of birth may be different, but we're all equal in death."

Makarov wiped a hand across her face and walked away.

Valdar's gaze ran over the many dead, and found that he agreed with her.

****

Durand's Eagle hovered over the beach near the wrecked ace. Her ship's thermal cameras showed the broken Toth fighter in a cooling patch of burnt-out grass, a blob of heat still in the cockpit. She eased her fighter forward until it was over a small clearing a hundred yards from the water. She landed slowly and opened the canopy.

The engines whined on idle as she swung her legs over the cockpit and landed with a gauss carbine in her hands. She powered the weapon and switched off the safety. Her feet crunched against blackened, long-bladed grass, wisps of flame and smoke dancing around her as she walked to the Toth fighter.

The smell of ashes mixed with salt air from the ocean.

The fighter lay nose-first in a driven pile of white sand and dark volcanic soil. Shards of the shattered canopy glinted in the sunlight.

Durand raised her carbine to her shoulder and stepped around the nose. Dried yellow blood stained the hull where it had run from the cockpit. The ace was there, crumpled against the controls, upper and middle arms broken and contorted, its snout tucked into an armpit.

Durand aimed the carbine at the ace and kicked the fighter.

The ace shivered, then turned its face to Durand. One eye was mangled, puffed and caked with dried blood. The other looked over Durand, struggling to focus.

It hissed at her, blood frothing over its lips.

"You know why I'm here?" Durand asked.

The ace let out a wet cough. A hind leg clawed at the side of the cockpit. A panel flopped open, revealing a pistol made of twisted metal cords.

"Fine by me," Durand shot the ace in its ruined face. The back of its skull splattered through the cockpit and it went slack. Durand shot it in the torso twice. Blood bubbled and spat from a perforated lung.

She spat in the dirt and turned back to her waiting Eagle.

There was no feeling of closure or satisfaction. Her heart beat cold.

****

Valdar's fingers typed against the holographic keyboard projected by his data slate. His complete report of his involvement with Fournier was almost complete. He'd spent the last many hours detailing every conversation, every fabrication, and laying out his confession to Admiral Garret. He'd felt a weight lift from his shoulders, like his soul was rising from a nadir of guilt and regret.

There was a knock at the door.

Valdar scowled at the door. He'd given specific instructions not to be disturbed.

A knock again.

"Later!" he snapped.

The door locks snapped open and it slid aside. Knight stepped into the captain's ready room and gave his commanding officer a respectful nod before closing the door behind him.

"Knight? You want to explain what the hell you're doing in here?" Valdar asked.

Knight reached into a back pocket and took out a small black ball. He tossed it in front of him and it hovered in midair. White light emitted from a ring around the center of the ball and a hologram of Marc Ibarra formed around the ball.

"Hello, Captain," Ibarra said. "We need to talk."

"What is this? Knight why do you have—"

"Oh, Eric here?" Ibarra pointed a thumb over his shoulder at the intelligence officer. "He works for me. Has for decades. I put him on this ship to keep an eye on Stacey. Who better than the counterintelligence officer to have on the payroll? Right? A whole 'who watches the watchmen' sort of conundrum for you."

Valdar looked at the screen with his confession, then at Ibarra.

"Now you're starting to get it," Ibarra said. "I know everything, Captain. Every little talk you had with Fournier. Every directive from Garret that you muddled before giving it to Hale. I know Fournier swore up and down that your conversations with him were secure. I let the old governments think they could talk without me knowing, gave them the illusion of control, but so long as I have one end of a secure quantum communication channel bugged, they really aren't so secure."

Valdar glanced around his room, then glared at Knight, who shrugged.

"That's right. I've had your office wired since before you ever set foot on this ship," Ibarra said. "But I'm not here to gloat. I'm here to thank you."

"What?"

"Yes, to thank you for being so honest and…honorable." Ibarra said the last word like it left a bad taste in his mouth. "I knew I could count on you to do the right thing—as far as you're concerned—and go along with Fournier. Feed me his entire plan so that I could twist it to my own ends. You see, Captain, I've been at this game longer than you've been alive. Just because someone's working against me doesn't mean I couldn't find some use for them. And you served a great purpose. Not sure how we'd ever have taken out the *Naga* without sneaking a bomb on board."

"You used me," Valdar said.

"Well, all I had to do was listen and pull a couple strings here and there," Ibarra said.

"Don't think you have any sort of power over me," Valdar said. "I'm sending my confession to Garret in the next few minutes."

"Why would you do that?" Ibarra cocked his head to the side. "Your secret's safe with us."

"It's the right thing to do," Valdar said slowly.

"Nonsense!" Ibarra rolled his eyes. "You did us a great service. Helped win the battle, all that. If you hit send, Garret will take this ship away and he'll build a jail just for you…or a gallows. Why don't we skip all that mess and make a deal?"

Valdar rubbed his thumb against his forefinger. He was tempted to reach out and send the file with a click of a button. Confessing would mean humiliation, the loss of his ship and what little he had left after the Xaros invasion. Ibarra put his hands on his hips and smiled like a huckster.

"I'm listening," Valdar said.

"*Don't* say a word to Garret," Ibarra raised a finger next to his face, "or anyone else for that matter, ever. It'll stay our little secret. You're far too useful to me on this ship than you'll be if Garret gets wind of what you did."

"'Useful to you'? I tried to help Fournier because I thought he was doing the right thing for humanity, not what you wanted to do. You think I'm going to be your pet?" Valdar asked.

Ibarra's face fell. "I respect you, Valdar. I really do. You remind me so much of myself when I was a young man, before I came to accept what must be done to save humanity. I think you could be the one to lead us all into a new Golden Age, if we can survive that long.

"The Toth attack taught me that our place in the galaxy is insecure, even with the Xaros sure to return. We have an opportunity, one I want you to be part of. We have access to a new planet, one far beyond the galactic rim. I'm going to send a small contingent of true-born humans to the planet in the next few weeks, then gravity tides will cut us off from the world for fifteen years. I want you to lead the second fleet, but we have to survive that long, and there are very few people that I trust anymore."

"Why would you trust me?"

"You are, at your core, a good man," Ibarra said. "I can depend on that, and the colony to Terra Nova could be our last chance to survive. We should survive the next Xaros attack with full, unfettered proccie production, but they're coming at us expecting to fight whatever survived the Battle of the Crucible. The third wave will be exponentially larger, trillions of drones to smother us into oblivion. Not even the tacticians on Bastion have ever figured out a way to survive the full force of the Xaros.

"We can't have another internal division like Fournier. That's why I need you working on my side from now on. In return I'll send you off to lead a colony of true-born humans—without meddling from me or Bastion."

Valdar considered the offer, then deleted the

file he'd prepared for Garret.

"There, you see," Ibarra looked over his shoulder to Knight, "he can be reasoned with."

"What do you need from me?" Valdar asked.

"In the future, I don't know yet," Ibarra shrugged. "But when I need you to jump, you better ask 'how high?' As for right now, I require penance, proof you really are on the right team. You're going on an assassination mission. You will kill Dr. Mentiq and end the Toth threat to Earth."

CHAPTER 20

Admirals Garret and Makarov watched as Stacey swiped through screens full of arcane coding language that neither of them could fathom. Ibarra's hologram sat on the empty plinth in the center of the Crucible's control room.

"We pulled the computer core from the *Naga* and a few other Toth wrecks," Stacey said. "Their programming language wasn't too difficult to crack. Lowenn brought back most everything Bastion had about the Toth. The hardest part for us to understand was their base twelve mathematics."

"You bought us all the way up here for a science lecture?" Garret asked.

"Hang in there, Admiral," Ibarra said. "It gets interesting."

"We found the virus the Toth sent that compromised our probe," Stacey said. "The probe will function as intended as soon as we're ready to reboot, but, while I was poking around that malcode..." She brought up a screen full of dense programming language and raised a palm just beneath the screen with a huge smile on her face.

"Am I supposed to notice something?" Makarov asked.

Stacey huffed and tapped her fingers against several parts of the code. "It's base ten! The same kind of math we, and every other ten-fingered species use, but wait, there's more! You see these command executables? They're not written in Toth."

"The Toth had help writing the code?" Garret asked.

"Yes, and here's where it gets weird," Stacey said. "The language isn't used by any species in the Alliance. We were about to give up when I saw these mentioned in Hale's summary reports." She took a gold coin out of her pocket and tossed it at Makarov, who plucked it out of the air.

Makarov examined the crude coin with the lion and seated man.

"It's Akkadian, from ancient Mesopotamia," Stacey said.

"The code or the coin?" Makarov asked.

"Both, but the language evolved somewhat in line with the pan-morphology theory doctor—"

"Fascinating," Garret deadpanned. "We care because?"

"Savages." Stacey shook her head quickly. "No sense of wonder or curiosity."

"Once we broke the code on the Akkadian language," Ibarra said, "it opened up the rest of the Toth records. Specifically, the location where Dr. Mentiq hangs his hat." Ibarra stood up and a planet appeared on the plinth behind him. Deep-blue seas covered most of the surface, and a single, small landmass surrounded a massive volcano.

"The Akkadian language code we recovered says this is a planet named Nibiru. Our tongues can't form the Toth word for whatever they call it," Ibarra said. "Dr. Mentiq has it set up as his own little playground and never leaves. The rest of the Toth come to him for everything."

"Wait, why are the Toth using one of *our* extinct languages?" Makarov asked.

Stacey and Ibarra shrugged their shoulders.

"Great, another cosmic mystery," Admiral Garret said, "keep this Akkadian business under wraps before I have to tamp out another conspiracy theory. All this is relevant, why? We just beat the piss out of the Toth. I doubt they'll come back for more."

"That's where you're wrong, Admiral," Stacey said. "The Toth that attacked us are a single corporation. There are hundreds more—some stronger, some weaker—but they will want the proccie tech, and they will be back in force."

"But the Toth are very set in their ways, thanks to the relationship between Mentiq and the overlords," Ibarra said. "He gave them their tanks, and in exchange he gets first cut of any new asset the Toth want to acquire. Try and shortchange Mentiq and he cuts the power to the tanks. So, once this Toth fleet is overdue to report back to Mentiq, he'll auction off the rights to Earth again."

"Chyort voz'mi," Makarov said as she pressed her fingertips against her temples.

"Why can't any species in this galaxy take a damn hint," Garret said.

"There's an opportunity in every crisis, Admirals," Ibarra said with a smile. "Every senior executive from the Toth home world will come to Tribute in the next few weeks for the auction. And we could be there."

"You think we can spare a fleet to attack that planet?" Garret said.

"We won't need a fleet. Mentiq doesn't let the leaders come to him in warships—puts him at risk." Ibarra waved a hand and the planet morphed into a large box shaped like the center of an extended accordion.

"That is the cloaking device from the *Naga*," Stacey said. "We found it mostly intact on the wreck. Lafayette examined it with the omnium reactor and was able to make some significant improvement. Turns out it's based on Karigole tech."

"What're you getting at, Ibarra?" Makarov asked.

"We send a single cloaked ship to Nibiru. Kill Mentiq and the senior overlords. That will throw the entire Toth race into chaos," Ibarra said. "End the threat they pose to us once and for all."

Garret looked at Makarov, who nodded.

"Which ship?" Garret asked

****

Stacey repaired the final piece of the probe's code and stepped back from the workstation.

"You want to check it over?" she asked Ibarra.

"I monitored it while you were working." His hologram paced back and forth in front of the central plinth.

"Why couldn't we tell the admirals about the override code the Qa'Resh gave us? Or about Terra Nova?" Stacey asked.

"The Qa'Resh gave us the code because the Alliance threw us under the proverbial bus. It was our way to escape the Toth. We tell them and they'll distrust the Alliance, and by extension, us. Your other modifications to the probe…excellent. I'll retain override authority. Bastion won't be able to lock us out ever again. I can open the portal to Terra Nova without the probe—or anyone else— able to stop me."

"But…why, Grandpa? Why does it have to be you?"

"So they," Ibarra pointed to a screen showing the Earth, "appreciate it. My goal, my only goal since the day that damn probe landed on Earth, has been to save humanity. We're not going to let the probe take that away from us or trust that Bastion has our best interests at heart. If we offer Phoenix a lifeline with Terra Nova, they'll be beholden to us. Our control will return."

"I don't like it," she said. "They're our people, not our pawns."

"Look what happened when we trusted anyone but ourselves," Ibarra said. "We almost lost everything a second time, and those that would survive would be slaves to the Alliance."

"Not everyone in the Alliance agreed to that. We have friends, those we can trust like the Dotok," Stacey said.

"Then you'd better convince the rest of the Alliance to stand with us," Ibarra said. "Now, let's reboot the probe and get you back to Bastion."

CHAPTER 21

Standish opened his foot locker and dug through a jumble of dirty clothes and even dirtier kit.

"Where is it? Where is it...ah-ha!" Standish stood up and brandished a loud yellow and blue Hawaiian shirt. "I knew I still had it."

"You aren't actually going to wear that on shore leave, are you?" Orozco asked. The Spaniard wore baggy shorts and an old-fashioned bowling shirt. He opened a pair of gold-rimmed sunglasses and slid them onto his face.

"I have been stuck on this tin can or neck deep in aliens trying to eat me for months, Sarge. Ibarra and his magical mystical construction robots rebuilt the R&R center in two days just so we, the heroes of Eighth Fleet, could get some time off. I am going to party like I just got my discharge papers." Standish slipped the Hawaiian shirt over his shoulders and tried to smooth out the wrinkles.

He looked in a mirror and raised an eyebrow at his reflection. "Irresistible," he said, emphasizing the second syllable.

"Standish, do I need to check your color vision?" Yarrow asked.

"And speaking of irresistible," Standish said, wrapping a lanky arm over Yarrow's shoulders and giving him a squeeze, "we're going to find you a girl with low standards and questionable decision-making skills. I will not have a virgin in my team. Your death would just be too tragic."

"Oye." Bailey stepped from behind a wall locker, wearing a safari jacket and khaki pants. She ran a comb through long dark hair. "The first thing he's doing is getting shitfaced with the rest of us. He's never actually drank alcohol. I bet he gets two shots of tequila before he's trying to hump a bar stool or passed out. Maybe both."

"Does no one want to go fishing with me?" Orozco asked. "I heard there are marlins off the coast of the Big Island this time of year."

"Fishing," Yarrow said meekly, "sounds

kind of—"

"New guy thinks he has some say in the matter!" Standish slapped Yarrow on the back. "It's called negative peer pressure, kid. We do it because we love you."

Cortaro, standing in the doorway, cleared his throat. He wore his shipboard fatigues, even though he was on the same R&R rotation as the rest of his squad. A grim-faced Lieutenant Hale, also in his fatigues, stood behind Cortaro.

"No," Standish shook his head in denial. He shook a finger at Cortaro. "No!"

Cortaro stepped aside and Hale walked in. He stopped in front of his Marines and looked each of them in the eye.

"We have an urgent mission. Shore leave has been cancelled," Hale said.

Standish fell to his knees and looked to the ceiling, "Why? Why, God, are you doing this to me?"

"Standish," Cortaro growled.

Standish's shoulders slumped forward and

his chin fell to his chest.

"What is it?" Orozco asked. He took the sunglasses from his face and slid them back into a felt-lined case.

"We're going to find the Toth leader and kill him," Hale said. "That should get them off our backs long enough for us to deal with the Xaros."

"The hits just keep on coming," Standish moaned.

"Get to the armory and suit up," Cortaro said. "Prep your chutes. We're doing a high-orbit low-opening jump over the California coast in three hours."

The team leaders left the barracks.

Bailey tossed her comb in her bunk and sat down next to Standish.

"Bullshit, is what it is," she said.

"Standish," Yarrow said, putting a hand on the Marine's shoulder, "you can get me drunk and maneuver me into sex I won't remember after we get back from the planet full of face-eating aliens."

"You promise?" Standish asked.

"Sure, why not." Yarrow took his fatigues out of his wall locker. "It's not like we're ever going on shore leave."

****

Stacey stood as her pod rose above the assembled ambassadors.

"Thank you for this chance to address our congress," she said. "Earth defeated the Toth armada. Every ship destroyed. Every overlord slain by our Karigole allies. We recognize the enormous sacrifice of our Dotok allies who lost many fine pilots in the battle, and the Karigole, who are the last two of their kind.

"We do *not* recognize the contributions of this congress. While many of you lobbied to support Earth in our hour of need…none of you were there. None of you stood beside us against a vile enemy determined to enslave and devour us. You can claim that you were simply following the rules of our alliance, that you fell sway to the words of a demagogue, but Earth will remember who stood with us," Stacey looked straight at the Vishrakath ambassador, "and who stood against us.

"Humanity will end the Toth threat for good, a task which we will carry out without your help or thanks," she said.

"No, unacceptable!" Ambassador Wexil's pod rose to face her. "You can't take it upon yourself to do something with far-reaching ramifications as attacking the Toth. They will consider it a provocation from the entire Alliance."

"I'm not asking," Stacey said. "I'm telling you what Earth will do. There will be no half measures in this operation. Mentiq will be killed. The rest of the overlords will die with him. If some part of the Toth can survive, I hope what remains learns to never anger us again."

More ambassador pods rose into the air, all demanding to be heard. Stacey looked up at the Qa'Resh face over the massive column in the center of the assembly. The face looked down at her, and she could have sworn it winked.

THE END

ABOUT THE AUTHOR

Richard Fox is the author of The Ember War Saga, and several other military history, thriller and space opera novels.

He lives in fabulous Las Vegas with his incredible wife and two boys, amazing children bent on anarchy.

He graduated from the United States Military Academy (West Point) much to his surprise and spent ten years on active duty in the United States Army. He deployed on two combat tours to Iraq and received the Combat Action Badge, Bronze Star and Presidential Unit Citation.

Sign up for his mailing list over at www.richardfoxauthor.com to stay up to date on new releases and get an exclusive Ember War short story.

The Ember War Saga:

1.) The Ember War
2.) The Ruins of Anthalas
3.) Blood of Heroes
4.) Earth Defiant
5.) The Gardens of Nibiru (coming April 2016!)

Made in the USA
Middletown, DE
10 September 2018